Dryad

SONYA SOLOMONOVICH

CONTENTS

1 AN INTEREST IN ALL THINGS HUMAN
(AD 2013)

"Solena!"

It was the voice of the Great Tree, a whisper and a roar all at once, thrumming upwards from the depths of the earth.

Around the giant trunk whose branches twisted into the sky, thirty young dryads danced, dipping low to the ground, then springing up, spinning round and round, even while they circled round the tree faster and faster. The High Priest stood in the centre of the circle, facing the Great Tree, a crown of roots and leaves on his head shaking in rhythm to the dance, while he chanted an ancient song invoking the spirit of the Great Tree.

He raised his arms sharply in the air, and the dancing ceased. The lithe, muscular figures froze, kneeling on the ground, their arms stretched upwards, the only thing moving was the sweat dripping from their glistening bodies. The onlookers — young dryads, greenish of skin, with bright golden, red or orange hair; infant dryads with flaming curls and leaf-shaped eyebrows; elderly dryads with faded yellowing hair, but with a strong and sinewy build as if they had been desiccated but not weakened with time — all stood frozen, breathless in anticipation.

They understood the word of the tree. It had answered even before the priest had a chance to pose the question.

The answer was disappointing to all present.

The priest sensed this, and he tried to complete the ritual as it had been planned.

In a voice suddenly made strong by the surging energy of the tree, he shouted words in an ancient language. His words were incomprehensible to most of the onlookers, but the barely suppressed anger in his tone was discerned by all.

"Who will journey to the human world and wreak havoc on all their plans?"

"Solena!" the tree replied again, the sudden boom of its voice making the priest stumble backwards.

Before he could fall to the ground, two of the male dancers caught him in their strong arms and set him upright. The priest heaved a deep sigh, adjusted his robes, and finally turned to face the waiting dryads.

"The Great Tree has spoken!" he announced. His voice fell back to its usual raspy timbre as he said the last words, "It must be Solena. She is the one who will save us from the humans."

A murmur spread among the crowd. It was growing louder when another old dryad spoke up:

"Quiet, all of you!"

He was not as old as the priest, taller and leaner but with the tell-tale yellowing hair of a dryad several centuries old. He strode to the front and stood before them, raising his arms in an appeasing gesture.

"Would you speak, Anastacio?" the priest asked.

"With your permission," the old dryad replied, bowing his head.

The priest nodded.

"Friends, I know many of you hoped to be given this task," Anastacio said, "Or some of you thought that your son or daughter would be best able to fulfill it. But we cannot contradict the Great Tree."

"But why Solena? The one who commits sacrilege?" a young female shouted. "Shame!"

"Shame! Bamboo forest!" The others picked up the cry. Bamboo was one of the most offensive plants to dryads: for some mysterious reason, it never bonded with them and survived perfectly well on its own.

"Mind your language!" the priest yelled.

"It is true, Solena is considered an outcast by many of you," Anastacio said, his tone acquiring an accusatory edge, "but I know her well. I have taught her many things of the forest, but when it comes to humans, she is far more knowledgeable than any of you, far more knowledgeable than I, though I have several centuries on her.

So who better to fulfill this task?"

The crowd still rippled with discontent, and a few scattered shouts of "bamboo" were heard.

"Thank you, Anastacio," said the priest. "Perhaps you will be the one to tell her of the decision, since she has not deigned to grace us with her presence."

"I would be proud to do it," Anastacio bowed once again.

The crowd of dryads dispersed into the dark corners of the jungle, murmuring but obedient. Dawn was breaking, and they returned each to their own tree, to tend to it and water it as the morning ceremony required.

***

Solena cowered underneath a human-made bench that stood a few feet away from her tree, sheltered beneath its shade. A few children had come by to pelt her with mud and shout something about her being the "chosen one." More mockery, no doubt. Later that morning, a few adults had also come to jeer and yell angrily at her. They would not come too close for fear of being whipped by Solena's protecting tree.

Hers was a gum tree with smooth gray bark, envied by many, and possibly a greater cause of her unpopularity with many of the female dryads than her passion for all things human. A dryad's good looks were important, but even more important for securing a good mate was the beauty of the tree.

Finally, she climbed up from under the bench, picked up her hand mirror and looked at her tear-stained face. She was past the point of outraged sobbing, and now only a dull pain squeezed her heart, sending a slow but steady stream of tears from her green eyes.

Two slender branches stretched from the lower boughs towards her. Their grey shoots were like fingers, which held a hair brush and a curling iron. They worked her long orange-red hair into large airy curls as the rest of the tree swayed and rustled soothingly. The small circle of a hand mirror lying flat and useless on her lap reflected nothing but branches and small segments of sky between them.

She would not have been so upset by the taunts, but another terrible occurrence had happened in the night, and had brought her back to the foot of her tree in despair.

Solena was awakened from her gloomy reverie when another lithe branch tapped her on the shoulder and pointed to her right. A familiar figure was approaching. Normally she would have stood up and ran to meet him, but now she only muttered something and made a vague gesture with the mirror.

Anastacio was slightly surprised but not too taken aback by her condition.

"Why so sad, Sol? Tonight is the Orchid Festival — oh I see."

She slid over to make room for him on the bench, and they sat side by side.

"Tell me about it, child."

"It was Tilio... I waited for him..." she sobbed, "I had asked him to accompany me to the festival. He said he needed time to think..."

"That doesn't sound right. Why would he need time to think?"

"I realize now he was just stalling... But I thought... well... he had kissed me. He was the only one I thought might take me to the festival. He is very handsome and talented, isn't he? A great dancer!"

"I have seen much more handsome and talented dryads. He is nothing special," Anastacio replied with a wink. "So what happened then?"

"Then... several days passed, and last night I went to look for him... and found him lying asleep at the foot of his tree with some unsightly dryad. No doubt he will ask her to be his mate. Ugh, she was like a bag of mismatched coconuts, all lumpy and hairy."

"Then he has already punished himself, hasn't he?"

The slightest of smiles alighted on her lips, then she fell back to sobbing.

Anastacio sighed. "You make me wish for the four-hundredth time that I'd been born four hundred years later... Sol! This is nothing at all. It simply means fate has a different plan for you."

"But why? I want to find a mate more than anything... well, almost more than anything."

"Any you will. Fate has someone better in store for you, my dear. In the meantime, this old dryad is grateful for the time you spend with him."

"I will always have time for you, Anastacio," she said. "Even if I do find a mate, which is probably impossible. Do you want to see my new arrival?"

"I certainly do," he said. His dark eyes twinkled beneath their curtain of yellowing eyebrows. "If you would help me ascend to your celestial palace?"

Solena hastily wiped away her tears with the back of her hand and sprang up from the bench. Anastacio's climbing speed was no match for hers; he could only watch as she jumped up and gripped a branch, swung herself up, nearly ripping her flowery human summer dress as it snagged on a twig. She freed herself and continued the climb, leaping and gripping like a flying squirrel.

She was nearly obscured from his sight by a winding staircase of branches when she arrived at the tree house. He saw her take a second to survey it proudly, then she was inside, and a swing was lowered down to him. He sat on the wooden plank through which a rope had been threaded, and she worked quickly as the other end of the rope was threaded through a pulley system — like the tree house, it was one of her creations. The pulley was not truly necessary, for she could have just as easily pulled him up with the rope alone: she was the same size as an average human female, but being a dryad, had five times the strength.

Anastacio stepped onto one of the branches that supported the tree house and ducked inside. He found the usual chest of drawers filled with human clothes. On top of it was a stack of magazines, which ranged from the likes of Human and Cosmological to Motorcycle Monthly and Martial Arts Enthusiast. However, Narcissism Carnival was her favorite. They often wrote about royalty of all kinds, and their stories were much more in-depth compared to, say Humans or WE.

Anastacio sighed, knowing it was not going to be easy to make her understand the nature of her mission. Solena was oblivious to him, rifling through another stack in the corner.

"Aha! Here it is!" she cried, brandishing a slightly dog-eared Narcissism Carnival.

"Where did you get that?" he asked.

"Traded it from a city woman."

What she usually meant by this was that she stole the magazine and replaced it with some other offering, such as fruit or flowers from the forest. Dryads are forbidden to steal outright, and it was said that they lose their magical powers if they do.

They sat down on two damask cushions, and began to leaf through the glossy pages.

"That's Meryl Streep, she's supposedly an old actress for a human — just sixty!" she explained. She had a keen, childlike interest in all things to do with humans, especially with Hollywood or the British Royals. She wanted to know everything about Princess Diana and her tragic death, a sad human fairy tale. Princess Kate and Prince William's glamorous and drama-free life did not hold the same attraction.

Anastacio supposed that the time he spent with her was possibly her happiest because she loved sharing her human artefacts, and he was the only one who cared to indulge her interest. He himself had always loved the forest and was not eager to explore beyond it, but he felt ignited by her passion and understood the attraction that the humans' short, fragile, and dramatic lives held for her. Perhaps it was because they were practically the opposite of the dryads that they fascinated her so much.

"And that's Rodney Love," she continued, "Some sort of corporation guy. He's not bad looking but his story is pretty boring."

"Wait!" Anastacio said, laying his wrinkled hand over the image of the businessman-adventurer with a surfer's haircut and preventing her from flipping to the next page. "It was this man I wanted to talk to you about."

She looked up at him in surprise. "What about him?"

"He is the head of the Timber Corporation. The High Priest had a vision of this man. The vision told him that this Timber Corporation is planning to destroy our forest. This morning, at the Rite of the Great Tree we asked how to prevent the disaster from happening, and the Tree replied we must send someone to the humans to undermine their company from within and prevent them from invading our forest."

"Just one dryad?"

"Someone who knows more than any of us about the humans," he gave her a meaningful look.

She jumped up with a scream of excitement. "Me? Me? I was chosen?"

"Yes," he said, smiling. "But you were not chosen just so you could prance around in human clothes and play with their technological gadgets. You are meant to undermine the humans. Do you understand?"

"I'm not going to prance!" she cried. "I'm offended that you would think that."

"I didn't mean to say that you would prance," he corrected

himself, "but you know what I mean?'"

"Of course," she said, "They must be stopped from cutting our trees or we are all doomed."

"Exactly."

"But what if... it is not really the humans who are to blame?"

"I doubt that very much."

"Most humans are against cutting trees, or so I've read. They have these... protesters."

"Protesters!" he scoffed, "What do they ever accomplish? They act like would-be dryads, singing and dancing round the trees, but they don't have our powers, and they don't even have the power to sway other humans."

"But there are others," she said, "those who support what they call 'minorities' like dwarves, elves, animals, and us."

"Maybe so," he said, "I have heard of new human laws that encourage them to employ minorities. But I do not think this would help us. You must go disguised as a human. No one must suspect your true purpose. I will give you spells to help you blend in and gain their trust."

"But what exactly will I do?" she asked.

"You must... what's the human expression?.. Get a job!"

"So... I must live as a human?" she asked, not quite believing that her dream was coming true.

"Yes," he confirmed.

"Will you come with me?"

"I would not be of much help," he sighed. "You must go undetected, and you would best blend in on your own. But I will give you some spells... Do you have a blank piece of paper handy?"

She grew sad at the thought of parting, but she passed him a pure white sheet of paper.

"When you told me about those things they call resumes, I thought up a little spell."

He waved his hand over the paper, and strange blue markings appeared on it.

"What does this mean?" she asked, examining the strange marks, which looked like dryad runes rather than human writing.

"This resume will get you a job. It will look like the perfect resume to a human, no matter what kind of a job you're applying for."

"That's amazing!" Solena cried. "I always wanted to work in

marketing. It seems very glamorous. I just wish you could come with me… but I know you'd miss your beloved forest."

"I think you will miss it too," he noted.

"Well, maybe a little."

She climbed down from her tree house later that night, having packed her favorite reading materials and human clothes into a small suitcase. Anastacio had already left; she didn't want him to see her off for fear of becoming too emotional. Here, at least she had one friend, but in the human world perhaps she wouldn't have any. She pushed the thought away.

The usual forest noises surrounded her. The crescendo calls of nighttime birds and insects blended with the exploding crackle of frog song. Solena sighed, a flood of regret washing over her at the thought of leaving, at the thought of how little others would miss her, or she them. But the human world awaited. Aside from small forays into the cities and villages, she had never truly experienced what it was like to live among them.

Solena had never been very interested in magic, but there was one magical spell at which she excelled. As she walked away, she began changing into a human form.

The green eyes of a dryad would be a tell-tale sign. They were round and luminous like a cat's. But that was not the only point in which they differed from human eyes: her eyes seemed to have a life of their own, as if one could see green leaves stirring gently in the breeze within them. Her skin was of a pale green hue, and her hair bright orange.

As she walked on, she changed her eyes and hair to dark brown, her skin to olive tones that were natural to humans of that region. Wearing a human summer dress, she walked away from her forest without looking back.

2 FATHERS AND SONS
(AD 2013)

Gregory Love was dozing over the newest issue of *Narcissism Carnival* when Rodney came into the office. It was a vast office, somewhat gloomy, housed in one of those New England buildings from the times of Nathaniel Hawthorne, but with a touch of playful summer light filtering through the maples outside the picture windows. The old man in the throne-like Victorian armchair looked slightly too small for it, shrunken as he was with age. He also looked insane because he was dressed in a suit that was several decades out of date, but Rodney was used to these eccentricities.

Rodney Love, heir to a billion-dollar empire, had flown in on a red-eye from L.A. to Boston, summoned by his father without any explanation. Not that this was unusual. The main office of the Timber Corporation was in Boston, while Rodney always preferred living on the West Coast. After some wheedling, he had been allowed to open some offices in California, where he enjoyed looking, feeling, and acting like the prototypical surfer boy. However, Gregory Love insisted that they talk face to face whenever there was anything vital or even not-so-vital to be discussed.

Rodney looked at his father, and a sudden emotional pang shot through his entire body. The old man never used to *doze*.

Just as he decided to leave — he didn't want to embarrass his father by catching him napping — the wrinkled eyelids lifted, revealing a clear, cold, alert gaze. Suddenly, Gregory Love no longer looked pitifully small for his chair. He looked like some kind of scheming, covetous gnome-king.

"Thank you, Rodney..." he said with his usual wry tone, "for not disgracing me as much as I thought you would."

"Always a pleasure," Rodney replied, tugging the brim of an invisible hat.

"You actually spent some of the interview talking about business and only a small part talking about your new age nonsense."

"What do you mean by new age nonsense?" Rodney asked, settling into one of the uncomfortable wooden chairs that faced the gargantuan desk.

"You know very well. All this stuff about 'aligned with your destiny.' You sound like a recovering alcoholic. I can't believe you would spout such hippie crap in front of reporters. You must get it from your mother."

"Right, I get all my hippie delusions from Mom, who runs charity fashion shows to benefit starlets who are suffering because they are not quite yet superstars. For the last time, Dad, I'm helping to run this billion-dollar company of yours... and at times I even enjoy it: I'm hardly a hippie."

"You sure like to act like one. Hell, what do I know? Maybe that's the image you're trying to sell, and maybe it's even working. I don't know anymore. It's all about the internet and public relations and yoga retreats these days... Maybe it's good that I'm on my way out."

Rodney approached the desk and leaned almost beseechingly towards his father. "I know you think a lot of it is hippie crap, but there are some real things out there that could help you. Some remedies from the Amazon—"

"Haven't you eaten enough shit already?" the old man said sharply, "Remember the 'muscle enhancers?'"

"I was nineteen then. Can't we get over that?" Rodney remonstrated, slumping back into his chair.

His father was rarely this rude and obnoxious in front of anyone but himself, Rodney knew. Even now, maybe it was the cancer talking, but deep inside he knew that his father always spoke to him like this, without respect. Despite being just over thirty, Rodney felt he was doomed to be perpetually a shiftless teenager in his father's eyes.

Gregory shifted the topic abruptly.

"The reason I called you here is the time machine."

Rodney grinned excitedly. "Is it ready?"

"A smaller version of it, anyway. I'd like you to fly down to Colombia and give it a test run. Do you think you could take a few days off from sun tanning and whoring?"

"I'm your man!" Rodney said, brightening up.

He had supposed his father had him fly down there only to have someone to grumble at. He had done it before!

"By the way, Dad, I haven't done any whoring in many years," he noted, "In fact, there's a wonderful girl—"

"Just don't screw up," Gregory added, raising a gnarled finger and pointing it at Rodney, "This is expensive equipment. Cut down the lumber, bring it here, and don't get sidetracked into any adventures."

"I still don't think it's the most brilliant idea: lugging huge pieces of timber here from another time period. Seems like a waste of a time machine."

"It may be the only way to get timber since these damned environmental laws have been instated."

"I thought you were going to do something more exciting, like go back to your beloved '20s."

"I may yet, my boy. I wish I could have lived in a time when big businesses could buy human babies and make them into soap for all anyone cared. There wasn't any TV or internet to inform anyone."

"That's disgusting!"

"Well, I exaggerate," Gregory added conciliatingly, "But not by much."

Rodney allowed himself to heave a deep, long-suffering sigh only after he left the room. *I know you don't see very much of yourself in me, father. But I'm more like you than you think. I can be a high-stakes player too, and I'll prove it to you. I'll prove it by saving your life.*

3 A DEPRESSED DRYAD
(AD 2013)

There is nothing like a depressed dryad to drain the life out of a place. The dryad's aura being much larger than that of humans, her despondent condition permeated the entire room, and other clients of the little cafe, no matter how lovely their day had been, felt a slow flood of despair oozing into their hearts. Of course, the fortune teller felt it most of all.

It was a type of establishment fairly common in L.A., a cafe with a vaguely eastern flavour, decorated with fat Buddhas and fantastic dragons with fake rubies for eyes. The spicy smell of Indian chai filled the air, and the owner, a plump, friendly and Buddah-like Chinese woman oversaw everything with her shrewd gaze.

Solena sat at a small, wobbly table in the corner, facing Gaby, the middle-aged fortune teller who looked like a cross between a gypsy and a department store manager. The mystic's hands were burdened by giant rings, her neck decorated with colourful beads and strange pendants, but her sensible JC Penney top contradicted these occult symbols.

"What kind of divination would you like to do?" she asked matter-of-factly.

"I don't know," Solena shrugged, "Whatever you think is best."

The fortune teller was her last resort. She had used up all of Anastacio's spell to get a mid-level marketing job in the Timber Corporation. Now it had been six months, and the head of the department, an unpleasant human with a body odour problem, simply saw her as one of the cogs in the wheel or whatever it was humans said. No matter how much excellent work she did, Mr.

Peters did not acknowledge it.

"Tea leaves," Gaby said decisively. "I think it's the most suitable for you. Can you bring us a cup of tea?" she asked the proprietress.

Solena drank the steaming black tea, liking the taste, though it was different from brewed maté leaves to which she was accustomed. The leaves on the bottom formed a fairly regular pattern.

"That's not going to work," the fortune teller said. "Where are you from, dear?"

"A small village in Venezuela."

"Ah, that's why. This type of tea divination will not work for you. Cecilia, do you have any mate leaves?"

Solena grew even more despondent, and a long-haired young man sitting at a nearby table suddenly felt he could not handle the weight of his guilt stemming from his inaction while those corporate assholes were destroying the planet.

"I can't take it anymore!" he cried, briefly attracting the attention of all the other depressed patrons. He quickly paid his bill and ran off to enlist in a Greenpiss (an organization named after an inside St Patrick's day joke) expedition against whaling.

The cafe owner handed Solena a cup of maté, brewed the traditional Argentine way, the dryad noted, in hot but not boiling water. She quickly drank it, savouring the familiar bitter taste.

"Now I have something to work with," Gaby said.

She looked at the wild patterns of the leaves.

"You're connected in a way with those leaves and with trees," she said in her matter of fact department store manager voice. "You're some kind of environmental activist?"

"In a sense," Solena smiled.

"You have a big project in mind, but it's not taking off."

"Right," Solena said, surprised.

She trusted the magic of dryads, but did not know humans could command magical energies as well. She could not tell whether the fortune teller was using the human art they called logic or just picking up vibrations from the air. Either way, it was impressive.

"Something is holding you back. You are depressed, my dear."

"I've been in the same job for several months," Solena replied, "I *have* to get promoted. I can't afford to lose any more time."

"But there's something else too, isn't there?"

Gaby peered into the tea leaves and saw something: an elongated shape flanked by two rounded shapes. "A man? And he's a real dick, by the looks of it."

Solena nodded. Her eyes seemed to grow bigger as they developed a moist glaze.

"Forget about him. Here, have a tissue, my dear. He was not right for you. The man you must seek is... well, he's not yet appeared..." she frowned at the swirling leaf pattern, "Oh, this is confusing. You sort of know him, but he has yet to appear in your life. You will know him at once, though he will not know you at first. But you have to be strong. You always have to be strong at the beginning of a relationship."

Solena sniffed into the tissue, nodding her agreement.

"Now, about that job, have you talked to your boss?"

"No." Solena sobbed, "I don't think he will listen. I'm just some Latina to him. He doesn't see I have better abilities than most of his people."

"Then you have to talk to the higher-up boss. And polish your resume, that never hurts. Bring me your resume next time, and I'll take a look at it. I used to work as an employment advisor."

"Really?"

"Yes, really. I don't know why people are always surprised to hear that. It's not that different from being a fortune teller."

"Okay, I'll bring it tomorrow," Solena said, somewhat stunned.

"And don't be depressed. You know what you should read? *Positive Attitude* by Teddy Goldman." She peered into the cup again, "And I think you're going on a cruise soon, so that'll be nice."

***

It was easy enough to find the fortune teller's recommended literature, *Positive Attitude*, in the self-help section. Solena devoured it in one sitting, and soon she craved more of the same. She realized she had just discovered a new kind of literature, perhaps even better than her previous favorites. Here there were no stories of moody heiresses and treacherous playboys. These weren't stories at all. They were things you could use in real life, like secret weapons or magical spells.

Solena soon returned to the book store and found that Teddy Goldman had written books on practically any subject, from the secretes of Thai kickboxing to workplace strategies. He had started out as a martial arts champion, then began to gain fame as a fitness trainer, and finally as a self-help writer. And from what Solena could tell, his self-help writing really was helpful.

Solena began to jog almost every day. She had previously seen no sense in doing a workout while living in the forest, although it was a human rite that intrigued her. Climbing trees, running, and dancing had been quite enough to keep her active, to have that feeling of immeasurable strength coursing through her body. Now that she lived as a human, it was impossible to be active at a dryad level throughout the day. Now she had a full time job, and there were meetings to be sat through, reports to be written, applications to be approved. It seemed never-ending. So in the evenings she once again turned to another Teddy Goldman book on personal fitness and went for a jog or a bike ride followed by calisthenics training.

The fortune teller was also true to her word and made some amazing changes to the resume, "inventing" a few volunteer positions here and there, but mostly just re-wording everything into the latest business-speak. Suddenly everything Solena did was "dynamic" and "results-oriented," with specific numbers and statistics to prove her accomplishments.

After a few weeks, she felt she was ready to be promoted.

***

She knew Rodney Love would be visiting their branch sometime that afternoon, so she sat around in the lobby, stalking him, a file with her resume and all her latest work tucked under her arm. It was tricky business, because trying to avoid Mr. Peters, the foul-smelling marketing boss, was an art in itself. He had some kind of sixth sense that told him when employees were slacking off. The lobby was very open, with no hiding places, and somehow she thought crouching behind a plant would not make the right impression on one of the major players in the company.

So she sat on a bench, trying to look busy reading her files, looking up now and again.

He appeared, quite alone and in a good mood by the looks of it, striding across the lobby with a spring in his step.

"Mr. Love! Mr. Love!" Solena shouted, hurrying towards him before he had a chance to get into an elevator.

He was even better looking in real life than he had been in the magazine, she noted as he stopped and turned toward her. The features were no longer glossed over with makeup, and she could see an interesting pattern of fine lines that gave charming nuances to his expressions.

It suddenly hit her: the fortune teller's words. She would know him at once — of course, because she had seen his picture in the magazine! And he would not know her. Not yet, anyway.

"Hello, Mr. Love," she said, "Sorry to intrude on your time, but I work here at Timber Marketing. My name is Solena Rodriguez."

"Very glad to meet you," he smiled charmingly, "Please call me Rodney. What can I do for you?"

"I have some great marketing ideas, which I would like to show you, and I would like to apply for a position on your executive team," she blurted out, trying to project a "positive" energy as the Teddy Goldman book had taught her, "Here is my resume and the marketing copy."

He took the file from her and glanced through it, though his eyes kept straying upwards to study her face.

"If you don't mind my asking, where are you from?"

"A small town you've probably never heard of, somewhere on the border between Columbia and Venezuela…" she replied vaguely.

"But your accent, which sounds lovely by the way — I just can't place it. It's not even the accent, it's the intonation. Very musical."

"Well, I am also half… French," she improvised. It wouldn't do to tell him it was a Dryad accent.

"Do you like French food then?" Rodney suddenly asked, "Now you'd think a guy like me is only good at counting profits, but I can cook some fine examples of French cuisine. You see, my own ancestry goes back to France. Would you like to join me at my house tonight?"

She remembered Teddy Goldman' advice from the book *How to Get a Man and Keep Him.*

"I'm afraid I can't," she said, "No offense, but I hardly even know you."

This was a stunning blow to Rodney Love. He tried to look furtively in one of the mirrored columns of the lobby.

"Yes, you are very gorgeous, and there is no food stuck between your teeth," she said with mischievous humour, "That is not the issue, Mr. Love— Rodney. I'm just a woman who respects her own boundaries."

He suddenly laughed. "All right then. Friends first?"

"Yes," she said.

"Can I take you out for dinner as a friend?"

"Yes, that would be very nice. And what about my work?"

"We'll look at it over dinner, of course."

It was then that her supervisor, the body-odorous Mr. Peters had to show up. As soon as the elevator door opened to reveal his pear-shaped form, he stomped his foot as if about to discipline a misbehaving dog.

"That's where you are, Solena! I haven't seen you in the office all day. Do you think I pay you to sip lattes and make chit chat with other employees?"

Rodney had his back to the man, and he slowly turned towards him with a smile.

"I'm sorry, I didn't realize *I* was an employee of *yours*, Mr. Peters," he said.

"Oh! Mr. Love, I didn't realize it was you." Peters instantly started sweating, which did not help the body odour in the least.

"That's all right. I was just going over some marketing proposals with Solena. She has done a fine job, and I partly credit you with developing such a fine employee. Keep up the good work, Peters!"

"I intend to, Mr. Love," Peters smiled obsequiously.

"Oh, and I hope you won't mind me stealing Solena from your department. I think she'll be more useful to me in executive."

4 ANOTHER DAY AT THE OFFICE (AD 2013)

Solena heeded the advice in the relationship book and made her presence somewhat scarce as far as Rodney Love was concerned. They were already working together, and he was also relentless in asking her out. She usually accepted only one out of three invitations, invoking the right to work out in the evenings. And the more she avoided him, the more he chased her. Now it was too late to invent a fictional boyfriend. She was afraid of where this was going, for the human was so genuine and trusting, it was a shame to take advantage of his good nature.

"I know you need your exercise to keep that gorgeous body of yours fit," he said one day as they were both leaving the office, "How about I join you? I'll just run beside you, and you won't even know I'm there. You can still do exactly the same workout."

She smiled, appreciating his effort, "All right. Meet me by my place at six thirty."

She never let him inside the house in all the six weeks that they had been dating. It would be just the kind of opportunity he needed to seduce her, and Teddy's book clearly said she must drag out the courtship for as long as possible. And what then, she wondered. Would she take the final step? Can she stop him from cutting down the forest without completely betraying him? The book, of course, said nothing on that subject.

On the one hand, she was happy: this was something like a fantasy she had dreamed when leafing through her magazines. She was beautiful and wore all the latest fashions and had a human boyfriend. Not just any human, but one of the handsomest, richest, and most glamorous men in the world. As if that wasn't enough, he even had a charming personality.

On the other hand, he was very likely behind the threat that the prophesy spoke of. Would there come a time when she will have to choose sides? In any case, that time was not yet approaching.

When the red convertible pulled up to her apartment complex, she was already waiting outside, doing some stretches. She had resolved not to feel guilty; after all, it was not her fault this man found her attractive, and that she found him not only attractive but also fun and friendly, perhaps the first friend she has made since Anastacio.

"I'm ready to go," he said. "Keep in mind, I trained with an Olympic track coach."

He didn't wear any kind of aerodynamic or high-tech jogging gear, just a simple pair of shorts and a t-shirt. For a millionaire, he was pretty down-to-earth.

"Should I be intimidated?" she asked.

"I know you're never intimidated, you Amazon. Just don't get mad if I outrun you."

She laughed. "That will never happen."

Solena set a good pace. She did not expect him to keep up for long: her previous workout buddies usually found some sort of excuse not to run with her again because she always unintentionally showed them up. Most humans could not run at her pace for even half of her usual distance without complete exhaustion.

Rodney jogged by her side, making jokes, his breath regular and steady. They had made it deep into the park, following a gravel path lined with palm trees. Solena thought of running for five more miles just to see if he could keep up, but she remembered Rule Number Three: Lose the small battles in order to win the big battle. That was actually from one of the combat books, but she felt that somehow it applied here. Besides, she was enjoying this running side by side. The rhythm of their feet on the path keeping perfect time together, their legs straining and pushing back and flying forward at exactly the same moment. Their breathing was one and the same.

Solena began to slow down as she neared a familiar tree, the four mile marker. He slowed his speed to match hers.

"Are you getting tired already?" he teased.

"No, I'm just letting you rest."

"I'm fine. In fact, I'll race you to that tree. Ready?"

He sprinted forward, and she followed with her usual ease. A burst of energy, and she was running beside him full-out. The tree was only about sixty feet away. Solena could have easily passed him, but she slowed down a jot, pretending to struggle, and Rodney sped up even more, passing ahead of her.

Just as he was a few steps away from the large palm tree, he suddenly stopped, clutching his side.

"Damn cramp!" he shouted.

Solena was running too quickly to slow down at this point, and she made it past the tree by sheer force of inertia.

She jogged back to him, as he slowed down to a walk now, still holding his hand to his side as if in pain.

"That's it, no more running for me today."

"You are a good actor," she said, folding her hands across her chest in a defiant attitude.

"What do you mean?"

"You let me win, didn't you?"

"No, not at all."

She glared at him.

"Even if I did, it would have been the gentlemanly thing to do," he shrugged nonchalantly.

Solena let out a scream of frustration. Somehow, he must have known she was letting him win, and that was why he took it out of her hands. He lost, yet he obviously did not feel emasculated because he remained in control of the end result of the race. She had been completely outmanoeuvred, and the part of her that wasn't furious was rather impressed.

"Now I know you did it," she said, "You're such a jerk, Rodney!"

"Let me make it up to you," he responded readily, "Let me take you out to dinner. And then we'll go dancing."

"Oh, so you think your devilish cunning will be rewarded with a dinner and dance date?"

"I hope," he said with that sweet look in his eye that was impossible to resist.

Dancing... it was one of the dryad skills she had never quite mastered. Come to think of it, she had not completely mastered any dryad skills. Dance, music, magic. She had never had the confidence to completely throw herself into these arts. The only one she had been really good at was climbing. Yet on that day, she suddenly felt it was all within her power.

When they danced amid the bright quickly-changing lights it was like the music she had heard in mountain villages she had sneaked into, the human music she adored. Now it was ten times louder, with a stronger, faster beat, and she found herself falling into it, letting the music take hold of her and effortlessly transform her feelings into dance.

...so much so that when he dropped her off at her apartment and asked if he could come in for a drink, she said yes.

Her place was inundated with luxuriant potted plants. It was just a small one-bedroom, and the living room and kitchen were not separated by anything save a few leafy vines that hung from the ceiling. There was a bookshelf with a few magazines, biographies of actors and actresses, classic novels, and combat and fitness training manuals by Teddy Goldman. Of course, she had prudently hidden away the relationship book. Solena hardly ever read the celebrity news anymore, focusing mostly on self-improvement, physical and intellectual.

"Jane Austen, huh?" Rodney picked up a random book from the middle of the shelf.

She shrugged, "Just trying to be well-rounded. When I was young, all I cared about were fashion and gossip magazines, but I've been reading a lot of classics lately."

"And Teddy Goldman!" he cried. "Of course, I could smell him all over you. I always suspected you liked a manly man."

"Actually, I think I've been trying to become one," she said with a laugh.

"You'll never succeed," he teased, and stepped closer to hold her, "You have a very feminine..." he wrapped his arms around her waist, "...body."

"Do I?"

He kissed her. "Am I... almost as manly as Teddy Goldman?" he asked.

She giggled. "Yes, almost."

He took it as a signal and picked her up and carried her into the bedroom. There was moonlight and a touch of golden lambency from the streetlights outside her window. A siren sounded briefly in the distance, and then there was silence. The only thing they could hear was each other's breath.

It was amazing, the human ritual of removing clothes... Dryads did not wear many garments, so they never took as much time divesting as humans did, from what Solena had seen in the movies. He lay her down on the bed and lowered the shoulder straps on her dress. She pulled him towards her and began to unbutton his shirt. Then his undershirt formed another pleasant obstacle. He grinned, happy to help in her efforts. Layer by layer, he came unwrapped, more and more of his skin revealed itself, bronzed by the California sun and illuminated by the moon.

Soon their breath and their rhythm matched once again, just like when they had been running, only better.

She had felt that pleasure with a dryad, but only because she had liked his looks and given in to impulse. This was different. She felt she knew this human almost better than she knew herself. She knew that behind his façade of wanting to be in charge of everything and everyone, he had a kind, gentle soul.

That was why she knew he was going to be moving so slowly and carefully, all of his great strength focused on giving her pleasure.

There was another sensation, aside from the physical, of ethereal energy flowing into her. Maybe this was true love, and this was what she was meant to do? Unite the humans and the dryads. It felt so right.

That night, she dreamed she was walking through the forest with Anastacio.

"What should I do?" she asked.

"I don't know. I'm not really Anastacio, I'm just a part of your psyche."

She looked around at the forest. The trees seemed hazy, and she realized she was in a dream.

"I don't care!" she said, "Somebody's got to advise me."

"I say wait and see. You don't know what this Rodney fellow is up to. The more you learn, the more you'll know about how to stop him."

"Right now I haven't got a clue."

"Did you tell the real Anastacio you're involved with the human? You could try to send him a message. Maybe he will have some advice."

"I... don't know."

His image seemed to blur as if she was seeing it through an aquarium. She wanted to talk with him more, but the dream ended, and she was awake beside a beautiful, peacefully sleeping man.

The next day, they drove to work in different cars, deciding it was not yet time to let their relationship out in the open. Solena arrived just a few minutes after Rodney, and he greeted her in a casual tone, adding a little wink when no one was looking.

"How are you doing today?" he asked.

"Just wonderful."

"Good. I have a little surprise for you."

"Oh?"

"I want to introduce you to our newest employee, Tyler."

He showed her into a spacious office, and Solena stopped in the doorway. A mud-coloured alligator lay on an inclined settee behind a desk. His peculiar perch allowed him to extend his stubby arms toward the keyboard and mouse. From what she could see, he was actually calculating data and arranging it into pie charts. Solena uttered a small exclamation of surprise.

"What? So I'm a minority! Big deal!" the alligator said in a southern accent. "The assistant vice president is a dark elf, and nobody says nothing."

"Actually, the assistant VP is human. Although I admit he does look like Lord Voldemort," Rodney said with a smirk. His secretary was approaching with a bundle of files under her arm. "Well, I'll let you two get acquainted. It seems I have another crisis to deal with."

"Okay, I have to ask," Solena said when they were left alone, "You are an alligator, right?"

"Last time I checked."

"How are you able to *talk*?"

"Practice," the alligator shrugged its scaly shoulders, "anything is possible with practice. That's the Teddy Goldman method."

"You read him too?"

"Oh yeah, great stuff. The only human I respect."

"Still, I can't believe they put you in executive," Solena mused.

"I should take offense at that. Sure, I'm not as pretty as you, but—"

"That's not what I mean. They usually just have white guys here, and a very small percent of minorities."

The alligator grinned, a bloodcurdling sight.

"You know that saying, 'so-and-so is a shark'? Well, they obviously value sharks around here, and the only thing better than a shark is a croc! A *real* croc. Imagine you're negotiating a deal with me: I've always got a great argument that will top any of yours."

She raised an eyebrow. "You can bite me in half?"

"Exactly," Tyler affirmed.

"I don't even have to say it. They feel it in the pit of their stomachs. I wouldn't actually do it unless someone really pushed my buttons, but it's some sort of primal fear that most humans have."

A knocking was heard on the door, and a balding, stressed-out clerk hurriedly entered with an envelope.

"For you, Mr. Alligator."

"Wait for an answer after you knock!" the alligator yelled, "Next time I'll bite your head off if you walk in unannounced."

"Yes sir!" the clerk hurried out of the office.

"Though I don't mind if I encourage it," the alligator said with a grin. "But you're not afraid like the others. You are not..."

"Shhh!" she hissed, slamming the door shut. "We can talk about that later."

"It's all right, all the offices here are soundproof. I was going to say, you aren't human, are you?"

"No."

"You're in disguise, and that can mean only one thing. You're a dryad on a mission."

"How do you know that?" she asked breathlessly. If the alligator was completely loyal to Rodney Love, her cover would be blown. "Maybe I'm just an elf who doesn't want to 'come out'?"

"No, you smell like a dryad. A dryad working for a timber company... Seems a little suspicious..."

"And you? Are you on a mission?"

"Let's just say alligators have their sources too. The Alligator Alliance keeps a watchful eye on human activity. Maybe we can help each other when the time comes."

"The time for what?"

"I don't know. All I know is there is a very important project. Rodney has not disclosed it to you yet, but I have a feeling he will. Just don't tell Maxwell, even if he's not a dark elf. I don't trust that creep. Although, we can't be sure that he's not the one who cooked up this whole scheme in the first place..."

"What scheme are you talking about?" Solena demanded, "I want to see some proof!"

"Proof, huh?" the alligator reclined in his settee, somehow managing to balance on his tail. "All right!"

He bent towards the computer screen once again. Instead of the pie charts, he now brought up a different file, one that was labeled "Time Boat."

Solena saw pictures of the boat, which looked like a small white pleasure boat that a billionaire might own for personal use. Then there was the diagram of a bigger boat and of a barge for transporting timber.

"These are supposed to be time boats?" she asked the alligator.

"The others aren't built yet, but this little one is going to be tested... by us!"

"You're joking?"

"Tyler does not joke! Except on rare occasions. Look here!"

He opened up another document that looked like a detailed itinerary for travel to Columbia, and thence... to the year 1694. Solena kept rereading the line:

'Departure: May 16, 2013 Arrival: May 16, 1694'

"What do you say to that?" the alligator asked.

"Well, a fortune teller did tell me I was going on a cruise..."

5 ANCESTRY (AD 1694)

Roger de St. Amour was the most notorious Sorbonne-educated pirate that ever sailed the stormy waters of the Atlantic. Even if erudition was not usually the most prized quality for a captain of a two-masted brig, he knew that curiosity, coupled with a quick and disciplined mind did not hurt at all, and a learning opportunity could very quickly lead to a financial opportunity.

The things he saw in his spyglass told him there was something to learn, and therefore most likely, a profit to be made, if he moved quickly. He could not believe his eyes, yet he saw men who looked like Englishmen cutting down giant trees a few dozen feet from the shoreline. Their attire and the tools they used were unlike anything he had ever seen.

The *Belle Catherine* was about to drop anchor in a sheltered cove several scores of miles north of Santa Marta, and St Amour had expected to find the place as pristine as usual.

"Lieutenant Jackson!" he cried.

"Here, sir!" his Jamaican lieutenant approached. He too sensed something was about to unfold, and had already hung a machete and a cutlass crosswise on his back. The man himself looked like a deadly weapon despite his calm demeanour. He was all muscle, six foot four, with a chiselled face that gazed at everything with fearless indifference.

"We will go ashore. Prepare the longboat."

"Yes sir," Jackson said in his usual calm and dignified tones.

St Amour was about to call for his second lieutenant but for a moment could not recall the man's name. The second lieutenants replaced each other so quickly, with some unfortunate accident always befalling the man who occupied that unlucky rank. It was not as privileged a position as that of first lieutenant, but St Amour knew that no one would dare vie for the position of first lieutenant because Jackson would certainly see to it that the foolhardy contender, rather than himself, met with an unfortunate accident. Jackson was a runaway slave, an African descendant born in the colonies, far from the refinements of the Sorbonne, but St Amour realized the man had a natural aptitude for command; he quickly taught him navigation and promoted him within a year.

"What was the name of that fellow?" the captain muttered, "The Irishman... O'Malley?!" he tried.

"Sir?" The second lieutenant appeared promptly before him, wearing a ridiculously wide-brimmed sombrero that protected his pale, freckled face from the merciless tropical sun.

"Lieutenant O'Malley, I'm leaving you in charge of the ship while I go ashore. Have an attack squad stand at the ready. If you hear gunfire, send them to assist us."

"Aye, sir." O'Malley went off at once to select the men who would have to back up the shore party.

St Amour did not trust O'Malley very much, but then again, he trusted almost none of his crew. The ones he did trust included Jackson along with six of the men who had sailed with him since *Belle Catherine*'s first voyage. One of these was a fierce Mexican, Carracha, the others were Frenchmen intensely loyal to their captain. After seven years of sailing the Atlantic and the Caribbean, almost none of his original French crew remained.

His loyal sailors rowed him to shore within minutes, and St Amour jumped gracefully into the gentle surf. Jackson stepped down very lightly for a man of his size and looked around.

"There is no boat by which they could have come," he said.

"I know, it is odd," the captain replied, "It seems incredible these Englishmen would have made their way here by land without being massacred. Something very unusual is going on here. We must be careful."

A strangely loud and obnoxious buzzing was coming from inland. Some of the French sailors crossed themselves.

"Come on then!" St Amour cried, seeing them hesitate, "There are men over there, I saw them clearly enough. It cannot be anything unnatural."

The pirates did not have to try very hard to hide their presence. The closer they came to the Englishmen, the louder the noise until it grew almost unbearable.

"Softly now," St Amour commanded, though he had to shout to be heard.

The pirates took their places behind various trees and observed.

Several of the crew crossed themselves again: the Englishmen were cutting down wood with strange instruments that looked like saws, except that they moved as if of their own free will. It was the saws that made the terrible noise as they sank swiftly into the tree trunks.

St Amour and Jackson were hiding behind a giant redwood.

"What shall we do, sir?" the lieutenant asked.

"My first thought was to ambush them, but I wish to find out more about them or we could be adventuring our persons needlessly. Do you see those fellows in green?"

He pointed to two men with what looked like giant muskets.

"I have never seen such trinkets."

"Perhaps it is best to talk to them," said St Amour, "Follow me."

He stepped from behind the tree and walked boldly towards the tree-cutters.

"Timber!" one of the men cried, and a giant tree tottered, falling irrevocably and terrifyingly towards the pirates.

Captain Roger de St Amour nearly met his end at that moment. He saw Jackson leap aside like a wild panther. He felt a branch sweep down within an inch of his face, and he sprang away just in time, rolling to the ground beside his lieutenant. He dusted himself off, and Jackson did the same, looking unperturbed.

"Ahoy!" St Amour cried, leaping over the fallen trunk and striding toward the surprised group.

The men in green uniform trained their strange muskets on him at once. A blond young man in an undershirt and sand-coloured breeches cut off above the knee held up his hand.

"No shooting, boys," he cautioned, "Remember, we don't want to kill somebody's great-grandfather."

Descending from a small rise, he approached the captain slowly, but when he got close enough to see his face, he stopped and stared, blatantly caught off guard.

"He looks like he could be *my* great-grandfather," he muttered.

St Amour did not see the likeness between himself and the stranger in undergarments, for he had never had much time for gazing in mirrors since he left France. His crewmen, however, had the distinct impression that they were looking at twins, save the only difference that their captain's hair was jet black instead of blond.

"I am Captain Roger de St Amour!" he said in flawless English, "From the sound of your accent, you are American colonials. I wonder what brings you here?"

"We're felling trees, as you see," the blond man replied. "My name is Rodney Love. And you're right, I am American."

"I am curious, by whose permission are you here? Have you made truce with the Spanish?"

"My guards are permission enough."

"Are those weapons of yours very powerful?" St Amour asked with feigned naïveté.

"Maybe you'd like a demonstration?" the man laughed.

"Preferably not on a live target," St Amour said quickly.

"Gary, Cal, show him what you've got," the blond man signalled his guards.

They aimed at a nearby tree trunk, and both guns fired together. St Amour stood frozen in awe, though his mind was already racing: the muskets kept firing without having to be reloaded. They struck up a horrendous racket, and the previous noise of the saws was nothing compared to it. The shooting continued for half a minute until the tree was thoroughly riddled with holes.

"*Sacre bleu!*" muttered the French pirates.

"*Madre de Dios,*" said Carracha.

Even Jackson opened his mouth in amazement.

"Well, Captain St Amour? What do you think of our permission to stay on this land?"

St Amour gave him his most charming smile, "You are right, Monsieur. You have all the permission you need. Carry on! It was a pleasure meeting you, but now we must retire to our ship."

"Have a nice day," Rodney Love said, grinning.

The pirates retreated cautiously, not turning their backs to the dreadful contraptions and the brawny men who wielded them. When they thought they were out of range, they breathed easier and hurried to their boat. It was only when they were on the beach that they heard a cry behind them.

"Hold on, sir!" It was one of the lumberjacks, running clumsily after them. "Mr. Love wants to invite you to dinner."

6 A FEAST IN THE JUNGLE (AD 1694)

"Do you not find it peculiar, Captain, that my name, Love, is the exact translation of your name from French?"

"Not exact!" St Amour corrected, "You forgot the 'Saint'."

"Yeah," Rodney Love smiled, "I'll bet 'Saint' was removed in tribute to American practicality."

They sat around a tall fire, using some newly cut logs as benches. On Rodney's left hand side was a wiry little man who seemed full of pent-up energy. He had been introduced as Stanley Pitchard, a lawyer. St Amour was inwardly laughing and contemplating of how little use the lawyer would be to Mr. Love in only an hour's time. Just after he had accepted the invitation to dinner, he had swiftly scribbled a note to O'Malley to be ready to attack upon his signal. He took only Jackson with him to dinner, and the black giant sat proudly beside him, eyeing everything with curiosity, an unusual state for him to be in.

"Rodney, I really would advise you not to go into particulars regarding our... let us say, our origins," the little man advised.

"It's all right, Stanley," Rodney said, "Captain St Amour is our guest, and possibly even a relative."

"I'm just saying, Rod. You brought me here for legal advice, and I am giving it."

"I do appreciate it, Stanley."

On Rodney's right hand side sat a beautiful woman. St Amour guessed that she was at least part native, though she wore the same strange clothes as the others. She seemed troubled by something.

"If you don't believe me, look in a mirror," Rodney went on. "Sol, you have one?"

The native woman reached into her bag and pulled out a tiny makeup mirror. She passed it to St Amour.

"Have a look at yourself, captain," she said.

St Amour looked at himself, then at the American. He muttered an oath, then looked into the mirror and up again.

"Well, perhaps you are a relative," St Amour said at length, "but if you seek my alliance, I must decline, relative or not. I work only for myself — and the government of France, simply because I do not wish to be hanged for piracy. I am a privateer."

"We seek no alliance," said the woman, "But it would be nice if you did not spread the news of our being here."

"Oh, I am no friend to the Spanish," said St Amour. "You may count on my discretion. If you wish to rob them of their trees, I do not object to it one bit. Though I am curious..." He looked around at the lumberjacks enjoying their meal and drinks. "With all your wonderful tools and weapons, why do you not launch a more profitable venture than the cutting of logwood?"

"Our venture is profitable." said Rodney, sounding almost hurt, "You see, where we come from there are laws against cutting too many trees. Here, we thought we could do so unnoticed by the authorities. So far, no one has ever spotted us, except for yourself."

"But is it not dreadfully expensive to transport all of these trees to America? Though doubtless you have thought of that too."

"We have," said the lawyer quickly, "but Mr. Love is not at leisure to disclose our methods of transportation."

"Stanley is right. I have to leave that question unanswered lest it put us in legal difficulties."

"I suspect your vehicle is another American invention similar to those machines. Perhaps I should change my allegiance one day and relocate to the colonies."

"Then our ways will part, Captain," said Jackson. "I will not be an ally to a land of slavers."

"I think you will find, Mr Jackson," Rodney Love said despite the almost palpable glare of his lawyer, "that in the future slavery will be outlawed in America, leaving only a bad memory. There will be equality for men and women of all races."

"I doubt that," said Jackson, "But even if the curse of slavery was to be lifted away in America, it would take root somewhere else.

Slavery will always emerge when the strong triumph over the weak."

"You have a good point," Rodney said. "We're lucky then to be the strong and not the weak."

Not for long, St Amour thought, grinning, knowing that O'Malley and the rest of the party whom he had ordered to encircle the Americans were preparing to surround the camp even as he spoke.

After the pirates departed and Solena wrapped herself up in her sleeping bag, she returned to her uneasy thoughts. They had never really left her but were always there at the back of her mind. How was she supposed to stop all this from happening? She understood now that the Timber Corporation would never dare to cut down their sacred forest in the present century and that the destruction of the dryads would occur in the past, their trees cut down before most of them had even been born. Was she not merely helping the humans by coming here?

She winced every time another tree was cut down, but at least she assuaged the act by asking forgiveness and giving thanks quietly each time to the tree. If only humans remembered that simple rule as they had in the olden days, she thought, they would perhaps think twice every time they took something from the forest.

"That was exciting," Rodney said, thrusting himself down into his sleeping bag beside her, "How many people can say they've met a real pirate? And I'm nearly convinced he's my ancestor. I'll have to review the old family tree when we get back."

"It was exciting meeting a real pirate," Solena had to admit, "but I'm not sure I liked your relative. He's not like the noble pirates of romance books. There's something very dodgy about him."

It was past midnight, and Solena awoke slowly, coaxed from sleep by a gradually building whisper. It was as if many voices were speaking quickly in succession, and each knew exactly when to follow the other.

"Solena... Solena... Solena..." three different voices murmured, "You must save us... you are the one who will save us... "

The trees all around were swaying more and more wildly, though there was not a hint of wind.

"The other humans approach..." the trees whispered, "They surround you... they will attack..."

Solena rose up on an elbow and softly touched Rodney's shoulder.

"Rod," she whispered as quietly as she could, "It's the pirates.

They're going to attack us."

Rodney opened his eyes. It took him a few seconds to situate himself in the rainforest and to let her words sink in.

He saw to his despair that Gary, the guard who was supposed to be on watch, sat by the fire drowsily nodding off to sleep, heedless of the creeping shadowy forms of the pirates. The riotous calls of monkeys and other forest creatures drowned out the sound of the pirates' approach.

"Goddammit," Rodney whispered, reaching for his glock into the pack that lay beside him.

He fired a shot into the air, and the whole camp sprang to life. But it was too late: before Gary had a chance to raise his sub-machine gun, a pirate tackled him from behind. Gary was trained in hand-to-hand combat, so he quickly recovered, wrestled the pirate off, and got to his feet, but by this time St Amour's lieutenant had appeared from the dense forest cover and snatched up the coveted weapon.

Wanting to finish off the guard, Jackson pressed the trigger, but the gun did not fire. He had to reverse it to club one of the approaching lumberjacks on the head, and then tried hurriedly to find out what went wrong. There was not powder pan and no flint that he could see. He looked at the thing more carefully, and by luck his finger found the safety switch. He pressed it experimentally, then pulled the trigger again. The gun went off in a multi-shot volley, nearly staggering him backwards.

The other machine gun began to fire too as a guard fought for control of it against three of pirates.

Rodney aimed his pistol at an approaching dark shape and fired, but the shape sprang aside. He was sure he had still hit his mark, but the man stopped only for a second, and in the light of the dying fires Rodney saw that he had shot none other than St Amour himself. The captain clutched his left arm and shouted a French oath. He raised his own pistol and fired directly at Rodney.

Solena saw all this happen in a few seconds from the corner of her eye. She had no time to help Rodney because a horrid-looking pirate with an unkempt mop of gray hair advanced towards her with a cutlass. She had no weapon at all.

"Surrender, *ma belle!*" the pirate growled.

Before the pirate knew what was happening, she stepped to the outside of his blade, gripped his wrist and gave it a good twist, just like the Teddy Goldman self-defence book recommended. The blade fell to the ground as the pirate's face wrinkled into a grimace of pain. Solena kneed him in the stomach and picked up the cutlass.

She saw Rodney groaning on the ground, his shoulder covered with blood, its colour a glistening black in the dim light. St Amour stood over him with a sword in one hand and Rodney's pistol in the other.

Solena knew she had to defend him. She wasn't sure if it was her affection for him or the urge to defeat the pirates, she wanted to save him even though he was the one masterminding the tree-killing. She didn't think, just swung her cutlass at St Amour.

The pirate captain was almost unprepared. She could have had him, but he saw her just in time and offered a clumsy parry. It was enough to stop her blade. He pointed the glock pistol at her.

"A brave attempt, my dear, but I would not try my luck further," he said.

Solena looked around, and saw that Jackson and a short, thin pirate in a sombrero now held the two machine guns. The lumberjacks, most of them stunned from the battle, and the lawyer, still putting up a weak but stubborn resistance, were herded together toward the center of the camp. One of the guards, Cal, lay on the ground dead of a stab wound through the heart.

Solena kneeled beside Rodney to examine his injuries.

"Jackson, come with me," said St Amour, "Help Mr. Love to his feet. We're taking him with us. He is going to show us where they've hidden their transport."

"Like hell I will," Rodney growled.

Without a word, St Amour grabbed a pistol from one of his men and aimed at the group of lumberjacks.

"No!" Rodney yelled. "All right, you French bastard. I'll show you the boat."

"A boat?" St Amour queried, "I saw no boat. This better not be a trick."

"Of course you didn't see it, you seventeenth-century dumb ass. It's cloaked."

"Come on, and you better not be lying or we'll shoot this damsel, even though I would hate to spoil such beauty."

"I'm coming with him," Solena declared.

"You stay here," St Amour commanded, and motioned her to

back away with his pistol. "O'Malley, you take her and these fellows back to the ship. They will fetch a good price at the slave market."

"Aye, sir!" the Irishman replied eagerly as ever.

St Amour strode away followed by Rodney, who could barely walk but was supported by Jackson.

"Touch not the woman," St Amour said to the remaining pirates without turning.

"I hate to point out the obvious," Rodney said through clenched teeth as he was half-dragged by Jackson, "But it's ungrateful to double-cross us like this after having dinner with us."

"Mayhap I likewise speak a truth that is obvious to all," St Amour said, "But a man has to make a profit."

"I thought that being my ancestor you would be a man of honour!" Rodney exploded.

"Ancestor?! How can that be? We are about the same age. Your wound has produced a brain fever. You better not go completely mad before explaining to me your method of transportation."

"Even if I explained it," Rodney said scornfully, "you would never understand."

"And why not? I attended the Sorbonne, I'll have you know."

"Yeah, well I went to Yale," Rodney said proudly. He was dizzy with loss of blood and could barely string a sentence together, but it was a good time as any to stand up for the Alma Mater.

"Yale? Is that some sort of upstart colonial institution?"

"It sure is, and a hell of a lot better than your Sorbonne."

St Amour grinned. "Then why am I the one holding the pistol?"

7 PROSCRIPTION (AD 1694)

The two pirates and their captive were standing knee-deep in water, looking for the boat. St Amour still could not see it. Rodney reached into a pocket of his shorts and found a small electronic device shaped like an iPod. He pressed a button, and suddenly the outlines of a boat began to appear farther off, in deeper water. The image wavered, bobbing on the waters of the bay, revealing itself in diagonal stripes until finally the entire white yacht appeared. It was almost the size of the *Belle Catherine*.

"Well, how do we get there?" St Amour demanded.

Rodney pressed another button and a cloaked little motor boat appeared in a similar fashion close to the shore.

"There are no oars," St Amour commented, "Does this boat run by itself too?"

"You better believe it," said Rodney.

"Amazing, eh Jackson?"

"Let us try," Jackson said, "I'll believe it when I see it."

Rodney and the captain stepped gingerly into the boat, and Jackson gave it a great heave, then vaulted on board. The two pirates jumped in a startled manner as Rodney started the motor. The boat took off towards the looming silvery-white shape of the time machine.

They climbed on board the great white yacht via a small ladder on its side, and the pirates looked around with a sense of wonder. They could see right into the cabins, for their walls were mostly glass, and very high quality glass too, such as could probably be procured only in Venice, St Amour supposed.

There were little lights and instruments blinking and gleaming inside, unfathomable to either of them.

"Well, sir," said St Amour, "Show us the workings of this here boat. And how would you be able to haul the timber all the way back to your land?"

"The timber? That's simple. We would attach is to the boat and drag it behind us."

"All the way to North America? But it would rot away through such a long voyage."

"No, we don't travel through space. I told you already," Rodney grew more and more irritable as the burning in his shoulder did not relent.

Jackson gave a little start and gripped his machine gun tighter.

"What is it?" St Amour asked.

"I thought I heard footsteps," Jackson replied.

St Amour swiftly shoved his gun at Rodney's chest. "Is there anyone else on board? Have you led us into a trap?"

Rodney's only reply was a groan as the pirate's hand on his shoulder aggravated the wound. Rodney thought he could feel the bullet still embedded in there as the pain rose up and subsided in excruciating waves. Now all three could hear a slight noise: very light, very soft and slow footsteps from somewhere on the deck.

"Call him!" St Amour whispered ferociously.

"It's just my dog, Dobie," Rodney said very loudly with a nervous laugh, "Here, Dobie! Here, boy!"

The pirates waited tensely, but no dog appeared.

"He's very shy," Rodney said, "He won't come out because he can smell the two of you."

"Lieutenant, go find that dog and put a bullet in it," St Amour said. "Meanwhile, you will show me how to steer this boat."

"You're the boss," said Rodney as sardonically as he could.

They stepped into the cabin, and he turned on the lights, making St Amour look up open-mouthed at the ceiling, then pressed a button that lit up the control panel. St Amour did not know where to start.

"Why don't you explain what you said before, 'we don't travel through space?'" he asked Rodney.

"All right, I don't know if you'll get this, but we travel through time."

"Time?" the pirate asked dubiously. "Sure, we all travel *with* time. Time moves forward, and we all grow old. But traveling *through* time?"

He looked over the panel and saw the date May 24, 1694 on one of the indicators. Above it was the date May 24, 2011.

St Amour felt he was on the verge of a breakthrough. There was just one more little detail that had to fall into place, and then he would understand everything.

The noise of scuttling feet and a terrified scream came to them from somewhere on deck.

"*Mon Dieu!*" St Amour shouted.

Just then, Jackson was inspecting a staircase that led below decks, completely unaware that a giant reptile stalked him, hiding behind a stack of buoys. As soon as he turned away, it pushed off and shortened the distance between them with amazing speed. He reacted to the sound and swung around only to come face to face with an alligator's open jaws flying straight at him.

St Amour ran onto the deck and saw Jackson grappling with the beast, which held his neck and shoulder firmly in its mouth. His struggles seemed futile against the dagger-like teeth which had already drawn a massive puddle of blood from his weakening body. St Amour raised his gun to fire, but the creature saw him, its fierce eyes ever watchful. Instantly it released Jackson and in a spring-like motion leapt to the cover of the buoys.

"*Merde!*" was all St Amour could say.

He knelt over his mortally wounded lieutenant and barely suppressed a shudder. Jackson's breaths were wheezing spasms. His lungs must have been damaged, for there were stab wounds on his chest, forming a line towards his shoulder. His neck was the worst to look at: it was punctured in two places and the flesh gaped wide open, glistening with blood. St Amour took his eyes away from the wounds and looked into the man's eyes, wide open with shock.

"Captain," Jackson whispered hoarsely, raising a shaking hand in warning.

It was too late. St Amour was knocked down to the deck beside his fallen lieutenant. Rodney had gathered the last of his strength and tackled his enemy from behind, following quickly with a punch to the face while St Amour was still down. It was not exactly the time to play fair, Rodney told himself.

He reached for the pistol gripped in the pirate's hand and wrenched it away with the sudden strength that comes with desperation. Then he struggled to his feet, while St Amour stayed down, stunned by the blow. He looked up into the barrel of the gun.

"Wait!" St Amour raised his hand in an appeasing gesture. "I understand now. You come from a different time. I *am* your ancestor. I must be. If you kill me now, you will have never been born. I have no children as yet... that I know of."

"Goddammit!" Rodney shouted. "How do I know you're not lying?"

"You don't know," the pirate grinned, "But will you risk finding out?"

While Rodney stood in bewilderment, St Amour launched himself at his descendant, driving him back, seizing the gun hand and smacking it against the railing. He had overexerted his strength: the gun flew out of Rodney's hand in an arc and disappeared over the side with a small splash.

"You foolish lubber!" St Amour cried, "I'm glad I'm your ancestor and it's not the other way around because it makes no difference to me whether you live or die."

Rodney felt an iron grip closing round his throat. He tried to unclasp the fingers, but he had expended all his strength in that first attack, and the remains of his energy were flowing away with the blood from his wound. St Amour did not feel up to playing fair either, as he punched his adversary in the bloodied shoulder.

Rodney ceased his struggles, shuddering and closing himself up into a ball of pain. St Amour struck him savagely one more time to make sure he was completely helpless, then hooked an arm under his knees and pitched him overboard.

"Fine fodder for the sharks," he muttered, watching his supposed descendant disappear swiftly into the murky water. "Now, for that crocodile."

Drawing his cutlass, he stepped over to the pile of buoys where the animal had been hiding, but found nothing.

"Ah, curse him. I'll worry about him later," St Amour said, "Let's get you into the cabin, lieutenant."

Jackson was unable to hear him, being completely unconscious, or perhaps dead. St Amour felt his forehead, and found it deathly cold and covered with a mist of sweat.

He dragged the senseless body across the deck and into the warmth of the control room, formulating a plan as he went.

"So these fellows came from 2011. We won't go there," he pronounced, "How about a little farther into the future? Who knows what manner of machines are to be found there? And maybe there's hope for you, if their physician can work as many miracles as their lumberjacks."

He caught himself sounding sentimental, but could not help himself.

"I cannot lose you, Jackson," he said to the unconscious man, "You are the best lieutenant that ever sailed with me. I'm only saying this now because you're lying there senseless and cannot hear me."

Rodney sank into the deep, warm water. He tried to kick his way back to the surface but did not know whether he was going to make it. Darkness gathered round. Was it the darkness of the ocean or was he just losing consciousness? He thought he saw something hit the surface above him, an elongated shape that slinked into the depth. Then there was a blinding light from above: St Amour must have figured out how to operate the time boat. Rodney groaned with chagrin and passed out.

8 EARTHLY PARADISE (AD 2694)

Professor X129 paced the front of the classroom on his mechanical legs. This pacing was not strictly necessary: he could have simply stood before the large white screen at the front of the class, his monitor turned towards those of his students, and delivered the lecture, or even downloaded it to them. Being a teacher of ancient history, he felt it was appropriate to simulate conditions in classrooms of the era they were studying.

The language in which the lecture was transmitted will be translated here into English, but it was in fact a compilation of ones, zeroes, pluses and minuses. It was much more precise than English, but completely devoid of subtext and undertone. The "words" and their combinations communicated exactly what they meant without any emotional or imaginative connotations.

"This period in the cultural history of earth was called post-modernism," Professor X129 said in his soothing voice, "There are not many surviving sources from this era, but many theories have been advanced, claiming that there were multiple strikes by postal workers. But then, not content merely with going on strike, they began to seize power of all cultural standards, and soon all literature and painting was performed entirely by postal employees. As you can probably deduce from this, all art was rendered absurd and meaningless. One thing is certain, it was a dark time in mankind's history."

The students, like him, had computer monitors for heads, hard drives for bodies, and mechanical arms and legs that could perform a variety of tasks. The lecture was nearing its end, and many of their screens had gone black into power saving mode, their attention drifting.

The bell sounded, a gentle music that caressed the microphones.

"Class is terminated for today," said the professor. If he had been human, he would have been slightly annoyed that many of the students were in sleep mode, but as things stood, he had not been human for about a hundred years. All the knowledge in his brain had been downloaded into his present computer body as soon as the human body had begun to deteriorate.

He thought it would be a good time to recharge his circuits between sessions when he heard a soft whirring as a familiar screen walked into the classroom.

"P82! Glad to see you," he said.

He wasn't really glad, being unable to feel emotions, but it was a token of appreciation to a loyal former student. P82 was an above-adequate archaeologist, and from time to time she would return to her old instructor for consultation.

"Likewise, professor."

Her aluminum arms held a strange object. Professor X129 deduced that she had yet another complex archaeological conundrum for him.

"Let us perambulate to my office," he suggested.

They walked down the hallway through lines of orderly students who moved either on mechanical legs or on tiny wheels.

"I deduce that you wanted to show me something," Professor X129 said, sitting down in his chair as P82 took the seat across from him.

She put the rectangular metal box on the desk.

"It's a sample of ancient writing," she said, "Discovered on the western coast of South America near the ancient ruins of Santa Marta. I brought it to you because you are adept at deciphering ancient idioms. It seems as if it is a message of great importance, and it had been left there purposely for us to find."

"For us?"

"Yes, that is: for someone in the future. Or at least, what *was* the future to the individuals who lived in that era."

"And what era was that?"

"They were very exact about the era and even the date: May 16,

1694."

"This is interesting," Professor X129 affirmed, "What kind of message would they have for us?"

"A warning." P82 flipped open the box and revealed an archaic mode of communication: thin sheets made from tree pulp on which the message was inscribed in ink.

"To whoever finds this message," the professor read, "I would like to warn you against the coming of two men from our time: Lieutenant Jackson and Captain Roger de St Amour. They are dangerous pirates who have stolen a time machine from me. Please report them to the appropriate authorities and send the time machine back to me, Rodney Love, CEO of the Timber Corporation. Somewhere in Colombia, May16, 1694."

"As you can see," P82 said, "there are quite a few ancient idioms that are not in any of the databases, but I hope that with your powers of deduction and your considerable knowledge, we can decode them."

"Yes," the professor said thoughtfully, his circuits whirring and ventilation system powering up in preparation for heightened activity, "These terms: 'dangerous', 'pirate', and 'timber corporation' are almost incomprehensible. But as for the rest of the message, it seems a time-traveling device has been removed from somewhere. Could this be a hoax? I have never encountered such a thing as a time travel machine. How is it possible that someone from that remote era contrived to build one?"

"What is a 'pirate' according to your calculations?"

"Pirates? The word is very ancient and holds many connotations. The closest definition I have been able to infer is 'a glamorous, freedom-loving music producer.'"

A messenger robot rolled into the office, distracting them from the riddle.

"Urgent email, Professor X129," it said, "You are requested to inspect live organic human form, arrived at South American Metropolis 4001, hospital facility 3794, condition weak but stable."

9 MYTHICAL CREATURE (AD 1694)

Solena was the first to have her hands bound behind her back with a hemp rope that cut against her wrists. The lumberjacks and the indignant attorney were likewise being fettered all around her.

The gray-haired pirate stood by as she was being tied, leering at her in a particularly disgusting way. He approached her, but the pirate who was doing the tying yelled at him.

"Hey Lelouche, the captain said not to touch the lady. She's for him."

"He won't know the difference," the grey-haired one replied in his gravelly voice. "I'll only touch her a little bit."

His hands reached for her breasts and he leaned forward to kiss her, but instead felt sudden blunt trauma. Solena's forehead had collided relentlessly with his nose with such strength and speed that he was lying on the ground before he even realized what happened and heard the jeering and laughter of his comrades.

Solena took advantage of this brief moment and ran for the cover of the trees, her hands still tied behind her. It was awkward, and she had to kick a pirate out of her way and send him sprawling to the ground, but she made it to the nearest pair of trees.

"Help me!" she cried.

The amazed pirates and lumberjacks and the incredulous lawyer stopped what they were doing and watched as two tree branches leaned down and untied her bonds, just as human hands would have done.

"Witch!" cried Lelouche and some of the others.

The pirates began crossing themselves assiduously.

"What are you, witch, mermaid, or banshee?" asked O'Malley, who was well versed in mythical creatures.

"I'm a dryad!" she roared.

The pirates were still stunned, and Solena swooped down upon the one she had kicked. He was still lying on the ground clutching his belly, and could not offer resistance when she quickly snatched up his pistol and his cutlass.

Panic spread among the pirates as she advanced slowly towards them.

"Release the captives!" she ordered fiercely.

"Hold your ground, lads!" O'Malley commanded as the others seemed torn between obeying her and running for their lives. He made the sign of the cross, but it had no effect. The dryad still advanced menacingly towards them.

What O'Malley didn't know was that dryads were not allowed to kill. If they did, they would immediately lose their magic. The anger in Solena's eyes seemed murderous enough to him.

"Hold your ground, I say!" he cried in a slightly more high-pitched tone.

Of course, Solena was not prepared to break the rules, but she did call upon the few dryad magic skills she had, hoping she was not too rusty.

The Irishman raised his pistol as she came almost within point blank range. A loud crack overcame all the usual forest noises, but everyone could tell that the sound was not quite right. It seemed somehow muffled.

Instead of a bullet, a single green leaf fluttered out of the barrel. The pistol itself changed shape, transforming almost instantly into a thick, crooked branch.

O'Malley cried out in panic and let it drop to the ground, where it immediately took root and grew into a tiny sapling.

The lumberjacks were nearly as frightened as the pirates had been.

"So what?" Solena shrugged, "So I'm a dryad. The assistant vice president is a dark elf, and no one says a word."

Solena gathered even more of her magical energy, and presently Lelouche's pistol and cutlass likewise turned into pieces of wood.

The lumberjacks, some of whom had not been tied up yet, took the opportunity and began to pummel their would-be captors. O'Malley ran at Solena, cutlass drawn. She stepped aside and parried his predictable attack. The sword was not a familiar weapon to her, but she knew the basic principles of Aikido and Jujitsu from her Teddy Goldman books, which came in handy in any kind of fight.

She wanted to be careful not to kill him, so she kept parrying and dancing round her opponent, not really attacking but rather feinting to keep him occupied.

In the meantime, the lumberjacks had taken heart. Some used their fists, others powered up their chainsaws and advanced on the pirates in a none-too-friendly manner. Their renewed fighting spirit turned most of the pirates to flight. The Irishman presently saw this.

"Oh, Jeezus!" O'Malley whined, and retreated after the others.

There were no casualties this time.

"Solena, you saved our lives," the lawyer finally murmured.

"I just hope we can do the same for Rodney," she said.

A sudden, horrifying thought struck her.

"Um... everyone!" she said, "Don't tell Rodney I'm a dryad. I want to tell him myself... later. It's really a bad time."

"Well, what are we supposed to say about what happened?" one of the lumberjacks asked.

"You can take the credit for escaping from the pirates," she said, "I don't mind. Just be as vague as you can, I guess."

"I don't like this secrecy," said Stanley, "Mr. Love is legally entitled to this sort of information. Especially considering the suspicious nature of a dryad's presence in a lumber company... One might think..."

"Let's go look for him," Solena said, ignoring his implication. "Just try not to tell him too soon."

***

Rodney Love found himself carried face-down in the jaws of an alligator. There had been a small amount of water in his lungs, but this peculiar position helped drain the liquid, and he was breathing again, though most of it came out as coughing. Tyler crawled onto the sandy shore, carrying him in his mouth almost as gently as a mother alligator carrying her young.

Of course, Tyler had never been a mother, and Rodney was not exactly the size of a newborn, so he definitely felt the prickling and cutting of the alligator's teeth against his chest and back. He was in no position to complain, however, and this minor pain was something of a pleasant distraction from the throbbing pangs in his shoulder.

"The only thing to do," he said, "Is to go by land back to Santa Marta."

Tyler spat him out in surprise. Rodney plopped onto the forgiving sand, rolled over and lay on his back.

"You didn't know about my ingenious backup plan, did you?" he grinned. "There's another time boat patrolling the area in case this one should fail."

10 THE PIRATE AND THE PROFESSOR
(AD 2694)

Jackson awoke in a strange place, which was by no means unusual for him. But while other places he had woken up in held at least some things he could recognize, this one was truly impossible to understand. If he had ever believed in heaven, he would have thought he had somehow made it through those pearly gates. And after all, the idea of untimely decease was not unreasonable: the last thing he remembered was the gaping maw of a crocodile closing around his neck as if he were some helpless gazelle.

Now there was no pain, only a kind of numbness and even a subtly euphoric sensation, as if he had smoked of the hemp leaf.

Everything around him was white: walls, furniture, bedclothes, sheer curtains billowing in the gentle breeze. Everything was remarkably clean and white. The only non-white things were the machines. There were wires and tubes running from his body into the machines, and he considered being alarmed at this, but the euphoric mood prevented any such ambition.

One machine that was not attached to him was a box-like thing on metallic legs.

"Must be another American invention," he muttered, feeling the pain of the wounds in his throat. He wondered if he was in the land Rodney Love spoke of.

The thing sprang to life, the object that looked like a black mirror on top of the box lit up, displaying the picture of a woman's face. No, not a picture: this was much more precise... and it moved!

This was not a machine after all! Sorcery! Just as he had thought when he first saw Rodney and his men in the forest.

"How are you feeling?" the thing with the woman's face pronounced in a horrid, metallic voice.

Jackson shrugged painfully. "I'm alive. At least, I think I am…"

Then he promptly fell asleep, the effort having drained him completely. His sleep was dreamless, which was good.

When he awoke, the creature stirred once again, this time not speaking a word. It walked out of the room and promptly returned bearing a tray of food.

There was a glass of milk and a bowl filled with translucent red cubes. Jackson tried to sit up and noticed that this time it did not pain him as greatly as he would have expected.

"How long have I been here?" he asked.

"Three days," replied the magical-mechanical creature.

"I dare not believe it," he said. "My wounds seem almost healed."

"We have put you through an accelerated DNA-rebuilding process. It is a procedure unknown in your days."

"In my days?" he asked, poking the red cubes with a white fork made of some strange, flexible material.

"You have undertaken a remarkable journey. But Professor X129 can explain better than I could. He awaits in the next room."

"Who is he?

"A scholar."

"Bring him in," Jackson said regally, "I have never met a scholar."

The thing that walked through the room did not look much different from his "physician." A rectangular device on mechanical legs beamed at the confused pirate, the smiling countenance of a middle-aged man depicted on its screen.

"That is not how I pictured a scholar," Jackson stated.

"I understand you puzzlement, Mr…" the professor's voice was human, melodious, much better than the doctor's.

"Jackson."

"You see, my human body has long since perished, but this machine houses something much more important: my mind."

Jackson crossed himself and muttered something about saintly protection.

"It is not the devil's work, I assure you," the professor continued, "I do not mean you any harm."

Jackson suspected as much. But he also suspected that the creature wanted something from him. It was the only way to account for the kind, almost deferential treatment he received.

But it did not reveal its cards immediately, choosing instead to get to the matter in a roundabout fashion.

"Do you know what kind of journey you have undergone, Mr. Jackson?"

"I'm still trying to understand it. Last thing I remember was being nearly eaten alive by an alligator. I don't know where my captain is, but he must have found his way here somehow. Have you seen him?"

"Captain St Amour?"

"Yes, that's the one," Jackson lifted himself on an elbow.

"No, he refused to be detained."

"It sounds like the captain."

"His ship entered the port 2281, but he stayed only a minute or so, long enough to hand you over to another ship's crew, and they saw to it that you were delivered to this hospital. It seems he had no desire to report to port authorities."

"Where is he now?"

"Ah." The machine said.

"You think I would know?" Jackson smirked. "I don't even know where *I* am."

"That will come in time," the professor said, smiling. "There is no rush. The main thing is that you are here. I would like to come and visit you from time to time, if you don't mind. There are many things I would like to know."

"What manner of things be these?"

"I am very interested in your time period, the seventeenth century."

"My time period... of course!" Jackson sat up briskly, excitement making him almost oblivious to pain.

"You *understand?*" the professor lifted a well-groomed ethereal eyebrow.

"Of course I do, sir. Do you think me an oaf?"

"Not at all," the machine protested logically.

"Then it must be true... what Rodney Love said about the future. There will be an end to slavery in America." If the professor had been wearing a shirt, Jackson would have seized its collar. "Tell me: is there slavery in your time?"

"No, there is no slavery *per se*, but you must rest, Mr. Jackson."

"I must leave this place and see for myself," Jackson declared. He wrenched himself out of bed and made for the door, despite the machine's objections.

But before he could leave the room, he felt his knees giving way and crumpling, a sudden fit of dizziness overcame him, and he fell heavily onto the perfectly clean tiles.

11 NATURAL REMEDIES (AD 1694)

Tyler was still flabbergasted by Rodney's revelation when the rest of their company appeared on the beach. Solena ran towards Rodney and collapsed beside him in exhaustion and relief.

"Bad news," Tyler said, "The pirates have stolen our time boat."

The company was about to break out in varying degrees of panic, but Rodney Love forestalled it.

"It's all right, it's all right!" he raised a placating hand, "Remember the backup plan."

"There is another time machine off the coast of Santa Marta," Solena said uncertainly. The backup plan had seemed solid enough at the time they formulated it, but now it was almost as certain as a mirage.

"It's still a bit of a walk. How can we trek across the continent with you in this condition?" Stanley asked.

"Oh, I'll make it," Rodney replied, "I'm just going to have to make it because I won't rest until I settle the score with that double-crossing pirate."

"There are other factors—"

"Don't worry so much, Stan," Rodney said, "We can stop in a local village and quickly heal my wound with miraculous herbal medicines. Isn't that what adventurers in South America generally do?"

"I hope that's a joke," the lawyer rolled his eyes. "But without antibiotics in this century, herbal remedies may be all we have."

"*Natural* antibiotics," Rodney corrected. "Do you really think we humans invented everything? There are plenty of antibiotics all around us. I just don't know which ones they are..."

"I can find them," Solena said, and everyone turned to her. "But first we have to get the bullet out. Where's the first aid kit?"

Stanley brought the kit, but he looked in consternation at all the various implements it contained. "Does anyone here have any medical experience?"

"Cal had some basic training," Rodney sighed, "but I think he's..."

Everyone fell silent.

After a while, Tyler pronounced, "I could try to dig it out with my teeth."

"That's not quite what I had in mind," Stanley said diplomatically.

The lawyer took Solena aside. She felt a twinge of nervousness, suspecting that he wanted to talk about something that had to do with the secret to which he was privy.

"You have certain... dryad power?" he asked her.

"Yes," she agreed.

"Can you do anything for him?"

She had already thought of that, and the truth was, she didn't know.

"I see your hesitation," he said, "You still don't want him to know you're a dryad."

"It's not that," Solena replied. "I just don't know whether my powers are strong enough. I'm not that accomplished in magic, and I don't want to risk Rodney's life testing my ability."

"But what you did to save us from the pirates—"

"Was an act of desperation! We would have been doomed if I hadn't tried it. I don't know if I could do a repeat performance."

"You've got to try," he insisted. "If the bullet is left inside his body he might get an infection. Who knows where we can find help now, how long it will be before we reach the nearest settlement? He could die."

"Shhh!"

"Are you dividing up my property already, Stan?" Rodney called out, trying to diffuse the tension.

He could not have heard what they were saying, but the words caused Solena to think about the real possibility of Rodney dying. She looked down at the little lawyer, his sober calculating gaze, his pinched face. She had never thought very highly of him, but suddenly a new respect awakened.

He was right: if a piece of fabric got caught in the wound, it would likely get infected. There were no hospitals, no cities here — the nearest being Santa Marta, a hundred miles away. All they had was the tiny hope that Solena could use her dryad powers.

"Do you have an anaesthetic in that med kit?" she asked.

The lawyer nodded.

"Something that could put him to sleep for a while?"

He nodded again.

"Good. I will do it, but you must not breathe a word. I don't want Rodney to know anything about any dryad powers."

"We have a deal," Stanley pronounced.

He returned briskly to Rodney's side and began to take various implements out of the medical kit.

"Gary, you have some basic first aid training if I'm not mistaken?" he asked. "You'd be better at administering this."

"I sure do," the brawny guard stepped forward and began helping Stanley set up an IV system.

Rodney didn't like the look of the medical equipment.

"What are you guys going to do to me?" he inquired nervously.

"We're going to remove the bullet," Stanley said in a tone that precluded argument.

"Better out than in, I suppose," Rodney said.

"Don't worry about a thing, boss," Gary said, "You're going to be out cold for a couple of hours while we perform some field surgery."

"Have you ever done this before?" Rodney asked.

"I saw a guy do it when I was in the marines. Piece of cake."

"Maybe we better wait," Rodney suggested.

"It's going to be okay," Solena sat down at his side. "Gary will take the bullet out, and I will make sure the wound is bandaged up with those natural cures."

Rodney took a deep breath. "All right," he nodded.

Gary inserted the IV needle into his arm, and the anaesthetic began to drip from the plastic fluid bag held by Stanley.

"Count down from ten, boss," Gary said.

Rodney got only as far as six, then his eyelids fell shut.

"Yep, he's out," Gary confirmed.

"Now what?" Stanley asked.

Solena was confident in what needed to be done. "We go towards the river."

12 THE KNIGHTS (AD 2694)

Jackson dreamed. He was helpless again, just a little boy, crying. Burly men shouted orders in his face and when he did not obey, they seized and flung him to the ground and held him there, his face pressed into the hard dirt. His mother's plangent cries resounded in his ears as she was carried roughly by two men, and he knew he would never see her again. He reached out a hand, vainly trying to grasp at her flowing dress, but in a moment she was gone.

When he opened his eyes, it was strangely a relief to find himself in the weird, neutral room with the inhuman creature. In a way, the creature was more human than his masters had been, and he himself was no longer a helpless child.

Jackson yawned. The professor registered the movement, and his screen lit up.

"What did you mean?" Jackson asked right away, sitting up in his bed, "What did you mean when you said there is no slavery now "pursay?"

"Slavery has been abolished all over the world," the professor replied, "But in a way, you could say every sentient living being, every computerized being, all are servants of the Great Sissy."

"The Great Sissy? I like not the sound of that."

"She is a benevolent ruler."

"How did it come to pass that all the known world is subjugated by a woman?"

"It happened a long time ago. In the twenty-first century, Teddy Goldman was one of the most prominent leaders of the world. His values were physical fitness, improvement of the spirit, individual endeavour. But later in that century his cult began to lose followers, for war and pollution became too much a part of everyday life and people could barely sustain their physical bodies, much less keep physically fit and healthy. The Great Sissy offered them eternal life and freedom from their bodies."

"And that is how you gained your present form?" Jackson asked.

"Yes."

"How is this possible? How are you released from your body, yet alive?"

"My mind and everything it contained has been transferred to this machine. Of course, parts may malfunction and wear out, but theoretically, I could live forever."

Jackson shook his head as if he had too many questions at once.

"Whither did your soul go?" he finally asked.

"Soul?"

"This is only your mind in the machine, so where is your soul?"

"I doubt very much that there is such a thing as a soul. It did not separate from my body and fly up to heaven when the download occurred, if that's what you mean."

"Maybe not," Jackson insisted, "Maybe it is still inside this machine. Otherwise, how is it you are able to speak, think, and feel?"

"I do not feel," the professor objected, "That is, I have sensors that detect light and sound and so on, but I do not feel emotions as humans do."

Jackson accepted a tray with Jell-O and milk from a mechanical attendant who had just rolled into the room. Then he focused a penetrating gaze on the professor and said, "I don't believe you."

***

When he saw the professor next, on a quiet evening, the conversation became more personal.

"Where were you born?" X129 asked.

"Jamaica," Jackson spat out the word with such hatred that even the imperturbable machine seemed taken aback. It said nothing for a long moment.

"My parents were Africans," Jackson continued, "shipped to the colony of the white lords, to labour in their fields for them so that they could languish in the shade and count their gold."

"I am sorry," said the professor.

"You said you couldn't feel sorrow," Jackson said at once.

"Merely being polite."

It had become a game with them, the pirate trying to catch the machine displaying any signs of emotion at all.

"I still don't know what happened to my parents, where they are now. When I was seven, they were both sold to another master, while I remained at the plantation. From that day forward, I swore I would escape and find them again."

"And have you?"

Jackson shook his head. "I had no knowledge of where to look. The names of slaves are not important, and I doubt their new masters even knew their names when they purchased them. I did run away from the plantation, joined a pirate crew, then was recruited by Captain St Amour. Even if I had a clue to my parents' whereabouts, I don't know if I would dare return to Jamaica. I do not fear death, but I tremble at the thought of being recaptured and made a slave again."

He looked at the professor. "Do you never feel the urge to be free of this metallic box?"

"I do not see how. And no, remember, I do not feel emotions."

"So strange," Jackson said, "Is this the way all men are in your century?"

"I do not know," the machine replied, "There may be some organic humans yet extant, but such a thing is known only to the Great Sissy and her advisors."

"This is far worse than slavery," Jackson muttered. "I must return to my time or I too may lose my soul and be turned into a machine."

"No one will force you to undergo the transformation," the professor assured him.

Jackson grunted, unconvinced.

"If you truly wish to go back, you must make contact with your captain."

Jackson suspected a trap. It was very possible that Professor X129 was gaining his confidence in order to get to St Amour and the time machine.

"You suspect a trap," the professor said, "You suppose I am gaining your confidence in order to get to St Amour and the time machine."

"How did you know?" Jackson said, wincing.

"I read it in your face," the professor's own face displayed a brief but satisfied smile.

"That was a feeling!" Jackson exclaimed. "You smiled just then."

"No, it is merely the way I am programmed to simulate a human face. I did not 'feel' anything."

Jackson grunted again, still unconvinced.

At that moment the door flew off its hinges, and Captain St Amour himself, armed to the teeth, appeared in the doorway. "Attack that demon, Sir Lancelot!" he cried.

A tall armoured figure strode into the room. Jackson had never seen a knight, so to him it seemed yet another machine, though in human form, covered from head to foot in iron plates.

Jackson sprang out of bed, just in time to grasp the iron creature's arms as it raised a shining sword over Professor X129.

"No!" he cried, "This is a scholar!"

On hearing those words, the one referred to as Sir Lancelot hesitated. Jackson felt his arms slacken.

"If you would release me, good sir, I give you my word I will not harm the scholar, though I know not what it is."

Jackson let go, and Sir Lancelot lowered his sword as promised. "But you have a goodly strength, sir," Lancelot commented. "I dare say mayhap you would have stopped me bodily an you had the desire. After we leave this land of demons, it would be well for us to try a passage of arms, for I have not met my match in strength these many years—"

"We can talk about that later!" shouted St Amour. "Let us away from this accursed future."

"Such are my feelings exactly," said Jackson, "Adieu, professor. It has been a pleasure."

Jackson gathered up his clothes and followed the others into the hallway.

"No, take me with you," Professor X129 said suddenly.

"What, into the past?" Jackson asked.

"Yes, if that is where you're going. I must obtain a visual of it for myself."

"Take him along," St Amour said, "Who knows what magical properties this talking machine may yet possess."

St Amour and Jackson went first, followed by the knights. Professor X129 kept up as best he could on his little mechanical legs. They passed down the long, bleached hospital passages, encountering some mechanical attendants whom St Amour threatened with his pistols just in case. In one hand he held an ordinary pistol, while the other was of a strange design.

"What manner of pistol be this?" Jackson asked.

"It's what they call a laser. I obtained it from an armoury in this land."

"But did no one try to arrest you? And why is no one trying to arrest us right now?" Jackson looked about, almost offended by the machines' lack of interest in him.

"There are no armies here," St Amour explained. "With everyone transformed into a machine, what need is there to keep order among the populace?"

"And where did these fellows come from?" Jackson asked, indicating the knights.

"Why Jackson, have you never heard of Camelot? These are the fabled knights of King Arthur."

"Never heard of him."

"Hast not heard of King Arthur?" Sir Gawaine cried. "Tell him, noble Sir Roger!"

They came out into the strong sunshine, and Jackson was still amazed that no one had tried to stop them. The landscape looked startlingly different than the tropical rainforest that clothed the earth in the pirates' own century. It was mostly mowed grass, with a few perfect-looking ornamental shrubs and flowers.

"They are warriors from medieval England," St Amour said, "Sixth century, to be precise. Did you know, the American's boat can travel that distance in a few seconds? Not only through time, but through space. When I left you here, the only thing I could think of doing was to go back in time and try to see whether King Arthur and his knights truly existed. I was especially interested in finding Sir Lancelot, for he is a French knight and the most gallant and strongest of them all. And then it occurred to me, why not bring them with me? They are fond of going on quests, but only the bravest agreed to come with me after I described the dangers we are going to face."

"But what are we going to do with them?" Jackson asked.

"We could always use more men," St Amour shrugged, "The

second lieutenants are bound to keep being killed. And we could lose even more men very soon, for I wish to capture Rodney Love and learn all his secrets. It will be no easy task."

"Have we not already obtained the time boat?" Jackson asked. "What need is there to entangle ourselves further?"

"Ah, it is not that simple, Jackson. For you see, I have discovered that this time boat needs fuel to make its wonderful journeys. I understand not the nature of this fuel or where to obtain it. We must ask Rodney Love. And beyond that, who know what other wonders we might discover?"

They walked at a leisurely pace to the harbour and found the boat moored there. The other vessels were much larger by comparison. Apparently there were not many leisure boats in the future. The ships were built for transport. The harbor itself was not the seething, chaotic dangerous place of old. It was extremely well-regulated, with robots or computers gliding placidly along their assigned trajectories while loading and unloading boxes.

As they boarded the time boat, St Amour took the helm and steered the boat out of the harbour until they were out of sight of the shore.

Jackson and the knights sat on the benches in the cabin. Bursting with curiosity, the pirate asked to examine Sir Gawaine's sword, and the knight readily agreed. He seemed a jolly fellow, easy to befriend, and probably a good drinking companion. Jackson had never seen the like of the blade. It was covered with beautifully etched interlacing patterns, yet looked serviceable in battle. The guard and the pommel were engraved with the images of animals and leaves.

"I have worked in the smithy before," he said, "but this craftsmanship would have been beyond my skill."

"It is a rare blade, which the king himself hath given me for brave deeds. Sir Lancelot draws his only in battle, for it is a magical blade. It was given him by the Lady of the Lake."

Jackson glanced at the other knight, who sat calmly looking out the window, deep in solemn thought. The water was clear aquamarine, probably unlike these knights had ever seen off England's shores.

The boat began to accelerate. St Amour looked over his shoulder at them with a grin.

"Avast!" he said.

The boat reached an impossible speed, bumping along until it seemed to fly atop the waves. Suddenly, there was a flash, and they felt completely weightless as they moved through a stream of blinding light.

13 THE RETURN OF ST AMOUR (AD 1694)

Stanley and two of the lumberjacks accompanied Solena – they could not be certain of their safety, for they saw in their binoculars that the pirate ship was still at anchor in the bay – while Gary and the others watched over Rodney. The river was only about two hundred paces away, and soon they could hear its gurgle mixing with the murmur of the ocean.

She led them still another few hundred paces upstream through a tunnel of overhanging vines until they saw a brightly coloured bird digging for something on the bank.

"See where the macaw sits?" Solena pointed. "That's where our natural cure is."

She fished a small container out of her bag.

"Mud?" Mattheos, one of the lumberjacks, asked.

Solena ignored them and approached the bird. When she was almost within arm's reach of it, she leaned down and scooped up a large chunk of riverside clay into her container. The bird did not fly away. It gave her a sideward glance for a split second, then continued to dig with its curved beak, taking little bites of the healing substance.

"Clay," she said. "Where the macaw feeds, there you will find the healing clay."

By the time they returned, Gary had removed the bullet, and the lumberjacks were busy constructing a stretcher from the tree branches they had felled.

Solena daubed a generous amount of clay on the wound.

"That's the dryad magic?" the lawyer scoffed. "I could have done

68

as much myself."

Solena did not look away from her work, "I am not going to dignify that remark with a response."

Rodney was still unconscious, but breathing steadily. She bandaged the wound with gauze pads and adhesive strips, and Gary began to lighten the dose of anaesthetic.

Rodney muttered something, and his eyelids fluttered open.

"Water," he whispered. Then, looking about him at all the concerned faces, he made an attempt at a smile. "I'm alive! Aren't you all happy to see me?"

"I think soda is better for now," Gary said, giving him a can of ginger ale.

Stanley helped him sit up as he raised the can to his lips and sipped.

"Ah yes," Rodney said, revived by the sugar but still shaky. "Now to plot our new course to the time raft... But I just want to take one small detour."

"What are you talking about?" Stanley asked.

"You know, the detour I'd planned. We were going to take it anyway."

"But not now, when you're injured and we're pursued by pirates."

"And knights," Gary added.

"What?!" Rodney looked at the bodyguard, then looked to where he was looking.

About a hundred feet from them stood Roger St Amour, flanked by two knights. His usual pirate crew crowded behind them.

"Take cover!" Stanley cried.

A gunshot resounded through the jungle, scaring birds from their branches. An eruption of caws, twitters, and chirps followed as everyone ran for the nearest trees. St Amour had fired the first shot, but it whistled by without touching anyone.

Rodney was quickly hoisted onto the stretcher by the loyal lumberjacks, and moved into the natural shelter of the trees. The rest of the company likewise took cover.

"Surrender, Mr. Love," St Amour cried, "We outnumber you, and we have Sir Lancelot and Sir Gawaine."

"Why didn't you bring King Arthur?" Rodney shouted.

"He didn't want to leave his throne." St Amour replied with a shrug. "We also have fearsome weapons of the future the likes of which you've never seen."

"Oh really?" Rodney shouted, "You know I'm getting bored of you, St Amour."

For reply, St Amour fired the gun in his left hand directly at the forehead of one of the lumberjacks, who had been imprudently peeking from behind his tree. A red dot appeared where the gun was aiming, and then a sudden flash blinded everyone momentarily.

"Ow!" cried the lumberjack.

He tottered and fell to his knees; the laser had struck him square in the head.

Everyone froze in shock while the lumberjack raised a trembling hand to his forehead.

Suddenly, he said, "I'm fine... I feel fine."

Solena looked at his "wound" and saw that it was non-existent. The hair had been singed off in a circular shape, leaving a small bald spot right above his forehead, but there was no other damage.

"I think... It's a hair removal laser! Maybe it's the Silver-Glide! I've always wanted one of those," she blurted out. Then she recalled the danger they were in. "Pretend you're wounded! Let them think it's a real laser gun."

It was not hard to do, as the lumberjack was faint and weak-kneed from his recent shock.

"Let's get moving," Stanley commanded, "Hair removal or not, they still outnumber us."

Solena headed down a narrow trail. Gary and one of the lumberjacks picked up the stretcher and followed her.

"It costs 299 dollars," Solena muttered as she ran, "or six easy payments of $59.99. How did they ever get one?"

Solena dared to glance back.

She gasped: St Amour was not fifty paces behind them. At his side were his giant lieutenant and the two knights in chain mail, armed with swords as well as bows and arrows. The knights couldn't very well shoot anyone while running, but the pirates could, firing their pistols whenever they thought they had something close to a clear shot. It was only the tortuous nature of the trail that prevented them from getting one. She hoped they would run out of pistols, for they probably couldn't reload while running either.

Solena didn't like this situation. She knew that the lumberjacks could not run at full speed while carrying the stretcher. Sooner or later, the pirates would catch up. She let the others pass her, and Rodney called out to her as he was carried past, but she nodded to him reassuringly and moved to the back of their column. Keeping St Amour in her sight, she slowed down, backing away from him at a decisive walk. She began casting the spell.

Dryad spells did not have a standard incantation; the words had to be formed differently each time a spell was cast, for every single spell was different. The words came to her suddenly with great clarity. It was strange: she had never been good with magic, but now that her life and others' depended on it, the power came easily.

Her fingers moved as if of themselves, weaving patterns through the air and connecting the trees around them with barely visible lines.

She could see the faint strands of magic emanating from her fingers, upward, through the foliage. St Amour and his company also noticed that something was happening. Branches snapped out at them out of nowhere. Vines descended like stage curtains to block their path and screen the fugitives from their view. Jackson and O'Malley hacked furiously at the rampant plants, but inevitably their progress slowed more and more as countless vines entangled them and leaves clung to their faces. The knights suffered the most, encumbered as they were by their armour.

"The enchantress!" St Amour shouted, spitting out a leaf, "Shoot her!"

"Nay! Tis not meet to shoot a lady," Sir Lancelot began to protest, but the pirates all did their best to raise their weapons amidst the floral chaos.

Lelouche, who lagged a little behind the others, did not have to strive as hard against the forest. He leveled his pistol, and Solena saw it point at her, but all she could do was retreat at the same relatively slow pace for fear of dispelling the magic. The spell was almost complete: an impassible tapestry of branches had coalesced until the pursuers were almost completely halted. However, Lelouche had the advantage of being on a small rise of ground. Through the gaps, he could see Solena, the lawyer huffing and puffing just in front of her, and Rodney transported by his lumberjacks all following the same curving path. He pulled the trigger.

Another second, and he would have been too late. Another second, and the bullet would have lodged in a tree branch or in the earth. With many creaks and loud rustles, the branches and vines formed a solid wall before the pirates, blocking them completely from further pursuit. But the shot had been fired, and the bullet winged its way through the swiftly closing gaps.

Solena shuddered. She lowered her hands, still tingling with the magic, and felt that she was not hurt. Ready to breathe a sigh of relief, she turned to her company, only to find Stanley lying on the ground, panting, blood flowing freely from a wound in his chest.

"Oh, I am killed! A plague on both your houses!" he pronounced dramatically. "I've always wanted to say that as my final words. Did you know I'd been very active in the theater club when I was in law school?"

Solena couldn't help but smile faintly, but though he put a brave face on it, his wound looked hopeless.

"We've got to carry him," Mattheos suggested as the lumberjacks gathered around the wounded man. Rodney's stretcher was lowered to the ground to lie beside him.

Garry applied several gauze pads, trying to stop the flow of blood, but the bandages became soaked through almost instantly.

"There's no time to build another stretcher," one of the lumberjacks objected.

"We do have some time," Solena said calmly. "It will take them a while to get around the tangle."

"No, leave me," the lawyer said. "I'm going to die anyways; there's no point in carrying me anywhere."

"Okay Stanley," Rodney said, "Whatever you like, buddy. We can rest here if you like. We've got time."

"Everyone, leave me alone with Rodney," the lawyer said, "I want to say a few words."

Solena and the others walked off, leaving the two of them lying side by side.

Stanley's breath came in more and more softly until it seemed he barely had enough strength to talk. Rodney propped himself up on an elbow and leaned towards him.

"I wish I could have done it over again... I don't mean my whole life. I have no regrets. But the plays! I loved doing them. I played Mercutio, I played Iago... I was amazing as Iago. But the play runs only for a week, and then it's over. I wish I could do it one more time."

"I know what you mean," said Rodney with a sigh. "I've never been in a play myself, but I know what you mean."

"One last piece of advice, my friend," Stanley whispered.

"What is it?"

"Solena... she is hiding something from you. She must tell you herself. I promised... not to tell."

"I know," Rodney said, "I know."

A few seconds later, Rodney beckoned the others to come closer. Stanley was gone. His features had relaxed into an almost smiling softness, and he looked at peace, having fulfilled his mission insofar as he was able.

Mattheos muttered a soft prayer.

"We'll take the body with us," Rodney said. "Quickly, build a stretcher for him."

"Shouldn't we just bury him here?" Gary asked.

"No, we'll bury him when we get to our destination. It would be a more... appropriate place."

They covered the body with a blanket and hastily built a stretcher, then moved on. Now two stretchers were divided between Gary and the lumberjacks. Their progress was slow, but Solena was confident that the pirates would remain stranded for a good long time.

***

"A dryad, that's what it is, sure enough," O'Malley muttered, "I met one in the woods of Dun a Ri, only I didn't know it then. Tis the same impossible tangle, but the magic should run out with time; it does not last forever."

The forest had closed around them, so they could go neither forward nor back. A strange twilight descended: the branches closed off most of the sunlight. The company moved closer together, away from the trees which seemed to frown at them.

"A dryad?" St Amour asked. "*Sacre bleu!* I wish we could have taken that Merlin with us. We could use a wizard to counter her magic."

Jackson sat down wearily on a log. "Perhaps we are not meant to follow further."

"A knight does not give up the quest!" Sir Gawaine protested, "We must catch these rascals before they do further harm."

"But they are not—" Jackson began, then realized that St Amour must have told the story a little differently to these noble but slightly obtuse warriors.

"A wizard!" Sir Lancelot cried, "Of course we have no wizard, but we have a scholar. Is it not the same thing?"

"Well thought, sir. Unpack the scholar!" St Amour ordered.

Carracha, who had been burdened with dragging the padded box containing the scholar, untied the fastenings of the rough cloth wrapped around it, and lifted the computer out.

"The past!" it exclaimed, "I have more visuals of the past. If I had feelings, I would be excited."

"Good scholar," Lancelot addressed it in a formal tone, "I am Sir Lancelot of the Lake, and this is Sir Gawaine, nephew to King Arthur. We are on a quest to stop the time-traveling Americans. Mayhap with thy powers of light, ye may guide us to their lair?"

"I will try," the professor replied as solemnly. "Scanning for life forms... no, those are just monkeys... Ah, here we are. Twelve human life forms and one alligator life form proceeding west by southwest."

"Truly wondrous this, oh scholar," Sir Lancelot said, "Canst also divine what is their destination? A castle hidden in the forestland?"

"Yes," the professor replied matter-of-factly. "A castle populated by 221 humans, approximately 16.5 miles from here."

"That cannot be," St Amour said, "There are no castles this deep in the jungle. Your powers of perception must be skewed, old man."

"The scholar is right, sure enough, sir," O'Malley suddenly said. "There's a Jesuit mission that lies yonder in that direction. It's fairly fortified like a castle. Father O'Reilly, who was a friend of mine from the old country, said I can look him up if I ever was in need of spiritual guidance and the like."

"Why didn't you say anything, lieutenant?" St Amour exploded.

"I thought perhaps you could reason it out, and I didn't want to interrupt yous," O'Malley replied serenely. "Besides, there's no hurry now. I reckon they will stay there awhile."

"You reckon," St Amour scoffed. "Pack up the scholar. Onwards to the mission!"

14 PRIESTS AND ALLIGATORS (AD 1694)

The rain started without warning. One minute the travelers were trudging beneath the muggy closeness of the forest, and the next, a slew of water descended as if some angry celestial denizen had flushed a hundred toilets at once.

Solena was used to these sudden deluges, but the others were taken aback. They were soaked, blinded, and shivering in seconds. Rodney struggled to breathe, turning his face away from the downpour. Solena had been walking in the tail of the column to look out for pursuit, but now she joined Gary at the front.

"Are we close to the mission?" she asked.

"It should be another five miles," he replied, consulting his compass.

"Then maybe we should wait it out."

They sheltered beneath a wide Ombu tree, its branches spread generously to shield the entire company, with only a few rivulets tricking down the branches here and there.

"So you're probably wondering why we're going to the mission?" Rodney asked Solena.

"I'm too tired to be very curious, but yeah, I have been wondering about it."

"The monks there have concocted some kind of miracle cure," he replied, "I've read about it. I need it for my father."

"Is that why you arranged this whole expedition?"

"No, my father arranged it, but that was my reason for coming here."

"You wanted to cure him?"

Rodney nodded. "He's got liver cancer. But there's a special plant these Jesuits used. I suppose they learned about it from the natives."

As soon as the rain stopped, they moved on. It was strange, but Solena felt she recognized some of the scenery, as if she had seen it in another lifetime. Though it was not so surprising: she had walked through this same forest in her century. She was approaching the lands of her tribe.

But they were still a few miles away from the dryad lands when they reached the mission. It stood sternly in the middle of a clear-cut stretch of land. A high palisade surrounded it, the gates stood open, with natives streaming in and out carrying plantains, palm fruits, venison, and other supplies from the forest. By the time Solena and the others reached the gate, they had amassed a curious crowd who followed them at a respectful distance, probably because of Tyler. A few children ran ahead to spread the news to those inside.

Two native guards armed with muskets stopped them at the gate.

"What do you seek here? Who are you?" they asked in an old-fashioned Spanish that only Solena and Mattheos could understand.

"We seek shelter," the lumberjack replied, "We come in peace."

"Then enter," another voice called to them, and they saw a tall priest, with a jovial appearance despite black robes, hair, and beard, walking swiftly towards the gate and making sweeping gestures for them to enter.

"I'm Father Montoya," he said, "Enter, and follow me."

"You thought it was going to be a mom and pop operation, didn't you?" Rodney asked from his stretcher.

"I did," Solena admitted.

"State of the art," Rodney said contentedly, "I've read up on these guys."

It was true, she had expected a few impoverished fanatic priests with a handful of rag-tag native parishioners, but this was truly grandiose. The guards were armed with muskets. The mission buildings looked clean and well-kept, surrounded by lawns and flower beds. The priest who came towards them did not at all resemble a pious ascetic. He was a hearty-looking man in his forties, beaming with good spirits, his jet-black hair and short beard well-kept and glistening in the hot sun.

But Solena's attention focused suddenly on a woman watering the flowers from an earthenware jar. A woman... who was in fact a dryad in human form, like herself. Solena recognized her true form. As a human, she was astoundingly beautiful. Like Solena, she had taken on a human form that resembled the usual dweller of those lands: she looked like one of the natives, with the open, smiling, energetic countenance of the Tukano tribe. Her black eyes were very expressive, though they also seemed to hold some mysteries.

The crowd of spectators still followed them. Of course, many glances fell on the alligator.

"I'm not a wild animal," Tyler said as a precautionary measure, "I know you haven't heard of animal emancipation in your time period, but I hope y'all will accept me as an equal."

This caused more of a commotion than he had bargained for. Some natives froze in horror, others ran in search of weapons. Many of the women and children let out shrill cries.

Father Montoya, the only one not upset by the talking alligator, addressed the people in their language in an attempt to calm them.

Solena kept an eye on the other dryad, who took everything rather calmly too. She quietly spilled some water from the jar onto her open palm and splashed it on the ground, muttering a few words that were inaudible in the general commotion. Solena shivered slightly as she felt the fine fabric of the spell drifting through the courtyard. The people grew calmer and seemed to heed the priest.

"You are all welcome," Father Montoya said to the newcomers. "Bring the wounded ones inside."

"There's only one wounded. This one is dead," Mattheos said, indicating Stanley.

"Then we shall give him a burial," the priest said calmly. "Come."

They walked into the cool chambers, past the other dryad.

"Who is that woman?" Solena asked Father Montoya. "She seems different from the others."

"A lost lamb. Father O'Reilly found her in the forest."

Just as Solena had suspected, the other dryad was also masquerading as human and the priest had no idea about her true nature. It was strange, though. No dryad could be "found" by a human unless she wanted to be found. And no doubt, dryads were thought to be something akin to demons in this day and age. So why would one seek out the humans, especially religious ones? It seemed like madness. Surely, this one couldn't simply be curious as Solena had been.

The priest went about his business with practiced efficiency, giving orders to the natives and novice monks as needed. The lumberjacks were assigned Spartan but clean communal rooms, Solena was given her own chamber, while Rodney was taken into the hospital wing.

Solena was exhausted. Her dryad strength was usually equal to roaming through the jungles, but the tension of the chase, Stanley's death, and anxiety over Rodney's injured state completely drained her. She glanced over her surroundings: a desk, a washing basin, and a bed beneath a small window. Without bothering to explore her cell further, she collapsed on the bed and soon fell into a heavy sleep.

She awoke to the ringing of bells, and a knock on the door. She rose dizzily and opened it to reveal a young native novice monk.

"It is time for dinner," he said. "This way."

They were heading in the same direction as many other denizens of the mission, and soon the hallway was thronging with priests, novices, and natives, a stream of people spilling out finally into a large dining hall in which three long tables accommodated the mission's entire population. Father Montoya presided at the head of the main table, which stood perpendicular to the other two, waved her over to where some of the lumberjacks had already been seated. Tyler occupied a place not too far from their host, lying comfortably on a couple of chairs stacked with folded-up blankets. He was drinking something out of a coconut through a straw and conversing with Father Montoya, who as it turned out, spoke passable English.

Solena found a seat that Father Montoya indicated to his right-hand side, between himself and Tyler. As she and the rest of the crowd sat down, Father Montoya stood up and silence instantly filled the large hall. He recited a prayer in his silky voice:

"Bless us Oh Lord, and these thy gifts, which we are about to receive from thy bounty, through Christ, Our Lord. Amen."

The gifts were quite numerous and varied, though simply prepared, from large hunks of tapir and deer meat to yams, hearts of palm, and avocadoes.

"This is Father O'Reilly," Father Montoya indicated the priest sitting to his left.

"My name is Solena Rodriguez," she said.

"A pleasure to meet you," the young priest replied softly, though his cool tone belied his words.

Unlike the gregarious Father Montoya, he seemed detached and despondent. He was in his early thirties, with fair angelic hair and a thin but not unattractive face.

"You're from Ireland, right?" Tyler asked.

"Yes."

"Tyler, do you mind?" Solena asked.

The alligator got a little carried away with his meat and was shaking it from side to side so that Solena was spattered with sauce.

"Sorry," he said. Then he turned to Father O'Reilly, "My people are from Ireland, you know."

"Oh, whereabouts?" the priest asked, showing a speck of interest for the first time.

Solena gave Tyler a quizzical look while trying to wipe the sauce from her shirt.

"I know what you think," Tyler said after swallowing an enormous chunk of meat without chewing, "All Americans say they're from Ireland."

"No, I believe you," said Father O'Reilly. "Ireland is a wondrous place, and I don't presume to know half of what it holds."

"Tyler, what are you talking about?" Solena asked.

"When I say 'my people,' I mean the people who I was sold to after I was captured from my native swamps. For a while I was part of a traveling show, the main exhibit, you could say. Not many Europeans had seen an alligator!"

"And how did you come to be here?" Father O'Reilly asked.

Solena saw that she had misjudged the man. There was a quick-rising zeal hidden beneath the appearance of dull moroseness. But was the alligator drunk? And what exactly was the point of that string of fibs?

"I learned to talk, though kept it a secret from my owners, and eventually I escaped, stowing away on a ship bound for the New World. Eventually, I came to know these good people who sailed with me and are seeking a new home in these lands."

Solena finally understood: he was establishing a credible background for them. It wouldn't have been exactly prudent to say they had come from "the future." Apparently the lumberjacks were in on it too: she heard them in the background describing themselves as pilgrims, persecuted for their Catholic faith.

"I understand you were attacked by pirates?" Father Montoya asked.

"Yes," Solena said, "but hopefully they lost track of us in the jungle and gave up the pursuit."

"And if not?" Father O'Reilly inquired in his soft voice.

Solena felt a chill run down her spine. Somehow she knew the pessimistic priest had a point: St Amour wouldn't give up.

"If not," Father Montoya chimed in, "you will be protected in the mission. It was built to withstand greater assaults than that of passing brigands."

"Thank you, that is very kind," said Solena, "I hope it won't come to that, and I don't wish to bring trouble into this peaceful place. We will move on as soon as Rodney is better."

"Our best physician is looking after him," Father Montoya said. "Have no fear."

"I am sure that he will be cured by the grace of God, now that we have reached this holy place," Tyler added.

Solena could not believe how much Tyler was enjoying playing the role of a pious alligator. It seemed that the late Stanley was not the only aficionado of the dramatic arts.

"We do what we can," Father Montoya said, noting the compliment, "to spread the word of God to these tribes. There are still many who need conversion, and even this flock we have is sometimes uncertain about the true teaching. They still cling to some of their savage ways."

"They seem a good and God-fearing people," Solena remarked, trying to at least support Tyler, for it was impossible to outdo him.

"Look over there," he nodded to the far side of the table, "See how they avoid eating the tapir meat."

"Why? What's wrong with tapir? Have we eaten some?" Tyler asked, dropping his saintly decorum for a moment.

"Nothing is wrong with tapir," Father Montoya replied, "That's just the matter. According to their religious customs, some tapirs are like deities. They can only be eaten at certain times, otherwise the gods would be angered or some such nonsense. There is still much work to be done here."

"Nonetheless," Tyler declared solemnly, "the heart of any Christian alligator would be gladdened by the sight of this place,

Father."

After dinner they walked to the hospital wing, guided by Father Montoya himself, to find Rodney.

"Tyler, I never knew you'd been captured," Solena whispered.

"I wasn't. I made that up," he said. "I'm a free alligator, always have been."

15 SECRETS (AD 1694)

As they entered the hospital wing, Solena was expecting to hear Rodney chattering self-indulgently to whomever was in earshot, even if they didn't speak his language. She was surprised and unnerved by the relative silence. Two rows of beds stretched across the long hall, and an elderly native accompanied by two young boys hobbled from one patient to another, muttering something, but most of what she heard was the quiet conversation of several native patients. Rodney was lying by a small window, shaking with fever. He waved weakly to the approaching party.

"So much for the miracle cure," Tyler muttered, "Looks like they made him worse. Bunch o'quacks."

"He must have caught fever in the forest," Father Montoya said, "But fear not, we have an Indian medicine man who knows how to treat local diseases."

He waved the elderly native over to Rodney's bed.

The wizened old face crinkled in puzzlement as he looked at his patient. He asked a question in his language, which Father Montoya translated as, "Tell him about your hunting experience."

"Umm... we didn't hunt on our journey," Rodney said, "We already had food supplies with us."

"He means in general," Father Montoya said, "He needs to know this in order to find out whether an animal spirit is trying to take revenge on you. How has your hunting been?"

"Is this how he usually interviews patients?" Rodney asked.

"Yes."

"I don't know," Rodney shrugged, "I've never done any hunting in my life. Only surfing."

As Father Montoya translated all the words except surfing, which he pronounced in its English form, the old shaman grew even more puzzled.

"Surfing?" he asked.

"It's like riding the waves on a very small wooden plank, like the bottom of a canoe, let's say."

Father Montoya, no less puzzled than the shaman, translated these words. The old man raised his eyebrows, and the next few minutes were spent explaining the theory of surfing using folds in the blanket to represent waves.

At length, the old man made a pronouncement.

"He finds it very interesting," Montoya explained, "but it would not cause animal spirits to harm you. The only other option is that this is caused by ill will from an enemy."

"The bullet definitely was," Rodney said.

The shaman said something else.

"The evil is very strong, for it stems from your ancestors, many generations ago."

"Damn straight," Rodney commented.

"He will attempt to cast the evil spirits out," said Montoya.

The old man began to mutter something, his voice rising and falling abruptly.

As the chant continued, the shaman grew more and more forceful, his voice sometimes rising to greater volume as he thrust his arms away from Rodney as if casting out the evil spirit. At length, his words grew calmer as he completed the spell.

The shaman sighed, shaking his head, and said something to Father Montoya.

"Alas," said the priest, "he says it is beyond his powers."

"There must be something else you can do!" said Tyler.

"There must be other remedies," Rodney suddenly said with a strange certainty. Solena knew what he was driving at: if the legendary miracle cure existed, then this would be the time to bring it up.

Father Montoya fixed him with a long look.

"There is one other remedy," he said, "but it carries a heavy price which I'm not sure you'll desire to pay."

"Did you say 'price?'" Rodney asked, amused, "No price is too hefty for me."

"It is not in gold," Montoya said, "nor silver, nor other coin."

"Doesn't matter," Rodney insisted. "My father owns a great deal of property in America. I'll give you anything you ask for."

"If you are to know this cure, you must remain here with us for the rest of your life. For no one outside these walls must know about the cure. It is much too powerful. I foresee wars being fought over this land. Although many wars and battles have already been fought in these regions, they will pale in comparison to what could be. I hope..." he gave Rodney a piercing look, "you do not come here to take this remedy and try to make yourself rich by selling it. For this will bring nothing but ruin."

"Not at all," Rodney replied firmly, returning his gaze unflinchingly.

"And you?" the priest turned to Solena and Tyler. "Would you remain here, secluded from the world, for the rest of your days?"

"We would be glad to remain," Solena said, "to see Rodney get better would be worth it."

"It is not a decision to be taken lightly," Father Montoya warned.

"But a true Christian knows that his choice is always to stand by his friend, no matter what the consequence," Tyler intoned.

The priest breathed a deep sigh. He beckoned one of the boys who attended the sick ones.

"Call Raffaella," he decreed gravely.

As Father Montoya walked to the far side of the room to look at some patients with the shaman, Solena, Rodney, and Tyler were left alone.

"What the hell have you gotten us into?" Tyler asked in a loud whisper.

"I thought you were just doing your Christian duty," Rodney said, amused.

"My Christian duty is *not* to remain here for the rest of my natural life!"

"But Tyler, what were we supposed to do?" Solena said, "He needs this cure to live."

"Thank you, Sol. At least *someone* cares about me," Rodney said. "Besides, we'll find a way to get out of this place. They can't keep us here forever."

"They could keep *you* here forever," Tyler retorted, "An alligator can always slip out unnoticed, but you my friend... good luck! Have you seen how many guards they have? You think it's just a bunch of priests sittin' around and prayin'? These guys are more hardcore than St Amour and his band of dorks."

"And we're centuries ahead of all of them," Rodney said, rather loudly.

"Shh!" Tyler hissed.

Father Montoya turned towards them, but no one could tell whether he had understood what Rodney said.

At this moment, the other dryad walked into the room. Solena noted the way Rodney reacted to seeing her for the first time. He must have missed her when they first entered the mission, but now he looked stunned, and Solena made a mental note to reprimand him later.

"Raffaella," Father Montoya addressed her, "Would you say this man is beyond all help except for your cure?"

She glanced at him briefly. "Yes," she said.

Tyler snickered.

"What?" Solena whispered.

"Nothing. It sounded like a double entendre."

"No it didn't."

"What exactly is this cure?" Rodney asked.

"It is not too complicated," Raffaella said, looking at him directly for the first time.

Now it seemed even to Solena that some sort of double entendre was in the air, if not in their speech. Raffaella had the capability of seducing everyone in sight, even if it was unintentional.

"There is a medicinal root that I found in the forest," the dryad continued, "All we have to do is brew some tea, and let you drink it."

Solena nearly gasped as Raffaella took the plant from the pocket of her dress. The plant was one that dryads consumed regularly, but it had always been unknown to humans for only dryads could find it by following certain signs and portents. It was a root shaped much like a yam, but yellow with golden glowing overtones. Solena also noted the way Father Montoya's eyes almost seemed to glow in response.

"I will help you prepare it," Solena suddenly said.

"Of course," the other dryad smiled mysteriously.

She must have recognized Solena's true form also. It was about time they had a talk.

They walked down to the kitchens, which were nearly deserted at this late hour, and in any case, they could speak in the language of dryads. Raffaella blew on some coals that were still glimmering in the stove and filled a pot of water. As they waited for it to boil, both were hesitant to begin the conversation.

"Why do you give the humans the Poniato Root?" Solena finally asked. She realized it was not a very subtle opening, but it seemed like the wrong time for small talk.

"A strange question," the other dryad replied, still smiling in her Sphinx-like way.

"What do you mean?"

"We need it to save your human. It's the only way. I don't know why you would object to that."

"I'm not objecting," Solena said, "But I wonder why you revealed it to the humans in the first place."

"Why shouldn't I?" Raffaella replied calmly, "Do you think only dryads are entitled to it?"

She began slicing the root into thin slivers, her movements with the knife steady and precise.

"I never thought about it," Solena admitted, "It's just that it makes us different from the humans. We live a longer life because we eat the root. Are humans meant to live that long?"

"Why not?"

Solena didn't know what to say.

"Don't you want your human mate to live as long as you?" Raffaella asked suddenly.

"How did you know he was my..."

"Just a guess."

"I *see*," Solena said. "You have one too. That's why you live here."

It was the other dryad's turn to be caught off guard. She was silent for a while, as she threw the pieces of the root into the boiling water and watched it turn a pale golden colour.

"We better get this to your friend," she said.

They found the others still waiting by Rodney's bedside. No one was going to miss the miracle cure. As Rodney sat up to drink the brew, Solena watched jealously, an unpleasant scenario unraveling itself in her head. She knew she ought to be glad of Rodney's recovery, but at the same time she couldn't help visualize how grateful he would be to Raffaella for providing it. This miracle cure was not just for him, she remembered, it was for his father. That was why he had risked his life, to bring the "miracle cure" back to his time. And here was another dryad making that dream come true. How ironic.

The effect was almost instant. The two dryads were not as filled with wonder as the others, for they well knew how powerful this plant was. As soon as Rodney had drank half the cup, some color returned to his face.

"These guys are definitely hardcore," he said.

16 MIDNIGHT IN THE GARDEN (AD 1694)

Father O'Reilly was composing musical notation for the children's choir when he suddenly found that night had fallen. He would become so carried away that he never noticed the arrival of dusk until it became impossible to see what he was writing. The noise of insects grew louder outside his window.

He lit a candle, but he hated writing by candle light, and sat at his desk thinking over the strange events of the day instead.

A quick and soft rapping sounded at his door, and the receding sound of footsteps. He did not get up to see who it was. He knew. It was a signal that he had heard and obeyed many times. He waited a few more minutes, then raised the hood of his robe to cover his head and left his cell.

A few seconds later he was in the garden, looking for that familiar form, and she soon appeared, like a shadow separating itself from the tangle of trees. It was Raffaella.

"I couldn't wait to see you, John!" she cried.

He smiled at her complete lack of coquetry. "I couldn't wait to see you either, my dear."

"There is so much I have to tell you."

"Truly, these newcomers are a strange lot," he said, finding her excitement contagious.

"Yes, and more strange than you know," she continued, "Come, let us to our usual bench."

They walked down the garden path, obscured from sight of the main building's windows. In the midst of the garden stood a small bench, and they sat side by side. Father O'Reilly was careful not to sit too close to the dryad. He knew it would be the end of him.

"That Englishman had a very strong fever, and I cured him with the Poniato Root," she began.

"So I heard."

"It reminded me of when I first met you in the forest."

"You saved me," he said, inadvertently taking her hand.

"You see," she continued, almost breathless, "*She* is a dryad too, and they're together. What other reason would a dryad have to leave the forest?"

Father O'Reilly was silent, and she paused also as she tried to look into his pensive blue eyes. Finally he returned the look, trying to make his delicate face appear impassive, and she continued.

"You see, it is possible."

"But not for me, Raffaella," he said softly.

She stood up abruptly.

"Did Jesus save you in the forest?" she cried.

"Hush! We'll be heard. Perhaps, in a way, he did. He may have sent you to save me... and to tempt me."

"For someone who is so learned and wise, you sometimes say the most foolish things," she retorted in exasperation.

"Sh! Someone is coming." He squeezed her hand tightly, and prepared to flee.

"No, it would be suspicious if we go together. You stay," she said, "I'll hide." And in an instant she was gone, just a shadow among the trees.

Father O'Reilly began to pace, dissembling a peaceful evening walk and trying to will his heart into beating slower.

A man appeared. At first it seemed to be one of the natives, but theirs was a lean and wiry physique. This one looked taller and more muscular. In addition, he wore nothing but a sort of undergarment made of leaves round his hips. The stranger looked angrily at the priest, but said nothing. It was a dryad, Father O'Reilly knew.

"Raffaella!" the male dryad said, "I know you're here."

"Who are you?" Father O'Reilly finally demanded.

"Anastacio," the dryad replied proudly.

Raffaella emerged from the shelter of the trees. "Anastacio, you can't be here!" she exclaimed.

The male dryad came closer, towering over both of them.

"Neither can you. I've come to take you back to the forest."

"I told you, I'm happy here."

"With him?" he gestured unceremoniously at Father O'Reilly, "He's a human, and a priest. This is not in accordance with dryad or human laws."

"What difference does it make to you?" she asked, "I've already told you I don't love you anymore. Even if I were to leave, I wouldn't leave to be with you."

"But you said—"

"Those words I spoke were in jest," she fired back.

The male dryad didn't look convinced by this pronouncement.

"Perhaps you ought to leave," Father O'Reilly said, his voice quiet but firm. "It is taxing enough trying to keep one dryad's presence a secret."

"Fear not, I will not stay in this monastery. My home is in the forest. As hers should be," he pointed sternly at Raffaella.

"That's not for you to decide!" she retorted.

"We shall see," Anastacio said ominously. "I can leave now, but I will return. I will not allow this madness to continue. By the Great Tree, I swear it so."

He strode away and soon they lost sight of him in the darkness. Raffaella looked after him, fuming, while Father O'Reilly sought the bench for support. In his mind, he agreed with Anastacio, but his heart suddenly begged to differ.

"Let us return to our cells," he finally said.

No one had witnessed the scene. No one but a large alligator hiding in the shadows of the rosewood trees.

***

Solena woke up at dawn, but it was not due to the sunlight streaming through her window. It was the blanket, being dragged away by something. Something with teeth.

She sprang quickly to the floor in a fighting stance, prepared for action, but realized it was only Tyler.

"Fif ofer dryaf if ufto no goo," he said, then he spat out the blanket. "This other dryad is up to no good."

"I knew it!" Solena said.

"She met that priest, Father O'Reilly in the gardens."

90

"Aha! This is interesting."

"She's in looove," Tyler cooed. "She tried to convince him they could be like you and the boss man."

"And Father O'Reilly is in love too?"

"He put up a formal resistance, but I could tell he was ready to crumble. It's just a matter of time."

"But he's a priest."

"I know," Tyler said with glee, "It's like one of those crazy reality shows. And just when things couldn't get weirder, another dryad jumped in. He literally jumped in over the wall. And she was all like, 'Anastacio, I don't love you anymore.'"

"What?!"

"So then he had to leave," Tyler continued, wrapped up in his narrative and not noticing Solena's utter shock, "but not before swearing revenge in the best Mexican soap opera tradition."

"Anastacio?" she repeated.

"Yeah, that was his name, I think."

Could it be the same Anastacio? They were so near the lands of her tribe. And he may have been already born by then... She didn't really know how old Anastacio was. Dryads were never strong with arithmetic.

Solena sat down on the bed. "This is very weird," she said.

"Tell me about it. We really need to get out of here. But don't you worry, Tyler has a plan, and it's a darn good one."

"Well?" she asked, rubbing her temples.

"We've got to get in touch with St Amour. Maybe he'll get us out of this place."

"*That's* your plan? I don't think St Amour is the 'Forward, to the Rescue!' type. He was trying to kill us, remember?"

"I'm not so sure he was trying to kill us. I think he wanted to see what other cool gadgets he could take away from us. That man has a hunger for knowledge."

"Good for him."

"I tell you, I see a lot of myself in him."

Solena got up and began to pace the room. "The one thing I can't understand is... why on earth would he bring Sir Lancelot?"

"I was wondering about that myself..."

"You know, maybe... no this is too weird," Solena began, "Maybe he thinks he's a good guy."

"Of course Sir Lancelot is a good guy, aside from a minor adulterous affair which we can disregard."

"No, I mean St Amour thinks of himself as the good guy in his own movie or story or whatever."

"Huh?" Tyler thought about this a moment, "Huh! That's why he got the knights!"

"He admires them, and he thinks he's a hero, like them."

"Human psychology is nice'n'all," Tyler interrupted, "but let's get real here: he's a bloodthirsty killer. However, I do think that if he's convinced we're more useful to him alive, he is less likely to kill us."

"That's the plan?"

Tyler swished his tail to and fro uncertainly. "Well, it's the beginning of a plan."

"What about the knights?" Solena mused, "Maybe they really are good guys. We could convince them to go over to our side."

"Right! Plant the seeds of dissention among the enemy, then make our stand here. If St Amour attacks, the knights will help us escape in the confusion."

"What about the priests and all the people here?"

"What about them?" Tyler asked, uncomprehending.

"They're good people, and I don't want to implicate them in this mess!"

"I'm not so sure. They're supposed to be followers of Jesus and they use shaman magic? It kind of calls into question their professional integrity."

"Whatever works, I guess," Solena shrugged.

"Exactly. In this situation, whatever works should be our motto. We should try out all possible solutions."

"Hmm..." Solena was almost convinced.

"Teddy Goldman' Combat Rule number 36..." Tyler began.

They said it together: "Always have a plan B!"

17 FRIEND OR FOE (AD 1694)

On the same morning, they buried Stanley. The miracle root having done its job, Rodney was already well enough to walk about the grounds, and he joined in the ceremony, as did the entire population of the mission.

It was a beautiful morning, the jungle mist melting away in front of their very eyes as if by magic. The sun shone gently, and the smell of damp moss and flowers intrigued the senses.

Solena found herself more concerned over the affairs of the living than the burial rites of the dead. She had two main preoccupations that morning. The first was Rodney, the second, Anastacio. It was strange, but as she watched the burial ceremony and half-listened to Rodney's speech ("He was a damned good lawyer, an excellent lawyer, who took relatively small retainer fees considering the caliber of work...") all she could think about was how to find Anastacio, if it was really him. But then she would become irrationally jealous of Rodney, even though she knew that Raffaella was much more interested in the priest, according to Tyler's story.

Instinctively following a compound of Teddy Goldman and *Cosmological Magazine* influence (which was still strong in her), Solena fled to her cell after the funeral. Raffaella may be ridiculously beautiful, but she was no match for modern makeup.

The hand mirror was produced. The cosmetics — there wasn't much, just the basic lipstick, mascara and foundation — were laid out on her bed. These would be quite enough: there was no need to go over the top. What she needed was a light touch, something subtle, not desperate. A bit of mascara. A thin layer of foundation that added an artificial touch that humans strangely liked to her already perfect skin. Some pink blush spread with light brush strokes around the cheekbones. It was all very well to feel confident on the inside, but it helped to look good on the outside.

And then, as Teddy Goldman wisely counselled, avoid the man in question while pretending nothing is the matter.

To occupy her time, she decided to satisfy her curiosity about the human culture of this strange microcosm. She sat down on the chapel steps and talked at length with a couple of teenage boys who spoke decent Spanish and could not repress how keen they were on becoming hunters. Tyler joined them, settling down in a shady spot beside the steps.

"So why is it that you can't eat tapir meat?" Solena asked.

Both boys' expressions suddenly acquired a grave and significant tenor.

"Tapirs are like people," the younger boy replied, almost in a whisper, his large black eyes becoming even more rounded.

"They are just like people," the other boy added, "They live inside the treeless hills, and they command other tapirs, who are their servants. Those are the ones we can hunt and eat, but only at certain times and after much fasting."

"What do you mean, they are like people?" Solena asked.

"They are like him!" they pointed at Tyler. "They go into their homes and drink beer and talk amongst themselves just like people do."

"And there is a special tapir drink," the younger added excitedly, "If you drink it, you will turn into tapirs, and you'll be able to enter their secret houses in the hills and see for yourself."

While Solena was thus occupied, a small man in a giant sombrero walked through the gates, demonstratively carrying a cloth in front of him, a cloth that was only notionally white. It was made of canvas, and covered with so many stains that it would have been wiser realistically to call it a muddy sort of gray.

The native scouts spotted him from afar, and by the time he made it through the gate, both priests were awaiting him in the courtyard.

"Greetings!" Father Montoya was the first to speak. "There is no need to bear a white flag. All who come here are welcome."

Father O'Reilly stood dumbfounded for a moment, then he

rushed towards the newcomer who dropped the white rag of peace on the ground and embraced him.

"Patrick O'Malley!" the priest exclaimed.

"John! So good to see you, my friend!"

"It's so good to see you, Patrick !"

He led the newcomer over to Father Montoya.

"This is Patrick O'Malley. We grew up in the same village together. With your permission, Father, I will show him the workings of the mission."

"Of course," said Father Montoya. "On such an occasion, you should find some fitting libation for your friend."

"Come on then," Father O'Reilly said, leading the negotiator-turned-guest to the cellars. "You won't find any Irish ales here, but this *chicha* stuff is not half bad. Let's have a drink."

After obtaining two flasks of the necessary liquor, they sat in the gardens, on the bench where he had sat with Raffaella the previous night.

"You seem to have found a peaceful haven," O'Malley commented, "And I'm sorry to disturb it."

"All is not as it seems," Father O'Reilly replied, "Truly, you don't know how glad I am to see you! I've been troubled of late, and it's good to find an old friend again."

"I don't suppose you'd care to unburden yourself?"

"I wouldn't know where to start."

"If regular folk confess to priests, then priests should also confess to someone," the pirate quipped.

"Ha! I wish it were that simple. Sometimes I think I should have been a soldier of fortune and you, a priest."

"Me?"

"And why not?"

"I can't read or write a word, for one," said O'Malley, "It's all bloody confounding to me."

"But I think you have the heart for it, Patrick. Truly you do."

"And so do you, man."

"Sometimes I'm no longer sure."

They sipped their beers.

"It's some girl, isn't it?" Patrick suddenly asked.

John looked up at him in surprise, then smiled sadly. "You *can* read, Patrick. You read me like a book."

"All men are easy to read. Always some skirt upsetting your good humours when she's least expected. My advice is, less women, more drinking."

They laughed, and kept the recommended course of action as their conversation flowed on, reminiscing about Ireland and the old days. Though their life then had been far from idyllic, it had acquired that strange patina of melancholy beauty when looked upon from a distance of so many years.

They walked through the school building, and briefly looked on the musicians teaching the children to play.

"These are the pupils I'm most proud of," John explained.

Two of the boys played violins, the others, woodwinds. It was a beautifully well-trained orchestra. The pirate looked on, not saying anything but evidently feeling much. He stood there until the students finished playing the piece, and his eyes had a wistful, melancholy look.

Finally, as they stood on the open plaza again and Patrick prepared to leave, they reluctantly arrived at the part of the conversation that both had been avoiding.

"Captain St Amour sent you to ask if we would give up the pilgrims?" John asked.

"Aye. He's fairly sure you will, though I'm pretty sure you will not. It's more in the way a formality."

"Then we are to fight?"

"It looks that way."

"I do not suppose I could dissuade you," the priest offered a rueful smile.

"You can certainly dissuade me, but not the captain."

"What does he want with these travelers?" John asked.

"Same thing as always," Patrick shrugged, "He wants to rob them."

"Well, we all have our various occupations, but I don't suppose I could persuade you to join us instead."

"I thought about it, of course," the pirate replied, "but at this stage it would be betraying my captain, and I cannot do that."

"I wouldn't expect any less of you, Patrick. And if things turn against you, at least you can always count on my friendship."

They parted with a sadness that John felt as almost a physical sensation. It was as if he was bidding goodbye to Ireland all over again.

***

Solena and Tyler had witnessed the coming of the pirate emissary. They had wanted to speak a few words with him too, but seeing how Father O'Reilly had greeted him and the joy with which the two met, no one dared to interrupt them.

Besides, Tyler had other plans. At nightfall, an alligator and a dryad crept softly from the lodging house. At first Tyler had proposed digging a tunnel, but since they didn't know exactly how deep the foundations of the walls went — and knowing the Jesuits, they were probably pretty damn deep — they decided to try climbing over the walls.

"This is where I saw that dryad guy climb," Tyler stated as they reached a dark part of the garden, away from the main gate and the sentries.

Solena was supplied with a long coil of rope that had been part of the lumberjacks' equipment. She wound it around Tyler's body and forelegs into a semblance of a climbing harness, then she scaled the wall easily using the rampant vines as handholds.

It was fortunate that the night was dark and none of the sentries were looking in their direction, for they would have seen the outline of an alligator hoisted up by a rope to the top of the wall.

Then in the same way, Solena lowered him down carefully and climbed down swiftly herself. The jungle noises grew strident in her ears as her pulse suddenly raced. Here they were, attempting to find a crew of pirates and somehow lead them into peaceful negotiations.

"This way," Tyler whispered, "I can smell them."

Pretty soon, Solena could smell something too — the smoke of a campfire and roasting meat. She could even hear snatches of words, music and laughter. They were approaching the pirates' camp.

"I'll see who's around," she whispered to Tyler.

"And if it's the knights, get them away from the camp. We don't want to be seen talking to them."

In a whirl, she was up in the tree branches, climbing silently towards the low glimmer of the camp fire. She had not done this in such a long time, but of course she had not forgotten how to climb with the stealth and swiftness of a dryad.

From a lofty bow, she looked down on the pirates' camp. There were about a hundred of them altogether. St Amour was asleep in a quiet nook by himself, his hand resting on the hilt of his cutlass. A few of the men were still awake, playing bawdy songs on a discordant guitar. The two knights were also sitting by the fire with the lieutenant.

Solena took further stock of them. Sir Lancelot was tall, dark, and handsome but not the least bit smug about it. He appeared the smarter of the two knights, though that was probably not saying much. Sir Gawaine looked like one of those happy-go-lucky fellows who were so much disposed to have fun that they came across as completely unhinged. Were these truly the knights of legend?

All three were having a great time as the lieutenant taught them to play cards. When he wasn't trying to kill anybody he looked kind of... friendly. Perhaps he too could be brought over to the good side, so to speak. She no longer knew whether they *were* the good side, considering Rodney's machinations.

She must have been looking too intently, for Lancelot felt her gaze and looked up at her before she could hide. Meeting her eyes, he dropped his playing cards.

"What is it, Sir Lancelot?" Gawaine asked.

"Methought I saw... the sorceress. Yonder in that tree."

Jackson leapt up, hefting his cutlass. "Let us report to the captain."

"Nay, let us not alert the others," Sir Gawaine suggested slyly, "For this could be an adventure worthy of only the bravest knights, such as we three."

"What about Sir Roger?" Lancelot asked.

"He is a brave knight and stout... but glory, when shared, becomes less glorious."

Jackson mulled it over. He was beginning to find the knightly conduct contagious. There was an adventurous streak in him, deep down in a place in his soul that should have been rendered inert long ago. That wellspring had nearly been dried out by the slave driver's whip and the life of toil and danger aboard ship. He had lived as an adventurer only because there was no other way for him, but now he was beginning to see that there was, strangely enough, *enjoyment* in it as well.

"Let us follow this adventure," he finally said, "to see where it may lead."

"Hurray!" the knights whispered.

Solena mentally thanked Sir Gawaine for making her task easier. She had leapt into the branches of another tree, and now she intentionally let the knights glimpse her once more.

"Over there," whispered Sir Gawaine.

She disappeared once again, camouflaged by the forest, then called out to them from the darkness. "Here I am!"

Despite his incipient romanticism, Jackson suddenly became doubtful.

"She's trying to lure us away from the camp. What do you suppose she wants?"

"No one knoweth. It's an adventure!" Sir Lancelot said, and they stumbled on through the entangling vines.

Solena landed soundlessly beside Tyler.

"Over here!" she called once again.

Presently, the trio emerged from the thicket of branches.

"My word, a dragon!" Sir Gawaine cried, pointing at Tyler.

"Are you sure?" Lancelot asked, "It is passing small."

"How large would you have it?"

"That's the alligator that nearly ate me for dinner," Jackson suddenly said. "I recognize it."

"I always thought I had a distinctive countenance," Tyler replied. "Wait a minute: how are you alive?"

"It speaks! Surely it is a dragon!" cried Sir Gawaine. "This is our chance for glory."

He drew his sword and began to charge. Tyler bared his teeth.

"Nay, first let us hear it out," Sir Lancelot reasoned, taking a stand between them. "Are you here to offer challenge?"

"On the contrary," Tyler said, "We're here to offer a peaceful solution."

"A dragon suing for peace? I trust it not," said Sir Gawaine.

"Look he's not a dragon, just an alligator," Solena broke in. "And I'm a dryad. I live in the forest and care for the trees. I'm what you would call a woodland fairy, not a witch or a sorceress."

"I put no trust in witches either," said Sir Gawaine, "They say they're not witches, but what if they *are*?"

"How do we know you speak sooth?" asked Sir Lancelot.

"Well... if I were a witch, I would have tried to kill you with my magic. Instead, I only covered up our tracks in the forest. That proves I'm a dryad, for dryads may not kill."

"That alligator tried to kill me, you can be sure of that, good Sirs," Jackson said.

"I don't have any rules against killing as I'm not a dryad!" Tyler remonstrated. "And besides, you were trying to kill me at the time. The point is, St Amour started all this. We hadn't done him any harm. In your chivalrous literature, *we* should be the ones you're fighting to protect. For look you, she is the innocent maiden, and I'm the innocent... reptile."

"Perhaps it is even so," Sir Lancelot spoke, deep in thought.

"Of course it's so!" Tyler insisted.

"Then Sir Roger has deceived us?"

The knights both looked at Jackson.

"Well, he is my captain, and I did not wish to betray his confidence... but in truth, he has deceived you."

"The blackguard!" cried Sir Gawaine. "I shall throw my gauntlet in his face."

"But that would be mutiny," Jackson protested.

"It's not the way," Tyler said. "What I suggest is that you three play along, for now. If St Amour attacks us, pretend you're still on his side. But if he successfully storms the mission town, then you could help us. We can escape together."

"Escape? Where to?" Jackson scoffed. "There is nothing but wilderness. Without the rest of the crew to protect us, we could be slaughtered by passing Indians or brigands."

"A knight may not be deterred by danger, Sir Jackson," Lancelot objected, "We must help them."

"Aye, we must help them!" Gawaine exclaimed with the same fervour he had displayed in trying to kill them not five minutes before.

Jackson shook his head. "That would be mutiny, a hanging offence."

"Look, just think it over," Tyler suggested. "We've told you our side of the story. Let your consciences decide the rest."

He and Solena retreated into the jungle. After once again performing the feat of going over the wall, they rested, panting, in the gardens.

"What do you think?" Solena asked.

"The knights will help us. I'm not sure about that Jackson guy. He might still be mad at me for biting him."

"How weird was that? They must really be the knights of the Round Table."

"I guess."

"But the story doesn't go like that... They don't just up and leave Camelot with some pirate."

"It didn't go like that *then*," Tyler pointed out, "but it does *now*."

"You mean, the course of history has been changed by that idiot pirate?"

"Well, first by us, then by the idiot pirate. After all, we started it by going back into a century where we don't belong. And now the Arthurian epics will read: 'And so Sir Lancelot and Sir Gawaine went forth in a magical ship and were never seen again.'"

"This is not good. Maybe this is what I'm here to prevent. Only I don't know how. Do you think we should take back the time boat and try to prevent any of this from ever happening?"

"Let's just get through this alive," Tyler decided, "Then we'll figure out what to do. I'm going to get some sleep because I have a feeling all hell will break loose tomorrow."

18 ALL HELL BREAKS LOOSE (AD 1694)

The morning commenced as usual. The birds twittered, the children sang in the chapel, the grownups drank beer, though a few men did occupy themselves with archery practice. Little did anyone know that St Amour would attack most boldly in broad daylight.

But before the action began, before anyone except Tyler even suspected it might begin, Solena finally ended up alone with Rodney. She had been bent on avoiding him, but as fate would have it, they came out of their cells at exactly the same time onto the wide expanse of the plaza.

"You're looking better," Solena said.

"Thanks. That native cure sure worked."

"Well, you got what you wanted. Though it's not a native cure, it's a dryad cure."

"I suspected it might be," Rodney said, "but one could never be sure. I read about this Jesuit mission where no one ever died. It was the strangest thing. Usually people died like flies, at least one person per day. But here... I thought it might be something supernatural, or at least homeopathic."

"We didn't have to go back in time," Solena said, as if in reproof, though she was not sure whether she was angry at him or herself.

"Why not?"

"There are dryads in our times too." Suddenly she knew she had to tell him. She took a deep breath. "I'm a dryad."

He showed no surprise. "I know," he said.

"What?!" She remembered Stanley. Surely his final words wouldn't have been about that. "Stanley told you?"

"No, I've known for a while. I did a DNA check on you when you started on executive."

"And you didn't say anything?"

"You didn't say anything," he countered.

"Well, I was trying to stop you from destroying the forests."

"And I thought you might be, so I decided it would be safer to have you close by."

"So this... relationship has all been a bunch of bullshit?"

"No, no," he said emphatically, "I like you! I mean, look at you: you're beautiful, you're sexy! I can't say it's *all* been bullshit, but let's face it, this whole relationship has been built on mutual lies."

Solena didn't know what to say to that. She was stunned, and even though she had known this all along, hearing it said out loud made it much worse.

But they were both interrupted the noise of grenadoes detonating nearby. Solena felt as if the sudden barrage of explosions erupting in the mission was just icing on the cake.

"That must be our friend St Amour," she said. "We should get to the armoury and find some weapons."

"Agreed."

By that time the pirates blew open the gate and roared into the mission, scaring the startled inhabitants. The native women, frantically grabbing hold of their children, fled to the church, and St Amour did not pursue them. He was looking only for Rodney and his companions.

However, the native men did not look kindly on this intrusion. The guards fired muskets, but the majority trusted their bows more and they let fly their deadly arrows upon the pirates. They stood on the roof, in windows, on balconies, hidden behind trees, or even up in the branches. St Amour rushed onward, cutlass drawn. He could hear the arrows whizzing through the air and his men falling beside him, but he didn't spare a second to look at the damage. Ignoring the native musketeers and bowmen, his eyes sought only Rodney Love and his companions.

"O'Malley, check these houses," he ordered, "the rest, with me."

The pirates followed their captain, occasionally stopping only to reload their pistols and discharge them at the natives. Several native men already lay dead on the dusty plaza. Dozens more suffered light bullet wounds and still fought on, emerging briefly from the cover of a tree or a balcony to release their deadly missile.

Lieutenant O'Malley and a few of his men entered the refectory, but found it deserted. Jackson and the knights followed him, hoping to find the dryad before St Amour did. As for O'Malley, he was more concerned with finding his friend and making sure he was safe. He urged his men onward with a feverish haste. They went to the next building and searched through the school rooms, finding nothing but frightened children and lay priests.

Seeing no sign of his friend, O'Malley ordered. "Let us search the grounds."

Raffaella had been watering flowers outside, but when the attack began, she hurried to the fathers' houses to search for John. Instead, she ran right into Father Montoya, who looked almost mad with panic, his usually perfectly arranged hair seemed to stand on end.

Father Montoya had made the mistake of trying to attack Lelouche with a pistol. Now he was shot in the leg and bleeding profusely.

"I don't want to die!" Father Montoya exclaimed, "Quick, give me the magic root!"

Raffaella herself was in too much of a panic to do anything. She ignored him, seeking someone else.

"Where is it?" Father Montoya cried, trying to search her pockets.

"What are you doing?" Raffaella exclaimed, not so much affronted by this but eager to get away.

"I need the magic root!" the priest protested.

Suddenly someone's fist put a stop to his search. He looked up to find that he had been knocked to the ground by Father O'Reilly.

"This is not the time or place," the Irish priest said, "We should be getting her out of danger."

He grabbed Raffaella's hand, and together they ran for the nearest building, which was the armoury. She followed behind in a kind of stupor, and Father Montoya got up and limped after them. But Father O'Reilly was not destined to reach the end of that short journey.

His hand slipped out of Raffaella's as he fell to the ground, struck down by a stray bullet. The dryad knelt beside him, her senses finally returned. She found the wound, all too close to his heart. He was already growing deathly pale, and she knew that his life force was draining much too quickly. Even dryad magic could not save him.

He looked at her longingly, and said, "Go, Raffaella, get you to safety."

She shook her head, tears now streaming from her green eyes.

Suddenly, he smiled.

"I don't regret..." he said. "I love you."

"I love you too," she whispered.

His eyes closed, and she could feel his breathing cease. The beautifully pale face now shadowed over with death, looked even paler and more ethereal than before.

The battle cries approached, but Raffaella was oblivious to her surroundings. It was just then that Solena appeared from the arsenal, armed with dagger and sword. Rodney followed behind her, hefting a musket.

"Oh my God, Raffaella!" Solena saw the terrible scene as she emerged into the daylight.

She rushed over to Father O'Reilly but saw that his spirit was departed. Raffaella sat helpless in a fit of tears.

The noise of fighting approached, and a few pirates could be seen scoping out targets from the cover of the porticos. Bullets began to fly.

"We've got to move," Rodney said.

Solena grabbed Raffaella and yanked her to her feet.

"No," the desperate dryad cried, "I can't leave him!"

"He's gone," Rodney said. "There's nothing we can do here. We'll come back for him later."

Together, they retreated towards the huts of the natives, some of whom were still trying to repel the pirates with bows and arrows. They arrived in the relative safety of the huts and collapsed, out of breath.

At this time, O'Malley finished searching the buildings and took his squad outside. But before he could give any more orders, his eyes fell on the prone body of his friend.

"What kind of villain would shoot a man of God?" he cried.

Ignoring the storm of arrows which rained down from the roof of the common buildings, he knelt down beside the body but quickly saw that it was too late to help. The plaza filled with smoke as the pirates returned fire.

Another shot rang out, and Patrick O'Malley fell to his knees on the dusty ground beside Father O'Reilly. A bullet had struck him in the back, and he knew it was no stray bullet this time.

"Maybe I should have been a priest," he muttered. "But since I'm not... a curse on whoever has killed me."

He collapsed beside the body of his departed friend.

"*Sacre bleu*, not again!" St Amour shouted as he arrived on the square and saw the dead body of his second lieutenant. "Everyone, with me! These scoundrels have retreated to a distant corner, and we'll have to surround them."

Solena and Rodney had gained a brief interval of rest, but a few sibilant bullets raised small, angry clouds of dust around them.

"I'm not really good with firearms," Tyler said, scuttling towards the hut behind which Solena was hiding. "If they come any closer, I could give them a fair fight."

The pirates were indeed coming closer. At first there was just five or six of them firing sporadically at the natives, but now St Amour was charging maniacally at the head of his entire forces. There was no stopping him.

"Retreat!" Rodney called, although the natives were already retreating.

They had to make their stand in the garden. Here were a few trees which provided cover, and perhaps some dryad tactics could be used to keep the pirates at bay. Beyond the garden was the cemetery, and even as the fugitives reached the shelter of the trees, they could see more pirates outflanking them and approaching them from the cemetery side as well.

Yet even as she ran, supporting the half-faint Raffaella, Solena saw something that nearly made her stop in her tracks.

A dryad was standing on top of the mission wall. His golden hair tossed about by the wind, his eyes gazing sternly on the field of battle, he was beautiful to look at, but it was more than that. He was Anastacio.

Other dryads soon joined him, climbing to the top of the wall holding generous lengths of vines in their hands, and they descended like a green wave upon the mission.

Just after Solena saw them, everyone else also noticed the dryads that were pouring down from the walls. Many of the natives who had been staunchly standing their ground against the pirates, screamed in terror and ran at the sight of these supernatural intruders. But their fear was unfounded, for the dryads swept past them and attacked the pirates, not with any weapons but with leafy vines, which they used like lassos.

These vines were infused with magic, for once a pirate was caught in the loop, the dryad released the other end of the vine, and its entire length entrapped the victim from head to foot in an unbreakable tangle of greenery.

Solena nodded to Rodney, and they used the distraction to break through the ranks of beleaguered pirates, who were too stunned or preoccupied to stop them.

"The sorceress is escaping!" St Amour shouted. "Bring her back!"

Instead of obeying, most of the pirates were succumbing to the dryad vines. As Solena, Rodney, Raffaella and Tyler drew level with Jackson and the two knights, who were still free, St Amour thought that their flight had come to an end. Instead, the way was cleared for the fugitives as Jackson seemed to inadvertently trip one of the pirates who aimed to block their path. Sir Lancelot and Sir Gawaine jointly tackled Lelouche, who was also intent on stopping the dryads' flight. Of course, no one could be blamed for attacking the vile Lelouche, even in the midst of battle with other foes, but this seemed a tad suspicious.

"Jackson, you side with them?" the captain cried, "Sir Lancelot, you too? Treachery!"

But he was even more upset when a troop of green people surrounded him. He lunged ferociously, but his sword arm was at once bound up in a sticky vine. St Amour raised his pistol with his left hand, but this too was entangled, and in a few moments he was wrapped from head to toe in vines, and he toppled to the ground, uttering outrageous oaths.

Solena reached the cemetery, where pirates were likewise being overrun by dryads, swiftly and loudly, the victims' shrieks of terror piercing the air. She came to a halt, knowing that the dryads would recognize her and Raffaella as their own kind. The two of them were nearly lassoed, but the attacking dryads stopped just in time. Instead, they threw their green twine at Rodney and Tyler, both of whom were instantly rendered helpless. Tyler looked furious as the vines pinned his arms to his sides and fastened his snout closed.

Another group of dryads appeared, carrying the lumberjacks and Gary, Rodney's guard, likewise securely tied with the green fastenings.

Everyone except for Raffaella, Solena, and the mission's inhabitants were captives of the dryads. Anastacio approached them, smiling grimly as he looked over the immobile collection of tied-up pirates and other creatures.

"This is very uncomfortable!" Tyler complained, "not to mention demeaning."

It was hard to tell how he managed to speak, for his mouth was held tightly by the vines. It was a triumph of the Teddy Goldman method.

Anastacio now stood facing Solena. Seeing the great bulk of his body so close served as final proof. There he stood, glowing with the energy of youth, almost nothing like the withered, lean dryad she had known, but his eyes were the same. He was indeed the Anastacio she knew, much younger and more... intimidating.

"Please," Solena said, "Let the alligator go. He won't harm anyone."

Anastacio looked at her with curiosity. Then he pulled lightly on the vines holding Tyler, and they suddenly slackened. He scrambled out of them and snorted with disdain.

"Let the alligator go?" Rodney mumbled, "What about me?"

"I'm mad at you." Solena said.

19 INTO THE DRYAD LANDS (AD 1694)

Father Montoya had finally tended and bandaged his wound. Now he limped nervously towards the dryads, accompanied by several of the native chiefs. The other natives also approached with varying degrees of caution.

Anastacio surveyed them sternly but not unkindly.

"You are in charge?" he asked Father Montoya.

"Yes, I am the only priest here. Father O'Reilly is departed, God rest his soul."

"I am sorry for your loss. We will see to it that these humans will not trespass on your mission again."

"Thank you, good sir," said the priest, clearly mystified by the dryad's provenance but too afraid to ask any questions.

The chiefs added their thanks in their own language, and Anastacio nodded and replied to each one.

"Raffaella must come with us," he said in a tone that precluded argument, "I hope you understand."

Father Montoya hesitated, at a loss for words. The chiefs and the elderly shaman approached Raffaella, asking her, "Do you truly wish to leave?"

"Yes," she said. "I belong in the forest, but I shall return for Father O'Reilly's funeral and mass."

"Of course," said Anastacio.

He then turned to Solena, curiosity again evident in his leafy-green eyes.

"We return to the forest," he said, "Do you wish to come with us?"

She nodded, dazed by the fact that he did not know her. But how could he?

"Thank you for helping Raffaella," he said. "Let us away."

He led the procession of dryads who carried their human prisoners through the devastated mission and into the jungle. Solena joined the rear of the column, still supporting Raffaella, with Tyler scuttling at her side.

That was all? A brief thank you? He might as well have written a card. She wanted to speak more with Anastacio, but he seemed so gloomy and unapproachable.

Suddenly she remembered the fortune teller in faraway Los Angeles.

A very fine prediction indeed, she thought, cursing the fortune teller for telling her all that nonsense "he won't know you, though you'll know him." Of course that was true for Rodney Love, but he was obviously not "the one!" Suddenly she realized it was also true for Anastacio. This strange young Anastacio. Maybe every male she met from now on would 'not know' her? How dreadful! It was not the fortune teller's fault after all for simply being the messenger. There was no one to blame but fate itself.

She suddenly realized he was devastatingly, and even demoralizingly handsome. No male dryad had a right to be so attractive, for it might make the females feel unworthy! The features of his face so gorgeous from any angle, yet rugged and masculine, reflected courage, intelligence, wisdom, sensitivity... in short, it was the Anastacio she knew, only much less wrinkly. And less friendly, apparently.

They entered the dryad lands of her clan. The land and the trees were somewhat different, giving Solena a strange but pleasant sense of déjà-vu. Some of the trees that she had known in her century were mere saplings here, and she was excited when she recognized one. The sapling actually wiggled its scrawny branches and she thought it may, in some incomprehensible way, have recognized her too.

Rodney, the lumberjacks, the pirates, and the knights were each suspended from a couple of vines and carried between two male dryads.

The procession arrived at a lithe, slender palm tree, which turned out to be Raffaella's. Curious females and older dryads thronged the new arrivals, pointing at the prisoners and chattering.

On seeing her tree, Raffaella heaved a great sob, fell to the ground, and recommenced weeping. Some females looked on, no doubt judging her for abandoning the tree in the first place, while others' gazes were filled with sympathy.

"So you've decided to come back and be a dryad!" one of the females jeered, "Might as well make friends with bamboo now."

Solena then felt another case of déjà-vu, this time not so pleasant. She suddenly recognized the instigator, a female she had known who was always making trouble, or rather will be making trouble for her. Magdalena was her name.

She was young here, but still just as unattractive as she had been as an old crone. Solena supposed she never had been very pleasant to look at. Of course it was Magdalena leading the crowd of catty females.

"Exile her!" Magdalena cried, "We must take this to the priest. Surely, he will exile this shameless weed who abandoned her tree."

Without thinking, Solena stepped in front of Raffaella and faced the group of accusers.

"If anyone's going to be exiled, it should be you, Magdalena. The only reason you find fault with other dryads is because you're a pain in the ass to everyone, including yourself."

This was so unexpected that it caused absolute silence to fall over the dryads, soon to be broken by small giggles from females, some of which included Magdalena's friends. Quickly incited to action, dryads regained their good temper just as quickly.

It was fortunate that the dryads did not have a democratic form of government, otherwise Raffaella would truly run the risk of being exiled. Instead, it was rather a peaceful form of anarchy; they obeyed only the Great Tree and sometimes the priest.

The priest arrived on the scene just in time. It was a different priest than Solena knew. He was middle-aged, and he reminded her of Anastacio too, not by his looks but by his kind expression and manner. He addressed her before any of the others.

"Where do you come from?"

"I come from the same forest as you," she replied, "My name is Solena."

The priest fixed her with a piercing gaze. "I don't recognize you. But you are welcome here. I am Venicio, the priest."

He looked over the strange assortment of prisoners. "*What* are all of these?"

Anastacio replied, "I cannot say with certainty, but they are all strangers to these lands, as you can see. When we came to find Raffaella, they were all fighting each other."

"Those pirates stole my time boat," Rodney volunteered, straining at his bonds, "And they've been trying to kill me ever since."

"What about you?" the priest asked St Amour. "You don't accuse the other man of anything?"

"I will not be judged by woodland creatures," St Amour replied with haughty dignity.

"Untie them," said the priest. "If you refuse my judgment, I will rule in favour of the other human," he admonished St Amour.

The prisoners, feeling their bonds loosen, stumbled up to standing.

"You will all remain here in the forest," the priest commanded, "until I see your dispute resolved and find you are ready to leave. For now, come with me."

"The sports!" the other dryads shouted excitedly thronging the priest, "Let the sports be the judgment!"

"Yes, I was just about to say that," Venicio responded grumpily. "These humans seem strong and healthy."

He led the way to a small grove where trees were spaced farther away from each other than usual, making a natural gymnasium for the dryads. Unlike humans, they did not actively try to "keep fit." They simply enjoyed frolicking among the branches.

The younger males and females leapt from tree to tree, spinning through the air as if the laws of gravity did not apply to them.

"Climbing! That is a task fit for a seaman," St Amour exclaimed.

"Because we do not expect you to climb with dryad ability," the priest spoke, "You will do this simple exercise."

He nodded to Anastacio, who stepped forward, his biceps shining like newly-waxed Ferraris. He leapt up, gripped a branch, and pulled himself up, performing a simple chin-up, then slowly, with no apparent strain lowered himself down. He did a few of these, then jumped back to the ground. The other dryads howled their approval.

"The first man who gives up and releases the branch will be the loser," said the priest, "Is that clear?"

"Yes sir," said Rodney, rubbing his hands together. "You've got

112

no chance, St Amour. When it comes to chin-ups, I'm practically a dryad. I practice these every day in the gym."

"I should like to see you practice them in a full gale while hanging on for dear life," was the pirate's reply.

The contestants were led each to his own branch, with a dryad standing by each one to count the number of chin-ups performed.

St Amour began at a brisk pace. Rodney's chin-ups were slow and controlled, almost as good as Anastacio's.

They ceased trading jibes and insults, both focused entirely on their task. Solena and her group cheered for Rodney, the pirates cheered for their captain, while the knights stood dumbfounded.

At last, Sir Gawaine said, "This is a trial of strength that we too could assay."

"Indeed," said Sir Lancelot.

They quickly stripped off their armour and found another tree whose branches were low enough for them to reach. Nobody saw them perform their own exercises, for the general attention was focused on Rodney and St Amour.

"They are not bad for humans," a male dryad commented.

"Fifteen," the dryad counting Rodney's chin-ups said.

"Nineteen," St Amour's attendant dryad said.

Rodney began to increase his speed. He was catching up to St Amour, who was very subtly slowing down. The pirate was not yet tired, but he had reached a point where the exercise ceased to be easy.

Sir Lancelot and Sir Gawaine were still going strong. Sweat trickled down Rodney's face, tickling his neck.

"Twenty five, twenty six," Rodney's attendant said.

They both arrived at thirty at the same time. Now they tried to keep pace with each other because both were feeling the strain, and the risk of faltering and letting go when the other had a higher score was too great.

"Thirty two," both dryads said at the same time.

Rodney knew he could usually do a maximum of thirty, after that he took his gym towel and headed for the steam room. But it seemed he was already in a steam room. The humid jungle air got more and more unbearable, his arms ached, and St Amour cackled gleefully with no sign of stopping. But maybe the pirate was just bravado-ing his way to victory.

Rodney rested his arms, releasing each hand momentarily and taking turns shaking them. Then he quickly did another chin-up to catch up with St Amour's thirty four.

But now the pirate too had to take a pause. They both hung on for a few seconds as the crowd grew tense. At this point Sir Gawaine had finished his fortieth one and jumped down to the ground.

St Amour roared and performed chin-up number thirty five. Rodney still rested. He wasn't sure he had another one in him. But at this moment the pirate released his grip and fell.

The crowd was silent, watching Rodney with rapt attention. He took a breath. His muscles crying out for help, he forced them to perform one more time. He was now even with St Amour. He had to do one more, but only made it halfway. His arms completely failed, and he fell, nearly collapsing as the dryad steadied him.

The dryads were confused.

"They are equal!" they cried, looking to the priest, "What now?"

"What now?" Rodney muttered with a grin, rubbing his biceps, "The pole vault or the trampoline?"

"We shall bring them to the Great Tree," said the priest. "The Great Tree will choose the righteous one."

"The Great Tree!" the dryads shouted, evidently happy with this decision. The entire crowd followed the priest, leaving the knights behind.

Sir Lancelot completed his fiftieth chin-up and alighted from the tree.

"Truly this is a manly pursuit that the knights of Camelot could learn."

"It seems no one has witnessed thy victory," Sir Gawaine said, looking round him, "I shall relate it to the company."

"No need," said Lancelot humbly, "But let us follow and see how the judgment shall conclude."

Solena edged her way through the crowd and suddenly beheld the Great Tree itself. She thought it would have been smaller, but when confronted by its leafy vastness she found it just the same as the tree she knew. She wondered if it had always been the same throughout time.

"Both of you, stand beneath the branches," the priest commanded.

St Amour grinned into his jet-black beard. "And so Roger de St

Amour, scourge of the Spanish colonies will be judged by a tree."

The two adversaries stood side by side.

"Moment of truth, St Amour," Rodney said, "I think the tree knows you stole my time boat."

But the tree did nothing yet. For a few minutes the priest waited, making a sign for everyone to be silent. Soon a strange stillness reigned. The tree itself was silent, almost palpably so.

"It speaks not," St Amour said, and his voice was startling in the stillness.

"It will speak soon enough," said the priest.

For a moment, his face was blank as if in meditation, but suddenly he looked up, pointing his leafy staff somewhere to the back of the crowd. The dryads parted to either side, trying to look to where the priest was looking.

Just then Sir Lancelot and Sir Gawaine were approaching the scene, carrying all the armor they had recently discarded.

"You!" cried the priest, and everyone now saw he was pointing at Sir Lancelot, "Come forward, and stand beneath the Great Tree."

The crowd gasped. Sir Lancelot looked bravely at the priest and came forward. The priest motioned for him to stand between St Amour and Rodney.

At once, a branch moved. It leaned down towards him and a cluster of leaves gently touched his head. Then the branch returned to its place and the tree was still.

"Sir Lancelot wins again!" Sir Gawaine shouted.

"He is a righteous man," said the priest, "Therefore it is up to him to dispose of this boat as he pleases."

A huge clamour went up, dryads cheering, people protesting.

St Amour and Rodney both looked at Sir Lancelot expectantly.

"I know not what to do with such a miraculous boat," Sir Lancelot admitted, "I shall need time to think."

"Then time you shall have," said the priest, "You will all be our guests, and when Sir Lancelot is ready to depart, we shall detain you no longer. But do not think of leaving the forest without my permission. Our guards are vigilant day and night."

And so the waiting began. Only instead of waiting, everyone began wooing Raffaella.

Solena found herself entangled in the situation when Raffaella was drawn to her, feeling that they both had an affinity for humans. The next morning Raffaella came to find her. Solena had been sleeping in the branches of a tree that reminded her of her gum tree, not far from where it would grow, perhaps its ancestor.

Raffaella appeared more composed, but still looked terribly frail. She kept her human shape, probably out of anger towards the other dryads who did not accept her, and Solena did the same in solidarity. Raffaella sighed and sat down, leaning back against the tree trunk. Solena climbed down and sat beside her.

"Are you well?" Solena asked.

"I don't know whether I ever shall be," Raffaella said. "I suppose you guessed that John... Father O'Reilly was very dear to me."

"I know," Solena said, "But it only seems like you will never be happy again. It will pass."

"Perhaps humans and dryads are not meant to cross paths," Raffaella sighed. "By the way where is your human?"

"We broke up," Solena said, "We had been deceiving each other all along, and it was time to end it."

For the first time, she had a quiet moment to think about the breakup, and it gave her a bleak feeling.

"It's a shame," Raffaella said.

"It was partly my fault."

"It's no use trying to allocate blame," Raffaella said in one of her rare moments of wisdom, "Sometimes I feel as if it was my fault about him... Father O'Reilly."

"No, how could it be?"

"He felt so guilty about his feelings of love for me, he feared God would punish him."

"I guess that kind of thinking can't lead to any good," Solena said.

"All he wanted to do was write music and spread the word of God. If I hadn't met him... he would have been dead either way."

"Why?"

"When I first met him in the forest, he was bitten by a poisonous snake. I couldn't let him die. I saved him. But if I hadn't met Father O'Reilly, we all would have been happy. Anastacio would have been my mate perhaps."

Solena felt her whole body tighten at the mentioning of his name. She didn't know why she felt so territorial of Anastacio, as if knowing the Anastacio she knew in the future gave her sole ownership of him. She didn't want anyone else to even say his name.

But here the dryad himself approached, and suddenly she was in a panic.

She jumped up and said nervously, "Well, I shall leave you two."

Anastacio opened his mouth to say something, but she fled.

Solena headed for the river.

She wasn't sure whether Tyler would understand about Anastacio, but at least she could complain about Raffaella.

Tyler was taking the opportunity to do plenty of swimming in the murky waters of a nearby stream, and they talked while he splashed and swished.

"It's not fair. She's too sexy!" Solena exclaimed.

She sat on the bank, twirling the stalk of a tall shoot of grass.

"They'll soon be bored of her then," said Tyler, "All sex and no substance."

"Besides, she hasn't even read any of Teddy's books. She doesn't have a clue."

A few hours later Solena returned to seek Raffaella and found her near her palm tree with none other than Rodney Love. Her first instinct was to run away yet again, but she decided to face them. After all, she wasn't doing anything wrong, and neither were they for that matter… though jealousy told her they might.

"Well, hello Rodney," she tried to sound friendly but it came out strained.

"Hello Solena," he was calm, his expression unreadable. "Long time no see."

"I hope you two are having fun," Solena said.

For some reason, his calmness was irritating.

"We are actually," Rodney said.

"This is the stuff of Shakespeare, isn't it?" Solena blurted out, "'A little month, or ere those shoes were old with which she followed my poor father's body…'"

"What the hell are you talking about?" Rodney asked.

Raffaella suddenly burst into tears.

"What's the matter?" Rodney was bewildered.

"It's just so sad that Father O'Reilly was killed!" Raffaella sobbed.

"Nice job!" Rodney said, glaring at Solena.

"I'm sorry," Solena said, sitting down beside her, "I don't know what came over me. I didn't even mean to say that."

"It's all right, I'm not angry," Raffaella replied, "But I just want to be alone now."

"Good night," Rodney said, "I hope to see you tomorrow."

Raffaella offered a non-committal sob.

20 THE STUFF OF SHAKESPEARE (AD 1694)

Raffaella spent the next day crying too, while Solena was slightly disturbed by her own urge to check on her every few hours. She'd felt bad about the Shakespearean outburst and rather than face Raffaella again decided to watch her from a distance. Finally she asked Tyler co come along with her, knowing the alligator's taste for scandal. If they spied together, it would make her feel less of a lunatic.

It turned out to be a good night for Tyler.

They stalked Raffaella's tree for a while. She didn't do much except half-heartedly sing a few hymns, then climb a nearby tree to fetch a coconut and drink the juice.

Tyler was on the point of giving up when he suddenly froze, and Solena had the feeling he smelled the approach of a human.

It was St Amour, his black hair and beard well combed, bearing a bouquet of wild flowers. Solena and Tyler exchanged the same raised-eyebrow look.

As the pirate presented his gift, Raffaella took the bouquet and threw it in his face.

"How dare you?" she cried, "Your men killed so many of the mission people. And for all I know it was you who shot Father O'Reilly."

St Amour looked duly ashamed and humbled, brushing away flower petals from his hair.

"Madame, I assure you I would never shoot a man of God," he replied, "I am a Christian. I likewise ordered my men not to raise their weapons against these holy men. But alas, their aim leaves much to be desired."

"You may paint it in rosy colours, but you are a godless man and a villain. Out of my sight!" she cried.

St Amour bowed and retreated.

"What on earth…" Solena and Tyler asked each other after they too retreated to a reasonable distance.

"St Amour?" Solena cried, "Not him too!"

"*Et tu St Amour*," said Tyler. "Well, it's not like you ever had a crush on *him* so that's okay."

"Definitely not."

"You do have a crush on that Anastacio guy, though," he noted casually.

"What? No! No, we're friends."

"How can you be friends?" the alligator asked, veritably puzzled, "You blush and run away every time you see him."

"We're friends later… in the future. He's older then."

Tyler took a few seconds to process this.

"Well, that doesn't mean you can't have a little fun with him now," he declared at last.

"Tyler!"

"I'm just sayin'. The pirates are sure having a good time, why don't we?"

It was a just remark. The pirates had fallen into complete dissipation since their forced invitation to stay in the forest. It had been a long time since they had access to so much free food and the company of so many females. It didn't matter much that they were dryads: the pirates made advances, and the woodland creatures encouraged them all, save Lelouche, who seemed to repel them with his leering manner.

"Besides," Solena continued, both opposed to and captivated by this line of thought, "if something did happen here… he would tell me about it in the future. He would have told me, that is."

"No reason you can't change the past. We've been messing around with it this whole time."

"He likes Raffaella," Solena offered another devil's advocate argument.

"He's going to have to get in line!"

Tyler's words proved to be prophetic. Over the next few days Raffaella was still beset by grief, but she was also beset by an array of suitors. Even a few of the pirates showed up, bringing flowers and apologies, though the stream of pirates soon dried up as they found satisfaction in the arms of other, more joyful dryads.

Raffaella received a visit from St Amour again, rather formally this time, but without breaking into a rage.

The next day, Rodney impressed her by letting her listen to his iPod.

It seemed they were unaware of each other's courtship. The only people who truly had a grasp of the situation were Solena and Tyler.

Soon the iPod battery ran down, and there was no way to charge it. But Rodney didn't let this daunt him in his courtship. St Amour would visit almost every day, taking care not to be too obnoxious with his attentions.

While he wasn't courting the dryad, he mused over the appointment of a new second lieutenant. Lelouche should have been next in line if one considered the order of seniority, but Lelouche, as everyone knew, was a complete blackguard even by pirate standards, and could not be trusted.

Too cowardly to be suspected of the murders, Leolouche was nevertheless not to be promoted.

The captain could not figure out who had killed O'Malley, but his suspicion fell on Carracha. Therefore he appointed Tessier a loyal, though dull Frenchman. If Carracha tried to kill him too, then he would know for sure.

In the meantime, he could not locate most of his crew, but that was only to be expected as they were on shore leave, as it were. Even Jackson seemed elusive. The usually taciturn officer spent much time with the knights and the professor, playing card games and pursuing feats of strength. Jackson and the knights also spent much time with the scholar, who was finally released from his travel case and could roam about freely. St Amour didn't know what to make of it.

Meanwhile, Tyler and Solena had taken to climbing trees – the alligator was hoisted up on a rope as they had done in the Jesuit mission. From a farther away and higher vantage point they could observe Raffaella and her admirers undetected. They even bugged a tree not far from her usual hangout so they could hear everything while observing from a safe distance.

"It's like watching daytime drama," Tyler said.

St Amour entered, carrying a bouquet of flowers.

"Madame, you look marvellous as always. Your grief becomes you," St Amour pronounced.

"You are the cause of my grief," Raffaella replied, "Why do you come here time and time again?"

"Have you not guessed why I come here?" he asked.

"No," she said flatly. She was not about to offer help, and he floundered, but only for a moment.

"Then let it remain a mystery," he said, sitting down at her side. "Even Leonardo da Vinci could not plumb the depths of all of nature's possibilities."

She darted a sidelong glance at him, her eyes quick as hummingbirds.

"You know Leonardo?" she asked.

"Yes, I even conversed with him a few times while studying at the Sorbonne."

She laughed. "Leonardo lived centuries ago. How could you have met him?"

"It just so happens I possess a magic boat that takes me anywhere I wish... even into the past."

"Your lies are entertaining. Tell me more."

"I may prevaricate a little," he admitted, "but they are not all lies. I did study at the Sorbonne. I give you my word as a gentleman."

"You are a learned man?" she asked, her tone growing warmer.

Solena could not believe this. It seemed there was some connection blossoming between them, and while Raffaella had tolerated Rodney and hated St Amour, suddenly the pirate was gaining ground.

"Someone's coming! Quick!" Tyler hissed.

But it was too late, by this time Solena too heard the very soft but unmistakable footsteps of a dryad through the forest.

Tyler panicked and scampered along the branch, as if in imitation of a squirrel. He slipped, and the canopy of leaves parted as he fell. Solena yanked on the rope that held him, but looking down she saw Anastacio's muscular form appear out of nowhere and cradle the alligator, who landed heavily in his strong arms.

"Oh, thank you," she said, then she climbed down, trying to think of a good excuse for climbing a tree with an amphibious creature.

"Much obliged," said Tyler. "We were just observing the uh... landscape."

If Anastacio doubted the veracity of his words, he did not show it. He released the alligator gently onto the ground.

"I have never seen an alligator climb a tree," he said, "Though come to think of it, I had never seen an alligator until I met you. But it seemed so unlikely... considering that crocodiles never do it. Is it something all your species do?"

"Naturally," Tyler said, "with the help of ropes, of course."

"I see," Anastacio said, raising an eyebrow.

"I'm off to the river!" Tyler exclaimed briskly. "Good day for a swim."

He scuttled off, leaving the two of them alone.

"It is none of my affair," Anastacio said, "but maybe one day you can tell me about why one would climb a tree with an alligator."

Solena smiled, "Maybe one day."

She wanted to talk to him so badly, but since it wasn't the same dryad with whom she'd shared so much, it was hard to know where to begin. Yet fortunately he carried on with the conversation.

"You seem as if you are from these lands, yet I have never seen you."

"Maybe you have," she said.

"No, I would have remembered such beautiful eyes."

He was flirting! Of course, it didn't mean anything. Anastacio always flirted innocently with everyone. It was his way. At the same time, she could see that he was anxious about something. He didn't look as stern as he had when she first saw him storming the mission, but she could feel that sternness hidden beneath his beautiful features like tough bedrock.

"Are you aware there are two dubious humans accosting Raffaella?" he asked suddenly. "I've watched them... especially the dark-haired one... what scheme is he working on, I wonder."

"I wish I knew," Solena sighed, "It's very annoying."

"You know more about him than I. Perhaps you could help me."

21 A NEW ALLIANCE (AD 1694)

It was not very often someone asked her for help. Sure, it had happened a few times at the office, but it was usually for some feat of agility like getting a piece of paper that had fallen behind the printer.

This was different. Anastacio needed her help with something important, something that was troubling him. He had never needed her help before, not even in the future when they were (or will be) close friends. It would be the other way around: she would always lean on him for support.

She was about to say something when he suddenly swooped away in a flash – she was still not accustomed to how swiftly he moved in this youthful body – he climbed atop a tree, cut down two coconuts and gracefully handed her one within a second or two.

This was just like the old days, except the old Anastacio was not nearly so sprightly. She couldn't help smiling, but she suddenly remembered that the only reason he needed her help was so he could safeguard his precious Raffaella. Still, it was a worthy cause; no one wanted to see Raffaella in the clutches of an evil pirate.

"You look thoughtful," Anastacio remarked, "What were you thinking about?"

"I was thinking that we must protect Raffaella. I was also thinking about whether St Amour is really hatching some plot or if his courtship is sincere."

"What does it matter? He's a human, and I would sooner not see him in Raffaella's company."

"You never liked humans much," Solena remarked with a smile.

"Like them? Why should I? They encroach on our lands and cut down forests."

"You don't know the half of it."

"I also know that being mixed up with them has brought no

happiness to Raffaella."

"I have been sent here to stop the humans from destroying the forest," she blurted out, mostly just to prevent him from going on about Raffaella.

"What? Sent here by whom?"

"By my tribe, and the Great Tree."

"Strange that I know nothing of this," he muttered.

"And why would the Great Tree tell you anything?" she asked, wanting to add 'you arrogant dryad' but seeing that he had already caught that unspoken sentiment.

He grinned. "Sometimes I talk to it at length. Sometimes it talks to me too. You are not the only one…"

"Why do you talk to it? Are you practicing to be a priest?"

"Maybe, I haven't decided yet."

She had sometimes wondered why Anastacio had not become a priest. He had the reputation of being wise and knowledgeable but not the title.

"These dryads can be so irritating," he said as if in answer to her unspoken question, "I do not think I would have the patience to deal with their petty quarrels. The priesthood is perhaps not for me."

Solena nodded, knowing all too well his irritation with other dryads, most of whom were immature and quarrelsome by nature.

"I just had a thought," Anastacio said, "If you are special, why was it the tree chose Sir Lancelot and not you?"

"You may recall it was the priest who called for Sir Lancelot to come forward. The time boat, it's more of a human affair. Sir Lancelot is the least harmful human of the lot, so perhaps that was why the priest and the Tree chose him…"

"And who is the most harmful human?"

"I wish I knew."

"Let's go talk to it," Anastacio suddenly said.

"The Tree?"

"Maybe it will tell us what to do about these humans. Maybe it will speak to you."

"Or maybe you just want to see whether I'm telling the truth about the Tree choosing me?"

"Maybe," he said.

As they walked together she noticed that playful grin was still lighting up his face.

The Tree stood encircled by its smaller brethren, yet somehow aloof of them as if voyaging in its own dream world.

"Wait," Solena said, putting a hand on his shoulder to stop him from coming closer to the tree.

She turned to face it, hoping for something to happen... after all, the tree had chosen her, spoken her name. She wondered now whether that was just a story made up by the tribe to get rid of her. A sudden feeling of paranoia washed over her, and she wondered how the tree was supposed to recognize her, three hundred years in the past. It had not chosen her yet, it doesn't know who she is. And yet, she felt that if it had recognized her once, it would do so again.

She moved towards it and it seemed a low throaty sound came from the tree, a sort of hum. She stood beneath its branches and turned about to look at Anastacio, who was watching her raptly.

A branch descended and touched her head gently just as it had done with Sir Lancelot.

Anastacio did not show it in a dramatic way, but he looked astounded. He continued to stand there with his arms crossed comfortably on his chest, but his eyes changed their expression to one of wonder.

"I must admit to a slight envy," he said, "The Great Tree has never shown me such a sign, though I have sat here for hours meditating, talking with it."

Solena shrugged. "You have always been interested in the ways of the forest, and I in the ways of humans. The tree has chosen me for my special knowledge."

Anastacio was about to ask a question, but instead he pointed behind her to someone approaching.

"Then I pray you, fair maiden, tell us what you know," a voice from behind her made her start.

It was Sir Lancelot accompanied by his usual retinue of Sir Gawaine and Jackson or perhaps Sir Jackson. It was not often that humans could surprise a dryad, and Solena realized that she must have been too involved in her conversation with Anastacio to have heard them approach.

"I have journeyed on many a quest and have faced many foes," Sir Lancelot continued, "Betimes an ogre would take on the guise of a fair damsel, and stranger still, betimes an illusory inn would turn into a fetid swamp, melting away like a dream before my very eyes... but I have never been on such a quest as this. A dragon becomes an alligator, a creature the like of which I've never seen, then a witch turns out to be no witch but a fair maiden of the woods, a scholar that lives inside a closed chest becomes my friend, and I am given charge of a magical boat with such powers as I can scarcely fathom... But strangest of all, I do not know what it is I seek."

"A knight always seeks the same things," Solena said. She had read enough human stories to know that. "To meet worthy adversaries, protect the innocent from harm, and restore justice."

"And yet, I do not know how to do all this in such a strange debacle. I know not who the innocent are and who are the oppressors. I feel as if within the blink of an eye this forest could disappear and become a cave, a castle, or perhaps my own bedchamber where I have been dreaming about all of these sundry adventures."

"I feel this way too," said Anastacio, "but fear not, you can trust in the dryads, and the Great Tree will never lead you astray."

"I believe it," said Lancelot, "And I hope it may give us a sign."

"It favours you... and Solena," Anastacio stated. "You have a good chance of receiving the sign you seek."

"I thank you for your help," said the knight. "What is the proper course then?"

"Sometimes it will speak if you sit before it, but ask no questions. Simply hold the question or circumstance in your mind, and the tree will reply." Anastacio suggested, then sat down before the tree and gestured for the others to join him.

Solena sat down to his right, trying not to sit too close. The knights sat on his left, with Sir Gawaine next to him and Sir Lancelot farthest to the left.

"Now be silent awhile," Anastacio counselled. "This will require patience."

And so they sat. Solena thought she could feel the warmth radiating from Anastacio's body next to her, though she sat a few inches away from him. She could feel the energy pulsating from him and also from the Great Tree. Closing her eyes, she tried to focus on the question, only there was probably more than one. It was not easy, but she stopped thinking about Anastacio and pictured the time boat.

She suddenly had a vision of the numbers 2013 as if they were entered into the time boat's control panel, the blinding light of time travel rushing past her, then another vision of the numbers 2694 and then...

She saw Anastacio beside her even though her eyes were still closed. He was surrounded by how own visions. He walked among skyscrapers, looking around him with astonishment.

In the next instant, she had another vision of her own – the J.C. Penney fortune teller, holding her hand and saying, "You have to be strong in the beginning of a relationship."

This was so strange it made her break away from the visions and return to reality. A relationship? Was the great Tree having a little joke? Could trees make jokes? But then if Anastacio would somehow be transported into her time...

"I understand now!" said Anastacio, who had also come back from the vision. "I understand why you are from these parts but unknown to us. That boat takes you from one time to another."

"I understand now too," said Sir Lancelot. He no longer seemed lost, but rather very certain and even inspired.

"By St Peter!" cried Sir Gawaine, "I can barely fathom it, yet methinks I can after all."

"I know now what to do," said Sir Lancelot. "Sir Jackson, I would ask your help on this journey, but it will cause you to break your fealty to your captain. Are you with me?"

"It seems my destiny lies with you," replied Jackson, "if what I saw is to be believed. I am with you."

"Good! I have a plan," said Lancelot, "There is to be a dryad festival three days from now. The pirates will no doubt drink their fill, and that very night we shall set out for the coast. If St. Amour decides to pursue us, at least we shall have many leagues' advantage. The boat is meant to go to the year of our Lord 2013 and return all of those who belong there to their rightful time. You, fair maiden, the alligator, and the sundry Americans. It is indeed your boat, but I feel my path is linked with it also. You would not take it amiss if I accompany you?"

"Not at all," said Solena.

"Let us meet here at the Great Tree," said Lancelot, "When the time is right."

***

Great crimson tongues of flame danced in the clearings. The dryads were burning deadwood on huge bonfires to celebrate the

Mango Festival. Although festivals were not rare, dryads rejoiced each time as if it were an annual occasion.

Solena recalled her lonely days of festivals when no one would dance with her, and now as she walked past female dryads swaying together with pirates and lumberjacks and as she headed towards the meeting point with Anastacio, two knights, and Rodney's crew, she hardly felt lonely. It was a strange feeling, this lack of loneliness, and she even thought it was much better than how she would have felt if this was a simple dryad festival at which she were to dance with someone, drink mango juice, and not have to fulfil a dangerous mission.

The path of action is its own reward, she recalled one of Teddy Goldman's aphorisms.

Rodney had been forewarned about Lancelot's plan, and so she expected him to be there, though she hadn't seen him all day and was feeling vaguely worried.

Solena felt the thrumming energy of the tree, even stronger on this night. There were five figures waiting for her there, in the gloom. Only five. That gnawing worrying feeling grew more persistent.

Anastacio, Sir Lancelot, and Sir Gawaine, Jackson, and Professor X129 were there, but no sign of Rodney or any of his people. She hadn't been sure whether Anastacio would show up, and her heart beat faster when she sighted him. After all, he wasn't the one going. Yet he had agreed to be there... probably to see them off and to make sure they would do nothing to harm his precious Raffaella.

"Good evening, Solena," said the knights.

Anastacio nodded to her, looking pensive and grim.

"You do not bring the Americans?" asked Sir Lancelot.

"I thought they would have been here by now," Solena said. "I told Rodney the time and place. He should have been ready."

Anastacio was strangely silent.

"He doesn't trust us," he suddenly said.

"Which means..." Solena began.

"He may have already set out for the boat," Anastacio concluded.

"I can't believe Rodney would just leave us here," Solena said. Maybe it was because of her recent spying activities that he decided to lose her, she suddenly thought. But then he would have left Tyler too... Though maybe not, because after all, Tyler did save his life.

"Tyler!" she exclaimed. "He wouldn't have left Tyler behind. And then, I think Tyler would have found a way to let me know what was happening. Something is wrong here…"

"Speak of the devil," Sir Lancelot suddenly exclaimed.

They heard Tyler approach before they saw him. It was the unmistakable sound of an alligator panting and running at a gallop.

"Bossman… in trouble…" he spat out breathlessly.

22 TOM SAWYER'S IDYLL (AD 1694)

Rodney Love contemplated the scene before him and a strange new feeling crept steadily into his heart. It was rebelliousness.

As a student, he had been a good boy. It may have occurred to him to become a pot-head, visit an independent art gallery, or wear a flannel shirt and march in an anti-war rally, but he knew all such initiations would be futile in the face of his father's iron will, and what was more, he didn't feel a pressing need for such things, being comfortable and having his future assured.

He may have felt a slight twinge in his early twenties when he was an exchange student in Australia for a few months. It was not exactly a fully formed plan, but there was the seditious desire not to go back to the States under the watchful eyes of his father but to assume a different identity and stay in the land of eternal sun and surf. Of course, it was in no way realistic and he knew it.

But now, here he was as far removed from the Timber Corporation as was humanly possible. There were beautiful dryads, pristine oceans, and granted he wasn't near a beach now, but the world was his oyster and surf boards could be crafted easily enough. Maybe the old man had sent him here on purpose as a guilt-free way of disposing of such bumbling offspring?

Rodney felt the call of the wild as the appeal of goal-oriented accomplishment receded into distant centuries, and the flames of rebellion rose high in his soul just as the flames of the dryad fires were rising amid the treetops, shooting out angry sparks and dancing to the wild drumbeats of the festival music.

"Dryads sure know how to party!" Tyler said settling down beside him.

"They sure do," Rodney confirmed, not taking his eyes off the perfectly built dancers.

"Too bad we'll miss the rest of it," the alligator said. "Are you all set, boss?"

"Tyler," Rodney replied with uncharacteristic pensiveness, "You saved my life."

"Yes, I did."

"So I'm going to be honest with you," said Rodney, finally looking over at the perplexed alligator. "I don't think I'm ready to go."

Tyler's jaw nearly dropped.

"Not ready to go?"

"You go on, tell the boys they can do whatever they like. They can go with the knights or stay here."

"Stay here?" Tyler echoed. "What about—"

"Work? Refrigerators? Macbooks and iPods? Are you going to look at me with those big black alligator eyes of yours and tell me that you miss that stuff?"

"I may not miss it now, but there will come a time when I will..."

"Look around you, Tyler. This is Paradise," Rodney insisted, "And the only way to lose Paradise is to be too damn stupid to appreciate it."

"You're really serious, bossman?"

"I believe I am."

Tyler spotted a small weak spot. It seemed Rodney was not completely resolved on the matter.

"What do you say, Tyler? Stay here, forget the twenty-first century. Who wants to die sitting at a desk? You're from the South, you know what Tom Sawyer said. I'd rather be Robin Hood for a year in Sherwood Forest than President of the United States forever."

"You haven't been elected president yet," Tyler remarked. "Have you been drinking this mango liquor?"

"Maybe a little," Rodney admitted.

"I better have some too," said Tyler.

He ran off in the direction of the liquor vats, muttering that this would be a good time to have a cell phone so he would be able to inform the others of the situation. But for now, liquor would do. A stiff drink was just what he needed to help him deal with things.

He took a gulp of the fiery liquid that was only slightly reminiscent of mangos. God knows what those dryads put in there, he thought. It did help in the Dutch courage department, and soon Tyler's anxiety all but dissipated. He was able to think more clearly and boldly.

He ran towards the throng of dancers and found the lumberjacks and Gary, who had also imbibed quite a bit of the liquor du jour. Partly with oratorical skills but mostly with threats of bodily harm, he got a few of them to break away from the party and follow him to where Rodney was enjoying his Mark Twain-inspired idyll.

To his chagrin, Tyler saw that Rodney was no longer alone: he was joined by Raffaella, who looked luxuriously sensual in her leafy woodland garb.

"Mr. Love," said Gary, "We're about ready to head back now. Aren't you coming with us?"

"I would love to," Rodney replied, "But there is nothing for me back in the States."

"Well, the boys and I want to go back, and I think you'll find once you return, it'll feel just like home again."

"Who are you trying to persuade, Gary? Me, or yourself? What do you have to look forward to? More work, retirement, sitting in front of a TV?"

"Yeah, I guess…" Gary said uncertainly.

Tyler shook his head. This was not at all going as planned. They were supposed to persuade Rodney, not the other way around.

"Are you saying you want us to stay here with you?" a lumberjack asked.

"It's up to you, the decision is yours," Rodney replied. "I'm just saying I want to stay."

"Should we take a vote or something?" Gary asked. "I don't want to go back all by myself."

"Have a drink," Raffaella suggested.

She was holding a large gourd filled with liquor, and she passed it to Gary.

"That stuff is good!" Rodney confirmed. "It's pretty much like whiskey with a sort of bacon flavor."

"That doesn't sound good," the security guard said, but he sniffed the drink and took a sip.

"Damn! It is good!" he exclaimed.

The lumberjacks all took turns imbibing and wanted to pass it to

Tyler, but he refused.

"I've had one to steady my nerves. That's all I'm going to have tonight. Somebody's got to be in their right mind for this."

"So, let's take care of this vote," Rodney offered. "Who's for staying here?"

He raised his hand, but he was alone in that. He sighed.

"Who's for going?"

The lumberjacks, Gary, and Tyler raised their hands.

"Well, that's it," Rodney concluded, "Everyone who voted for going is free to go. Everyone who voted for staying is free to stay. By the power vested in me as the former Chief Executive Officer of the Timber Corporation, I officially pass this resolution."

Raffaella stayed mysteriously silent, and Tyler didn't like it. She was smiling in a sphinx-like manner.

"Um... all right then, I guess this is it," said Gary, "We've got to go."

"Let's have one last drink then," said Rodney, "I'm going to miss you guys."

They passed the gourd around and each man grimaced as he swallowed the pungent liquid.

"I'm going to get the others," Tyler said.

"All right, we'll meet you back here," Gary slurred.

"I'll be back soon," said the alligator as he scuttled off.

He headed for the group of dancers to find the two remaining lumberjacks, but when he looked back at the group he was leaving behind, a shiver ran up his spine. Rodney was sitting back against a large tree, his head tipped back as if asleep. The others were lying on the ground, and one of the lumberjacks swayed and finally settled down next to Rodney using the tree for balance. Raffaella had disappeared.

"Wake up, people!" Tyler yelled.

He tugged at Gary's trouser leg and dragged him along the ground, shaking him, but the man merely groaned and tried to wave him away with a languid hand.

"I wasn't going to resort to this, but you leave me no choice."

Tyler bit Gary's leg, making a neat row of incisions down the length his calf. Gary uttered a faint groan, but remained asleep.

"The drink!" Tyler exclaimed. "It was drugged. Why would Raffaella do this?"

***

Eight men waited, warming themselves by a small deadwood fire. These were St Amour's most trusted sailors, Frenchmen such as Tessier who had been with him since the first sailing of *Belle Catherine*. Carracha and Lelouche had joined them too, having smelled the familiar odour of dissent. They were too unsightly to be favored by the female dryads and had no desire to stay in the enchanted forest.

"The more the merrier," St Amour thought.

He stood apart from the others, peering into the tangle of the forest, tapping the hilt of his cutlass.

At length, he saw her appear. A beautiful, long-haired, slender form born of the forest.

"All is ready," she said, running to his open embrace.

"And so am I, Raffaella," said the pirate. "Here are my most loyal men. We will make for the coast and sail away in the magic boat. Are you certain, my love, that you will not miss the forest of your birth?"

Her face turned hard for a moment.

"No," she said in a low voice, "They don't want me here, save perhaps Anastacio. I wish more of them were like him... But it doesn't matter. I love him not. I love you."

"Then let us away from here," said St Amour. "We'll have to break through the sentries, but after that it should be fair sailing."

"I know a spell that will charm the sentries," Raffaella said. "It is fair sailing from now on."

St Amour signalled to his men, and the small party raced off into the depths of the jungle.

23 THE SECRET LIVES OF TAPIRS (AD 1694)

"What is that hideous thing?" Rodney muttered as he awoke.

It seemed the night was still young – he could hear drums and music and voices off in the distance – but he had already incurred a hangover. And how had he managed to pass out surrounded by a herd of tapirs?

He had never seen one up close before, for they were shy and elusive creatures.

The tapirs slumbered in a hoggish mass all around him, uttering faint snorts. They looked like a smaller version of a hippo or perhaps a larger version of a pig with a long, protruding snout. Presently one of them awoke, opening its shiny little eyes.

"Get out of here, you hogs," it muttered.

"Talking tapirs," Rodney complained, "That's just what I need right now."

"Aaaargh!" the tapir that had recently talked now screamed.

"What the hell?" Rodney got up on all fours.

He sniffed the air. Suddenly so many new scents disclosed themselves to him it was as if he could see into the innermost recesses of the forest. Over there, a jaguar had just passed, scattering various birds out of the branches. And there, only a few steps away delicious berries ripened beneath drooping leaves. In far corners of the forest, other tapirs gathered.

Suddenly he understood why the tapir had screamed.

"Gary?" he asked.

"Yes," the tapir replied.

"You're a tapir."

"So are you, Mr. Love," said tapir Gary.

The others began to awaken groggily.

"Now what?" asked Gary.

"Well, I wanted to stay here in the jungle," said Rodney, "but not as a hog!"

"Those are the conditions that come with living in your paradise, as you call it," Gary scoffed.

The lumberjack tapirs also uttered a few screams as they realized their transformation, but for the most part everyone remained remarkably calm. Their minds now operated partly in tapir mode, which unless pursued by a predator, was always in an unflappably calm state.

A few of the lumberjack tapirs instinctively began to nose around the bushes, searching for fruits and berries to eat. Rodney tried to fight the animal instinct, but he couldn't be sure this wasn't all a hallucination or a dream, in which case, following dream logic, he had merely to do what's natural for a tapir until he woke up.

A small part of his brain was saying something about meeting up with the others and getting help, but it was soon silenced when a few real tapirs emerged from the bushes.

"Any good food round here?" one of them, a male, asked.

Rodney grunted noncommittally but it was obvious the other fake tapirs from his party were feasting on the plentiful berries.

"We'll take a quick repast, and then it's time to go," another of the real tapirs said.

Real tapirs can talk too, Rodney thought. Weird.

They feasted on the berries, which tasted good to his tapir senses and quickly relieved his hangover. But soon the real tapirs started saying that it was time to go to the cave, and they all loped away, the human tapirs following the real ones.

***

"Are you sure this is the place?" Solena asked.

"Yes, I've told you," said Tyler. "I left them here just a few minutes ago. They were all drunk and unconscious. Drugged, I think."

Solena, Anastacio, the knights, Jackson and Professor X129 all set to work examining the scene. It was dark, but the professor made his screen more luminous to enable them to see footprints.

"Methinks a herd of wild pigs invaded the place and carried them off," said Sir Gawaine at last.

"Or they were transformed into pigs," Solena suddenly said.

"The tapir potion! That boy had told us about it at the mission!" Tyler exclaimed, "It does exist! This means Raffaella has allied with St Amour."

"It also means we must catch them and quickly," said Anastacio, "they're probably on their way to the boat even as we speak. I knew that scoundrel was not to be trusted!"

"But what about Rodney?" Solena asked, "We have to help him and the others."

"They have been rendered helpless pigs and need rescuing," Sir Lancelot agreed.

"I don't see much of a difference," Anastacio shrugged.

"Nay, we cannot in good conscience leave them," objected the knight. "The boat is several days' journey from here. In that time, we will overtake St Amour. Let us first rescue the others."

Anastacio sighed. "Very well, I suppose we must."

"Can you see where they may have gone, professor?" Jackson asked.

"I can detect many tapir life forms, too many to investigate them all within the time allotted."

"That's all right," said Anastacio, "We will track them. Besides, I think I know where they have gone."
***

Through some sort of instinct from his new tapir form, Rodney sensed that this was the place he was supposed to go. A lonely hillside, aloof and brooding, overgrown with ferns and shrubs.

Tapirs arrived by twos and threes, sometimes alone, stopping respectfully before the hill. The ones from his group likewise stopped and walked to the hill in pairs. They seemed to disappear as soon as they reached its shadow, and neither Rodney nor his group could see where they went. At last, it was their turn.

They trotted towards the hillside, peering into the thick darkness, not seeing anything but suddenly smelling something. It was there, up ahead. Beneath some overhanging vines, there was an entranceway. Slivers of light beckoned the bemused tapirs forward. Rodney and his crew pushed the vines aside with their snouts and entered the cave inside the hill.

Before them was a magnificent dining hall. The light stunned him for a moment, but then he saw other tapirs, sitting around a long table that circled the whole cave. They were feasting, just like humans would have done. Plates were heaped with food, glasses filled with beer. With some sort of magic, lanterns glowed, green fires dancing inside them.

Rodney soon realized that there were two different types of tapirs. The ones sitting around the large table were human-like in their ability to sit upright and even use cutlery. Then there were the tapirs running around in the center of the room, entertaining the human-like ones.

Somehow Rodney knew these ones did not have the gift of speech like the other tapirs did.

They were playing something resembling a soccer game. A ball bounced and rolled from one side of the room to the other pursued keenly by the hippo-like creatures, each trying to take it away from the opposing team.

"Brothers and sisters, it is time for us to drink!" shouted the host. Rodney assumed it was the tapir king as he sat at an elevated table.

Despite their lack of opposable thumbs, the human-like tapirs somehow managed to use their odd-looking toes to pick up goblets and utensils. Rodney and his crew sat down and began to feast with the others. There were plenty of aquatic weeds and fruits as well as frothy, light beer. Part of him was terrified, but his tapir sensibilities forced him to continue as if this was something he did all the time.

Every now and then the soccer ball would fly onto the table, upsetting dishes or smacking one of the diners on the head, but this was taken as a matter of course and caused even more delight for the spectators.

The soccer game ended with a final goal and both teams left the "field."

One of the king's attendants rose to announce the next entertainment.

"Tonight is unusual," he said, "for as we sit here and make merry, our wizard informs me that there are a few among us who are not what they appear. For many centuries humans have tried to enter our stronghold by means of stealth, but we shall not let them leave, knowing our secrets. Find them out, my servants! Kill them!"

Other dumb tapirs were ushered into the arena. These looked

older and fiercer than the soccer-playing ones. Each was the size of a small horse, and much more pugnacious. They walked upright and carried spears.

Rodney froze in terror. He could barely contain his instincts, both human and tapir, which told him to flee at once.

The seekers clambered up to the upper level where the tables stood and began to sniff the air.

Rodney saw them slowly being drawn towards his group, whether by smell or some other sense, it didn't matter. He now felt certain they would be found out. He and his party grew more and more stiff in their seats, and the seekers smelled their fear. But finally Rodney sat up taller and heaved a deep breath. His human dignity won out, and he decided he wouldn't be afraid of these glorified pigs.

"Wait!" he said. "You don't need to seek us out. We are the humans, but we are not here to discover your secret. We were transformed into tapirs against our will."

"Humans," the king laughed, "always full of trickery. I know humans well enough: you destroy everything you touch. I will not believe you, for I cannot take that chance. My people must be protected. None of you will live to tell the tale of what you have seen here."

"I object!" said Rodney.

He was going to say more, but a spear flew at him, launched by the powerful limb of a tapir servant. Rodney pushed away from the table and fell backwards, throwing himself onto the floor as the spear hurtled by. It bounced off the wall with a dull thud.

A tapir's "hand" reached for it awkwardly. It was Rodney's hand. With a sort of thrill, he found he could hold the spear just as well as the tapir servant could.

"Stand aside!" he shouted to his crew as he took a run and hurled the spear at his assailant.

For a moment, the hall was terribly silent save for the whoosh of the weapon through the air.

"Kill them!" shouted the king.

Rodney's spear had nicked the tapir's back, drawing blood, but merely goading it on instead of wounding it. The same servant tapir was the first to begin the assault.

The lumberjack-tapirs ran in a blind panic. The hunter-tapirs chased them to the wild applause of the audience. But the strangest thing of all, Rodney was chasing the hunters. He felt an incredible blood lust surging up through his animal body. He refused to be the prey: he was the heir to a billion dollar empire, and he would not be killed here!

At this moment Sir Lancelot charged into the dining hall. He looked magnificent in his armor, sword drawn and at the ready. Every one of the tapirs was dumbstruck, for they never expected a human to enter unannounced, and in his true form.

He was followed by Sir Gawaine and the rest of the company.

"How do we know the true tapirs from the false?" the knight asked, stopping just for a moment to look back at Solena and Anastacio.

"I can tell which ones they are," Anastacio said, "Besides, look! They're running towards us."

He pointed to the madly dashing lumberjack-tapirs who were trying to escape their pursuers.

They ran past the astounded knights and out of the cave. Just as the last lumberjacks passed, Anastacio yelled, "Now!" and together with Sir Lancelot and Sir Gawaine they formed a solid barrier to the onrushing hunter-tapirs.

Sir Lancelot swung his sword, but the creature that charged at him swerved aside and was about to gallop on by when he tackled it and knocked it off its feet. Anastacio was unarmed, but he seized a tapir – an amazing feat since the creatures weighed over a quarter of a ton – and threw it at the other thronging animals.

"Go!" he cried to Solena, "You must make sure they don't get away from us again. We'll delay these tapirs."

Solena was about to make a run for it and pursue the escaping lumberjack tapirs, but something stopped her. She realized there was one human-tapir missing. She wasn't sure how Anastacio seemed to know them from the real ones, and there wasn't much time for a magic spell.

"Anastacio, where's Rodney?" she cried.

The dryad was engaged in wrestling a spear away from a hunter-tapir. At length, he pushed his foe aside and pointed to a raging tapir, careening about the hall, completely mad with bloodlust.

Solena was stunned for a moment. But she quickly gathered herself. It was no time to be indecisive. She leapt on top of the table and ran towards Rodney, who was lambasting two hunter-tapirs.

"Rodney! Rodney, snap out of it. We've got to go!" she yelled.

He seemed not to hear and paid absolutely no attention.

She dove from the table and tackled tapir-Rodney, knocking him to the ground. She hadn't been sure it would work, as the tapir was in a whole other weight category, but her flying tackle was enough to knock him off his feet. She rolled away, and saw that he regained his footing and still paid no attention to her: the real tapirs were closing in on him.

She could see out of the corner of her eye Anastacio and Sir Lancelot trying to break through the mass of tapirs to reach her. The tapirs were like a living sea of grey, bulging animal flesh. Anastacio's dryad strength made his attempts more successful, while Sir Lancelot, whose strength was incredible for a human, was failing to contend with such massive beasts. She saw a glimpse of him being knocked down by two of the charging animals, then she became too preoccupied as another spear-wielding tapir advanced on her.

She backed away slowly, trying to think of a strategy but not finding any weapon close at hand to counter the spear.

Rodney broke through the ring of his attackers at that very moment and his momentum was so great that he slammed into the spear-wielding tapir, jarring him for a split second. Solena lunged forward and seized the spear, twisting it out of the creature's hand.

Now Solena advanced more confidently, trying to reach Rodney once again, poking at tapirs that got too close with the dull end of the spear. She approached him just as he leapt onto the table, threatening the tapir king himself. Solena sprinted over and jabbed Rodney in the ribs with the blunt end of the spear. Tapir Rodney spun around to face her, and she held her breath.

He was either going to attack her in a fit of rage or...

He froze for a moment, and she thought she saw the light of recognition in his eyes.

"Time to blow this joint," she yelled, pointing to the exit.

Tapir Rodney nodded. With one of his hind legs, he flicked a dish at the king's head, then leapt off the table and charged towards the exit, Solena close behind him.

She didn't remember much about getting out of that cave except that it was terribly noisy and that clammy animal bodies crowded her on all sides, but soon Tyler appeared beside her, snapping his jaws at any who approached, and Rodney in his berserker state cleared the way forward. Somehow, Anastacio made his way to them and together they fought their way to where Sir Lancelot, Jackson, and Sir Gawaine, nearly at the end of their strength, were desperately striving with a horde of beasts.

Anastacio snatched them from the fray, and the next thing Solena knew they were outside in the warm moist air, running full-out until finally they realized the tapirs were no longer pursuing them.

The company walked on for a while, following the tracks of the human tapirs, until at length they beheld the entire group lolling about in a small clearing, watched over by Professor X129.

24 HE WILL BE SORRY (AD 1694)

Dawn was not yet ready to break, and the sounds of the forest were dying down as even the nocturnal animals seemed to need some rest. The weary group of humans and dryads finally caught their breath.

"What now?" asked Sir Gawaine. "Is there a counter-spell?"

"I think that potion will wear off," Anastacio said grimly, "though I don't know how soon. I suppose we can still travel, driving the tapirs before us."

"The poor things," Solena said, "they must be exhausted. I know I am. Maybe we'd better stay here until they do change."

The tapirs seemed to agree with her, for they were gathering beneath the branches of a tree and curling themselves up to go to sleep.

"Maybe they'll transform after they sleep," Tyler suggested, "That's what happened after they drank that potion."

"Now we have to wait for them to change!" Anastacio grumbled. "St Amour is making good progress, no doubt. Let's leave the pigs behind!"

"They seem more like cows," Sir Gawaine chimed in.

"Or very small elephants," said Sir Lancelot, rubbing his sword arm.

"In any case, it was a goodly adventure."

"We must all travel together or fail entirely," Jackson said. "I know these jungles. One false move and you'll end up with a poison dart in your neck or caught in a slave-trader's net. This lot wouldn't survive five minutes on their own, and we stand a better chance if we form a larger party."

"The let us rest," said Sir Lancelot. "God will direct things. I believe St Amour will not escape us."

"Perhaps you're right…" Anastacio replied. He seemed to have formed a grudging respect for this human.

Solena and the others settled down beneath the trees, and soon she was fast asleep. When she awoke, the faint rays of sunlight were piercing the treetops. She looked over to where the tapirs had rested, and found the lumberjacks and Rodney, back to their usual forms.

She noted that Anastacio was still sitting where she had last seen him, wide awake.

"You're worried about Raffaella?" she asked.

"I am. And also disappointed," he replied. "I doubt that human could have forced her to go with him. It means she left of her own free will."

"Then how can you ever bring her back?" Solena asked. "You can't force her to come back with you either."

"I don't know…" he said. "But I must find her."

"You're still not over her, are you?" Solena blurted out.

"I'm what?" he asked, not understanding the modern phrasing.

"You still have feelings for her."

"You still have feelings for that human," Anastacio countered suddenly.

"What human?"

She was taken aback, not knowing that Anastacio had somehow deduced she had been in a relationship with Rodney, much less had feelings for him.

"You know, the one you risked your life to rescue," he replied nonchalantly.

Rodney and the other began to stir.

"I'm going to kill him!" Rodney yelled, surprising the others and even to some extent, himself, "I'm going to kill that douchebag pirate! I don't care if he's my ancestor! I'm going to kill him even it kills me!"

This woke up Jackson and the knights. The professor's screen lit up.

"Rodney, don't be ridiculous," Solena said, yawning.

"He took Raffaella away from me, and I bet he was the one who convinced her to drug us so he could safely slip away in the night.

That unbelievable traitor!"

"I'd say Raffaella is the traitor," Solena objected, "She was the one pretending to be your friend and stabbing you in the back."

"Well, I can't kill her. She's cute," Rodney said, perplexed.

"I didn't say you should kill her," Solena replied, "Don't kill anyone, okay? Let's just get a move on. St Amour must be way ahead of us by now."

***

The next few days were spent in a relentless slog through the rainy, muddy vastness of the forest. They incurred a further delay as Rodney and the lumberjacks insisted on returning to the dryad forest to take their packs and equipment.

Fortunately, it seemed St Amour had not bothered to cover his tracks, and they could tell easily enough where he had passed as long as the trail had not been too washed out by the rain. Perhaps he knew that the path of his flight was predictable: he was heading back to the coast, back to where he had left the time boat.

The humans were completely exhausted by the long march, and even the dryads were feeling a kind of dull weariness. The trail was hot, but still they never seemed to catch up to the swift-moving pirates. Professor X129 had to be carried, and at times Tyler also would lay down in exhaustion, unable to tolerate such a fast pace over long periods of time. He was carried between four people in a sort of sling that was constructed for him out of canvass.

"I just realized something," Rodney said as they stopped for a night's rest.

The knights were busy organizing a fire and Anastacio was off procuring food. Rodney and Solena were more or less alone, save for a half-fainting alligator and the professor whirring nearby, though it was not clear whether he was in sleep mode.

"What is it?" Solena asked.

"The reason I had come here, the miracle root. I haven't got it. But perhaps you could show me how to find it…"

"I had thought about it," she replied. "But remember what Father Montoya had said. Wars could be started over this. Imagine if humans were to discover the secret of the root. I think it was very careless of Raffaella to reveal it, even to that small number of people in the mission."

"I know," said Rodney. "But if I only give one small piece of it to my father, he will be cured, won't he? And if I promise to keep your secret?"

"Perhaps..." she said. "I could give you some of the plant, though I can't show you how to find it."

"I'd be more than happy with that," Rodney smiled.

It felt a bit like old times, when they were still together.

"I'm sorry," he said suddenly.

"For what?" Solena asked.

"Well... you know, hitting on Raffaella so soon after we broke up. It was stupid, and she didn't even like me. I don't know what came over me..."

"Apparently you weren't the only one," Solena said.

"And then despite my being a jerk, you came to find me."

"The knights wouldn't let us off the hook about that," she grinned, "You know how noble they are."

At length, when the others were busy with food preparations, Solena slipped away into the thick of the forest. She said the magic spell for finding the Poniato plant, and found her magic powers had grown even stronger. Usually, it would take her a while to follow the golden threads of magic leading to the plants, and often her instincts were wrong. But this time, an amazing luminosity exploded before her vision, and she followed it for just a few minutes before coming towards the plant. She spoke words of thanks and dug up the root, concealing it in her pocket. She sliced it in half, and when she returned to camp, she furtively gave Rodney one of the halves as the others were preparing food or just dozing.

The next day, they could smell the ocean breeze in the air. It was so close, but the travelers were tense with doubts. Solena led the way, followed closely by Rodney, and they soon emerged onto that fateful beach where they had left the boat. The pirates' tracks seemed to be leading to that very same spot.

Looking over the vast expanse of water, she was not seeing what she had feared: a brighter spark against the far-flung sheen of the ocean, indicating the departing time machine.

"The time boat is gone," Rodney suddenly said.

It was the only conclusion to be drawn from the fact that the pirates' trail ended on the small stretch of sand where he and the others stood in consternation.

Rodney seemed angry, but at the same time strangely calm.

"Now I'll have to travel through time to catch that goddamned thug," he muttered.

The lumberjacks looked desperate and began cursing wildly. Mattheos and a few others sat down on the sand in exhaustion.

"The boat is gone?" Sir Lancelot asked. He seemed to take it in stride as Rodney had. "What shall we do, find another magical vessel?"

"No need," Rodney said, "I have the means to get us back to our time."

He dug around in his backpack and fished out a few electronic devices which he proceeded to connect with cables and arrange in a circular pattern on the beach.

"Boss, you had this all along?" Gary asked. "And you never told us?! Jesus Christ, I thought we'd be stuck here forever."

"I didn't want anyone to get any ideas about going back before it was time," Rodney replied, not looking up from his work.

The lumberjacks exploded once again with a new barrage of curses, but this time it was more in relief than anger.

Finally Rodney completed the circle, about six feet in diameter.

"It's going to be a small squeeze, but I think everyone can fit. Anastacio, are you coming too?"

"Of course," the dryad replied. "I want to help you find that pirate and free Raffaella."

"Knights?"

"How can we refuse another adventure?"

Everyone stepped within the bounds of the circle of wires, and Rodney pressed a button on his remote. With a sudden flash of light, everything whirled around, and a second later, they were back on the same beach.

"Did it work?" Solena asked. Then she suddenly realized that it did. The air smelled less pure, the wind coming from the ocean bringing not just salt, but other subtle odours indicating the chemical admixture the water had acquired in the twenty-first century.

Not only that, they all suddenly heard the sound of an engine overhead and saw a black helicopter hovering over the water a few miles away.

"That's the Timber Corporation helicopter!" Rodney yelled. "We're back!"

The black helicopter veered left, and they lost sight of it for a moment as it was obscured by vegetation, but then it reappeared, heading toward some small object out on the waves.

"Is that?..." Solena asked.

"It must be the time boat!" Rodney exclaimed.

The company ran along the beach to get a better view, but they were still too far away to be sighted from the helicopter, which seemed to be preoccupied with the boat instead.

"Hey! Hello!" Rodney waved both arms, "I'm right here!"

He was still ignored. Meanwhile, a few figures separated from the boat and seemed to be taken within the helicopter, which didn't linger and flew back the way it had come, paying absolutely no attention to the people and dryads on the beach.

"What the hell is going on?" a lumberjack asked.

Rodney was laughing. At first it seemed to the others it was some sort of hysterics, but as he sat down on the sand it was evident that he gave his whole-hearted enjoyment to this moment.

"Oh I see," it finally dawned on Solena. "They think St Amour is you."

"Now I don't have to kill him!" he exclaimed, "It's a win-win situation. He doesn't have to die, but man will he ever be sorry he met me and got himself into this."

"Are you quite sure?" Sir Gawaine asked. "I thought you were bent on killing him."

Rodney looked up at him with a wicked grin. "It's even better. They're taking him to my father."

25 SISSY INVESTIGATES (AD 2013)

Sissy Maynard gazed at her computer, comparing reports from different wacky news sites, ranging from those outwardly reasonable ones whispering of government conspiracies and the enslavement of the working classes to the really crazy ones claiming aliens had landed in broad daylight in Times Square. No matter how outlandish they were, the majority of these sites had a tiny jot of truth in them, yet they were blithely ignored by the general public.

So, for example, when yet another loner with too much time on his hands claimed he had captured video footage of a time machine/boat departing from some harbor in Colombia and disappearing into thin air, Sissy felt it safe to assume that rational people would ignore the report whereas she might find something useful in it.

Sissy was a stolid-looking sixteen-year-old girl, though at times she could be mistaken for a very short forty-year-old man. Any other high school girl with a plump, square-shouldered, and non-curvy physique and a flat, snub-nosed, unattractive face would be nervous about going to prom night, but Sissy was in fact looking forward to it. Even as she trawled the internet sites, her mother was busy in the hobby room making alterations to the dress Sissy had selected — it had not come in her size. This was the first time Sissy had ever shown an interest in any social gathering! Little did her parents know that this interest was due to the possibility of playing some very scientifically advanced pranks on the hated popular girls and their dates.

Sissy herself, of course, had no date. She spent most of her time at the computer, and as for the rest of her time, it was devoted to thinking, machinating, and plotting. Only a fraction of that thinking time was devoted to homework. Although she had the potential to astound the social studies teacher with an analysis of Marxist influence in post-colonial Venezuela or to propose an interesting alternative to string theory that would have been completely beyond the grasp of her physics instructor, she regulated her answers well enough so that all adults, including her own parents, were thoroughly convinced of her intellectual mediocrity.

"It's almost ready, sweetie!" her mother called from the other room. "Come try it on so I can add the final stitches."

Sissy sighed. She didn't like how she looked in dresses, but she decided to play the charade to the last detail. After all, she couldn't very well show up to the prom in her usual nondescript corduroy pants, hoodie, and sneakers. She trudged into the other room, and her mother, with a beaming countenance handed her the dress, a flouncy, silken, scarlet affair that Sissy felt was wasted on her.

Her mother left her to change, and as Sissy struggled with dress, the doorbell rang. It was Uncle Craig, who was due to come over that day for dinner. It was just as well, Sissy thought. She would tell him about the "time boat" incident.

Uncle Craig was a big, tall, blustering man. He blustered in, talking in his loud voice, just as Sissy got the dress zipped up in the other room. It fit as well as it ever would.

"Sweetie, come out and show Uncle Craig your prom dress!" her mother called. "Sissy, where are you?"

Sissy came out into the hall, looking like a frog who had accidentally fallen into a flower.

"Here I am," she pronounced glumly.

"There's my girl!" Uncle Craig enthused. He was one of very few people who were genuinely fond of Sissy. This was partly from familial affection — after all, Uncle Craig had no children of his own and would not likely ever get married since no one wanted to put up with his blustering ways — but Sissy suspected it was also partly because he felt he had "taken her under his wing" as it were. And as she had learned from reading *Le Voyage de Monsieur Perrichon* (she had taught herself to read in French, Spanish, Ancient Greek, and Chinese), people always have a greater love for those whom they help rather than for those who help them. It was an undeniable fact of human nature.

Uncle Craig was one of those men who thought they could handle every sort of conceivable problem or contingency by looking like they knew what they were doing and talking in a loud voice. He also applied this method to his work as a private investigator, while Sissy occasionally helped out with what he called "small administrative tasks," which were things like finding key evidence, analysing data, and extrapolating facts. In short, Sissy was the brains behind Maynard Investigations. She had been for the last two years, and she had done it so skilfully and manipulatively that no one, not least Uncle Craig himself, realized it. Her parents thought it was a great thing, Uncle Craig giving her a career boost and helping her learn new skills.

Being too gloomy to say much, she simply motioned Uncle Craig to come into her room.

"Don't work too hard, you two! Dinner will be ready soon," Sissy's dad said. He was frying steaks in the kitchen.

Still silent, Sissy motioned Uncle Craig to sit in the little swivelling plastic chair in front of her computer and re-played the video with the disappearing boat.

"Now," she said, clicking on another tab to open a different window, "Look at this article: Heir to the Love Empire Changed by Latin American Visit."

"Ok, I'll bite," said Uncle Craig, "What does this thing have to do with the other thing?"

Sissy sighed. She had expected he wouldn't get it at first, but it was still annoying.

"Don't you see, it's not him at all."

"It's not Rodney Love? Looks like him."

"Sure, he looks like him, but all the speech and mannerisms are different. And now he only makes public appearances when surrounded with a troop of bodyguards. He never used to do that. He's afraid of someone."

"Who's he afraid of?"

"The *real* Rodney Love."

"So you think he's been replaced?" Uncle Craig began to get excited. "And what does the boat thing have to do with it?"

"I suspect the boat is a sort of time machine," she said matter-of-factly, "Rodney Love must have traveled into the past (or maybe the future, one can't be sure) and been taken in by some rogue. This man who is now taking over the corporation has either had plastic surgery or is an ancestor of Rodney Love; that would explain the resemblance."

"Time machine? Sissy, you've been watching too much Dr. Who."

Sissy had foreseen this too. Would a grown man believe in a time machine even if the evidence was right in front of him? Of course not.

"Ok," she said, "even if there isn't a time machine, you've got to agree that there's definitely an impostor here."

"All right, maybe I agree..." Uncle Craig allowed. "But what are we supposed to do about it?"

"This gives us a great opportunity to work for him. No doubt he's scared the real Rodney Love will show up and expose him. We'll help him find and eliminate the real Rodney."

"Isn't that a crime? What about our professional integrity?" Uncle Craig asked.

"It will remain intact," she said coolly, "Because you see, we'll be playing both sides. We'll be *paid* to look for the real Rodney Love and eliminate him, but what we'll actually do is help him regain his inheritance, and then he will pay us even more money. We will be on the side of right and justice."

"Playing both sides, huh? I've got to think about this."

But thinking was not Uncle Craig's strong suit, so after dinner he decided to try Sissy's plan and see what happens.

What Sissy did not share with Uncle Craig, or indeed any other living soul, was that her real interest in this business was not with making a great deal of money, although that certainly wouldn't hurt, but of taking control of the Timber Corporation. World domination was at hand, right after prom.

26 THE DWELLINGS OF RODNEY LOVE (AD 2013)

They sat in an air-conditioned café, with accordion music playing softly on the radio, baristas grinding coffee, cups clinking comfortingly against saucers. Everything indicated a return to civilization... except the thought of St Amour in Boston, running the Timber Corporation.

They had caught a truck to Santa Marta, where Rodney sent his lumberjacks home with extra cash bonuses for all the trouble they had gone through. Now, it was only Solena, Rodney, Jackson and the knights, as well as Anastacio. The newcomers to this century gazed around them in wonder, and even Solena and Rodney felt unaccustomed to this city environment after such a long absence. The noises of cars, horns, and people's voices seemed jarring and chaotic.

Finally they took refuge in the café.

"There's nothing else for us to do," Rodney concluded, "We have to go surfing."

"You're going to let the pirate take your place?" Tyler asked.

"We should challenge the impostor to trial by combat," Sir Lancelot suggested, "Now that we know he's at your father's castle."

"Unfortunately, trial by combat is forbidden," Rodney replied.

"Forbidden?" the knights exclaimed, nearly upsetting their coffee cups.

"There are likely many things you won't like about these times," Rodney said tiredly, "But I suppose I have to except them and so do you, at least temporarily. As for letting St Amour take my place, I will let him do it, just for a while. I want him to experience life with my father. After three days or a week at the most, he will come to find me, begging to get him out of there. At first he may be blinded by power and could try to find and kill us, but soon enough he'll realize he can't make it in this civilization. We just need to hide out for a little while."

"You are certain the captain will surrender?" Jackson asked, "He is a very stubborn man."

"Not more stubborn than my father."

"So… we go surfing?" Anastacio asked. "How will that help?"

"Because it's fun!" Rodney exclaimed, "You'll see, you'll be a real natural at it. Riding the waves!"

"It has the sound of a most noble pursuit," said Sir Gawaine.

"I have a house not far from here," Rodney said conspirationally, "I'll withdraw a bunch of money just in case St Amour decides to cancel my credit cards, we'll rent a car – or a van," he amended, looking over the numerous company, "And hide out there for a few days. What do you say?"

"It is your world," Anastacio said, "I will put my trust in your decision."

***

"Jesus Christ, Rodney. Can't you be mature at all? It's like the time you came back after four months in Australia with an Australian accent. Now you've been in the 17th century a day and you're spouting Shakespeare?"

Gregory love was pacing his office feverishly. He looked pale and gaunt, but it seemed his fury had some sort of sustaining power that gave him amazing energy.

St Amour, still in his pirate attire stood before him. Raffaella was at his side. They had been taken here directly from the time boat, and the ride in the helicopter followed by a private jet had astounded them.

"I beg your pardon, sir," St Amour began, "But though to you it seemed a day, I journeyed for many weeks in the jungle. The hardship of the voyage…"

"All right, do your clowning if you like. Who is this?"

"May I present Raffaella. We met in the forest, and –"

"She looks like a hippie," Gregory spat out.

"Good sir, I know not what a hippie is," Raffaella chimed in, "but

I assure you, I am not one. I am a dryad."

"A what?"

St Amour said firmly. "Sir, this is the woman I want to marry."

"Well, get her cleaned up. You can't marry her with the both of you looking like that."

"Of course not, father."

"And what have you done with my employees? Gotten them all killed, I suppose?"

"On the contrary, father—"

The phone rang, and Gregory went over to answer it.

"Hello!" he barked. Someone talked at length, and Gregory listened until finally saying, "Okay, thanks for the update."

"I guess I was wrong – you got them back after all," Gregory said, "They've all reported back to their usual jobs. They must have used the backup device."

A shadow crossed St Amour's face as he heard this. It had to mean Rodney and his associates had other ways of coming back. Perhaps he had not seen the last of the pesky prince after all.

"What about Stanley?" Gregory asked.

"I'm afraid… he was killed while bravely performing his duty."

"Unbelievable!" Gregory yelled. "I send you back to an unknown part of the world, and you still manage to get into shit. I'll never find a lawyer to replace Stanley – or at least it'll take a while."

A heavy silence filled the room.

"Well, go on," Gregory finally said, "Get out of here."

"As you wish, father," St Amour bowed and prepared to go.

Suddenly Raffaella rushed over to Gregory's side.

"One moment," she said calmly.

Her hands reached out to him. Gregory's first instinct seemed to be to shrink away from her touch, but something, he couldn't have said what it was, kept him standing still. Her hands seemed to seek something, probing gently like a doctor's hands.

"You are ailing," she said.

Gregory snorted. "I guess Rodney told you. Not a big surprise. It's already leaked to the press, and pretty soon the whole world will know."

"I know something that will help," Raffaella said just as calmly. "I'll just need to brew a tea for you… where is the kitchen?"

"Now look here Miss," Gregory began.

Suddenly, she did look at him, meeting his eyes in a gentle yet assured way that for some reason made him fall silent.

"You will feel better soon," she said reassuringly.

"Well... if you insist," Gregory pronounced at length in a soft voice. It was the first time he had spoken without anger or accusation. "Though I have to tell you right now I don't believe in miracles."

He called for his secretary, who showed Raffaella the hot water dispenser in the kitchen, and presently Raffaella returned with the tea in hand.

"I wonder sir, if you would be so kind as to transport my men—" St Amour was saying as she entered the room.

"You mean those pirates? I've already given orders to transport them back to the 17th century where they belong."

Gregory took the tea absently as Raffaella offered it. He sipped gingerly, cursing at its scalding heat.

"I really don't think that bringing a bunch of pirates back here is an appropriate prank," Gregory added. "Really, when are you going to grow up?"

"So my men will not join me?" St Amour said dispiritedly.

"No, they've been taken back to that ship of theirs."

"*La Belle Catherine*?"

"Yes."

The old man took a few more sips.

"You know, this tea is..." he began, as his face gained a subtle touch of colour, and it seemed like a small spark was suddenly lit in his eyes. "I feel better."

"I'm glad," said Raffaella. "It will not work quickly, as you have been ailing a long time, but it will work."

"Thank you," said Gregory, nodding. "And Rodney, I know you mean well."

St Amour bowed. "Of course, father."

Instead of reprimanding him once again for his clowning, Gregory waved him away.

"Go on, son, get some rest. You've earned it. You too, Miss Raffaella."

"Where shall we go?" St Amour blurted out.

"How should I know?" Gregory said. "Go home, I guess."

St Amour stepped outside into the noisy street, not knowing

where his home was supposed to be. Luckily, a man in a black cap greeted him and ushered him into a large magical carriage, conveying him and Raffaella, to what he could only suppose was the abode of Rodney Love.

27 A SAFE PLACE (AD 2013)

Somehow it seemed wrong to try to take over the world before one had graduated from high school. It was all very well for Alexander the Great, who had been tutored by Plato himself, to start a military career at sixteen, but Sissy felt it was important to obtain a diploma if nothing else as an official sign of adulthood.

Still, even with the diploma in hand, she wasn't certain whether a teenager would be taken seriously by the head of one of the biggest corporations in the world. At first she had thought Uncle Craig would be able to bluster his way to see the big boss, but after that failed, she realized it was time to drop the blustering figurehead and finally take things into her own hands.

That was why she called Mr. Maxwell, an executive of the Timber Corporation. Nearly everyone in the world was reachable on Skype these days.

"Hello?" he said, his flat-nosed face appearing on her screen.

"Hello Mr. Maxwell. I was hoping to have a few words with you."

"I'm very busy. What is it you want, young lady?"

"It's simple. I know that you are in fact a dark elf, Mr. Maxwell. You faked your DNA test."

Maxwell suddenly turned even paler than his customary colour.

Sissy continued. "The scary thing about this brave new world is that any teenager with a spycam can have you by the balls... well maybe not just any teenager. I do very likely have the highest IQ in the world."

"What do you want?" Maxwell sighed.

"To see Rodney Love."

"Oh. That's all?"

"Yes, that's all."

"Suit yourself. Can I ask what your visit would be about?"

"Tell him it's about making more money than he has ever dreamed of."

"I'm sure he has dreamed of a lot of money," Maxwell replied contrarily.

"Tell him anyways." Sissy clicked the conversation off.

***

St Amour was just about to pour himself a cocktail when a knocking sounded on the door. Raffaella was off exploring the city, while he was catching up on work. The pirate was in a grim mood. It seemed the dryad was adapting well to 21st century life, while he was rather at a loss as how to handle it. He was eager to move on, but Raffaella was firmly against it.

He opened the door and saw that it was Maxwell, accompanied by some sort of youngster.

"Good day, Mr. Love," Maxwell began.

"Good day, Maxwell. Thank you for coming rather than sending an email. I grow weary of those things."

"My pleasure," said Maxwell, encouraged by this opening, "Mr. Love, if you could devote a few minutes of your time to Miss Sissy Maynard, I would be most obliged. She's my niece, you see, and she's working on a school project."

"Well, since you've come in person…" said the pirate.

Sissy promptly stepped forward, leaving Maxwell to go about his business.

"Won't you come in, Maxwell?" St Amour asked.

"No, sorry sir, I've got to run."

St Amour sighed.

"Thank you for seeing me," said the child. "I promise that what I have to say will be worth your while."

St Amour considered the young girl (or was it a boy?) before him, and thought that something had gone wrong with children's education in the last five hundred years. This child seemed well-behaved and yet at the same time condescending. It wasn't even as bad as the wild street children of Paris who would mouth off to their betters or even throw rocks at them. It was something else. This child was seemingly acting like an adult.

"Mr. Rodney Love, if that's what you like to call yourself," she said, "I have a proposition for you that you will find most attractive."

"And what is that?" he asked.

"I will make sure that your rival is eliminated."

"You know who my rival is?" St Amour asked, reaching for his cocktail nervously.

"Yes."

"And what's his name?"

"The same as yours."

"Huh! How do you know this, child?"

"I don't think you have a good enough understanding of modern technology," she scoffed. "Or a high enough estimation of my intelligence. I can see that you're not who you claim to be. At the moment, you find yourself in a position of advantage. I could help you keep it that way. For a price, I could eliminate your rival."

"And what is that price?" St Amour asked, amused.

"A share in the company and some control over its finances."

"Ha! I would never grant that to a child."

"I'm not a child," Sissy said, losing her composure for a moment. "I could help you make more money than you ever thought possible."

"And anyways, I don't want him eliminated at all," St Amour added.

"But you're an impostor!" she replied abruptly.

"Perhaps, although I admit to no such thing, I may need to be an impostor only temporarily." St Amour stated, sitting down and beginning to sip his cocktail.

Sissy thought over this for a moment.

"I see," she said, "This lifestyle doesn't suit you."

St Amour said nothing. He was beginning to feel alarmed as the girl's vast knowledge and insight.

"You could let me do all the strategizing, and I'll let you take the credit," she continued. "I know I look young, but I'm more intelligent than anyone you could possibly employ. I've got a plan for distributing and selling that botanical remedy that cured your father's cancer. All we have to do is supress the environmental groups. If you'll have a look at my website…"

"I hate websites!" the pirate cried at once. "Why is it that one cannot utter a word in this century without someone directing you to a website? You have harried me enough, young lady. Now get of my sight. I need to enjoy my drink in peace."

"What?" Sissy's calculating mind had counted on complete rejection as one of the outcomes, but she hadn't realized how much it would sting.

"I could call my guard, but it seems rather ungentlemanly, so kindly leave of your own free will."

Sissy's face turned rigid.

"All right," she said, "I'm leaving. But whoever you are, you better watch out. You've just made a very wrong decision. Although, in a way, it proves to be right…" she said, more to herself than to him, "I've worked behind the scenes long enough. It's time for the world to get to know the real Sissy."

Later that night, when Sissy had returned home, her parents noticed that she was dressed more formally than usual. In fact, her mother realized she had never seen Sissy in these clothes before: an expensive-looking blazer combined with well-ironed silky trousers and a crisp shirt.

"Did you buy these clothes, honey?" Sissy's mother asked.

"I did," Sissy replied with a business-like air. "I might be getting an internship, and today I had my first interview."

"Oh, that's great!" her mother exclaimed. "Arnold, Sissy's been to an interview for an internship."

"Good work, kiddo!" her dad replied from the kitchen. He was one of those dads who are gifted in cookery and was always puttering around with various recipes. That night he was making a royal dessert to celebrate Sissy's acceptance to Greenfield Community College – not that Sissy had any intention of going there, but she remained punctilious in the keeping up of pretenses.

However, after sitting through dinner during which her parents glorified the exciting vocation of accounting, Sissy suddenly felt her patience was at an end.

She needed to mobilize her troops that very night. These were a private army of professional paratroopers financed through Sissy's ingenious stock investments; they had been placed on standby the last few days because Sissy had foreseen the possibility of the fake Rodney Love's refusal to cooperate.

She suddenly felt an explosion of anger for all mankind, with emphasis on *man*. For years she had gone to school and toiled at her job, only to be looked on as a kind of quiet assistant. Of course, that had been part of her plan, but she also knew that if she continued down this path and even if she revealed her amazing intellect to the world, things wouldn't be much different. There would always be men who would love to take the credit for her work.

That night, her parents were intrigued and then alarmed at the sound of an approaching helicopter. Looking rather military in its camouflage paint, it landed on the soccer field just at the back of their house, the blades still spinning as it waited for someone.

Sissy sprinted out of her room, now dressed in combat boots and her hiking clothes, her big hiking backpack crammed with mysterious objects.

"Where are you going?" her mother stammered.

"It's part of the internship," Sissy called out, "I'll explain later."

The truth was, she didn't know whether she would ever come back to that house again.

28 TO SAVE THE ENVIRONMENT (AD 2013)

The hardest thing about finding a driver to take a whole company of knights, computers, and animals to Rodney's cottage was to trying to convince the driver that Tyler posed no threat.

Any van or truck owners they approached didn't want the creature in their vehicle.

When Tyler spoke up to remind them about animal emancipation, they usually ran away screaming.

At last Rodney considered going through with buying a truck outright, but he encountered a bearded man in a patched denim jacket willing to transport the whole company. When asked whether an alligator would pose an inconvenience, the man merely smiled in such a way that suggested that he was the bane of alligators.

In fact Tyler and the entire company were slightly apprehensive of their chauffeur. But it was the road itself that posed the biggest threat. The sizzling heat of the truck compounded with the relentless sunlight and combined with the jolting of the vehicle made the six hours of the journey pass as quickly as a never-ending dentist appointment.

The whole company was relieved when at last they pulled up to Rodney's cottage, said goodbye to the scary driver, and took in the amazing scenery that lay before them.

The sound of surf spoke eloquently of refreshing water. The house, embraced by greenery on all sides, beckoned with its coolness and comfort.

The travelers couldn't decide whether they wanted to eat, sleep, or bathe first. However, Rodney quickly ran into the house and soon emerged carrying swimming shorts for everyone and even a bikini for Solena.

"Do I want to know why this is here?" she asked.

"No," Rodney replied with a flirty smile, "You probably don't."

After changing, they walked stiffly down to the beach and plunged into the gentle waves. Their tiredness was instantly washed away, and the swimming and splashing was so unlike anything they had done in the past few days that it seemed heavenly. In his rush, Rodney had not thought of swimming goggles, but Solena enjoyed connecting fully with the ocean. When she emerged from the water, she saw a beautiful blurry reflection of the sun.

When they settled in for the night, Rodney allotted one of his guest rooms to the knights, one to Jackson and Anastacio, and one to Tyler. He seemed to hesitate about Solena's accommodation but she didn't give him any encouraging signs and there were others around so he opened the door into a small but cozy little guest room for her, retiring reluctantly to his own room. Solena was not blind to his momentary hesitation, and as she fell asleep she mused on whether she and Rodney could ever get back together.

The next morning, they surfed. Tyler found it hard to balance on the board, so he body-surfed instead.

The professor watched from the shore as the rest of the company enjoyed the sport. As Rodney predicted, the dryads took naturally to it. Their athleticism was far beyond that of the humans, and their balance and timing were perfect.

The knights were a bit daunted at first. Though used to facing many danger, they were unaccustomed to the menacing look of a six-foot wave that looks like it is about to crush them to smithereens. However, they were too invested in their reputation as the bravest warriors of Britain, and soon they were paddling fiercely into the oncoming watery giants, piercing them with the surfboards or ducking underneath, emerging on the other side in a wild upsurge of hair and water.

"Don't fight the wave," Rodney called to them encouragingly, "Be one with it."

They had all made it through the breakers and now they sat happily on their boards, looking out into the broad expanse of ocean before them. It seemed to Solena like a perfect photo op for

Narcissism Carnival. There they sat, a group of surfers all fit and good-looking, beads of water glistening on their skin, though the knights were perhaps a bit too pale. Tyler added a nice dash of wildness to the picture.

When she looked over at Anastacio, he smiled at her. It seemed like ages since he had done that after Raffaella's disappearance. But here he was, seeming like the old Anastacio she knew, and when their eyes met it was as if they had been friends forever. There was that old spark of understanding and affection.

Strangely, when Rodney caught her eye, the same thing happened. Was he trying to get back together? Is that why he wanted to take them all surfing in the first place?

But soon her mind stopped questioning as the rollers swelled on the horizon and the company hurriedly began to turn their boards towards the shore. One by one, they chose a wave and paddled full-out until the board rode majestically atop its crest, plummeting down and across it in plumes of spray.

***

Alex and Dave were roommates living in a quiet suburb of L.A. They had moved in together through a set of complicated circumstances, and only once they had done so did they realize that no two people were worse suited for co-habitation.

They were both environmentalists, but their characters were so different that this similarity did next to nothing to create harmony between them.

Alex used to be a Marxist, but he had found communism was going out of fashion as one world dictator after another surrendered to the lure of capitalism. Still, he yearned for some kind of revolution to stand behind. Or better yet, he longed to march in its front ranks. Then he realized the planet was overrun by nasty oil companies and mining corporations.

He had joined Greenpiss in the hopes of marching in its front ranks, and in a short amount of time, he became one of its leaders, though he still didn't find an occasion for marching. Most of his time was spent emailing people or soliciting them for money. He was that same long-haired young man who grew depressed from sitting in the same café as Solena and her aura of despondency, and therefore one could say his rise in Greenpiss was parallel to, and possibly triggered by the dryad.

His roommate Dave, on the other hand, would have been the last person to march at the front of anything. He too was a fervent environmentalist, but of a completely different sort.

He left his clothes out in the sun instead of washing them because using a washing machine was a cardinal sin and UV light destroyed all bacteria anyway. If left to his own devices, he would deposit all dirty dishes in the sink, submersed in murky water like remnants of the Titanic. Dishwashing was a waste of water and could only be done on extremely rare occasions when there was absolutely not a single clean fork, knife, or plate left in the house. Dave never traveled outside of the two-block radius of his house. This area contained a grocery store and a small street mall which catered to all of his needs. To go "beyond the pale" by foot would be an extreme physical exertion, and of course travel by automobile was out of the question.

He believed that taking no action was the best action and that if everyone lived like him, the planet would be saved. He wrote long tracts to that effect on his blog.

"I need a spoon!" Alex shouted from his bedroom. "Will you let me wash one lousy spoon!?"

Dave did not reply, for he was too busy composing a rebuttal to a comment someone had made on his blog post.

When the Aerospatiale Puma helicopter, began to land in front of their house, Dave immediately thought it was the government coming to capture him. They had read his blog and deemed him a particularly dangerous subversive thinker.

"You'll never take me alive, carbon fiends!" he yelled, hurriedly putting on his "battle gear," a protective vest woven from kale stalks and carrot peels which he hoped would be bullet-proof.

"They're not here for you," Alex said, rolling his eyes as he entered the room and witnessed his roommate's preparation.

"Then we'll fight together!" Dave exclaimed.

"It's a Greenpiss helicopter," Alex replied, "There's no need to fight it. They're here to take me on my first mission."

Sissy had managed to worm her way into Greenpiss in case the corporation route would not work out. Fortunately for her, the members of Greenpiss rarely met in person and corresponded largely by email, so no one suspected they were dealing with a sixteen-year-old. For the most part, they were a disorganized bunch who kept disagreeing about what their aims were, and when someone as organized as Sissy came along, they naturally followed her. Thus she became the Head Coordinator of Coordinators in a very short time.

These angry young activists were the natural enemies of the corporations, and all they needed was a practical leader and some fire power. If Sissy couldn't win world dominance the peaceful way, she would pit the two movements against each other and triumph over the wreckage.

Dave rushed over to the helicopter and the door was opened for him by a stocky man dressed in a green uniform with the Greenpiss logo on his chest: a pint glass filled with green beer pouring onto a brown sapling.

"Commander Sissy Maynard is leading a mission into the Amazon," the man informed him. "She has just departed from Boston with the vanguard forces. You are instructed to come with us as a high-ranking Greenpiss official."

"What's the nature of the mission?" Dave asked, stepping into the cockpit.

The helicopter began gaining altitude.

"The corporations have found out about a rare jungle plant that has miraculous healing properties," the officer reported, "They plan to clear the forest and displace all the local residents in order to collect and sell these plants. Our mission is to stop them and collect these plants for ourselves, in moderate amounts so that we can study them."

This was just the mission Dave had envisioned. A mission to punish the corporations and thwart their greedy efforts. A mission to allocate natural resources wisely, as only humans knew how. He was ready.

29 JOLLYROGER2013 (AD 2013)

Rodney was resting in his room after the great surfing day when his computer alerted him that there was an incoming Skype call.

Rodney looked at the screen. He had expected this, but still, a little suspension of disbelief was needed for him to answer it.

The call was from someone with the username JollyRoger2013.

Rodney answered the call and saw an amazing likeness of himself now that St Amour had shaved off his black beard, cut his hair, and wore one of Rodney's button-up shirts.

In the background was the living room of Rodney's apartment in Boston. So the old man was keeping him close at hand in order to sort out the consequences of the trip back in time, just as Rodney had expected.

"St Amour! Well, well. Enjoying being me?"

"In some respects, yes," said the pirate. "Though in others, your life is paltry."

"*Your* life is paltry," Rodney corrected. "It's no longer my life."

"Why do people see it fit to be so obsessed with showing each other pictures and words written on magical tablets? And why am I forever visited by emails? As if a man cannot mount a horse or one of those magical carriages and tell me his request face to face. Cowards, all!"

"Welcome to the twenty-first century," Rodney remarked with a smirk.

"And must I forever be attending these meetings where they talk of profit margins and revenue shares? It is enough to drive a man insane. Moreover, your father is an overbearing, short-tempered, toad-spotted, gudgeoning knave!"

Rodney tried very hard to repress a triumphant laugh.

"I resent these insults your hurl at my father," he said, "Though of course I don't expect an individual with a non-existent moral compass such as yourself to be capable of appreciating this gem of a man."

"I refuse to be taken for you," St Amour continued, "things cannot go on in this manner."

"Then tell my father you're not me."

"And face his biblical wrath? I think not."

"Miss Reilly is here, sir," said a disembodied voice that Rodney recognized as belonging to Peter, his chauffeur. Miss Reilly? Why did that name sound familiar?

In the background, Rodney saw Raffaella, in a delicate cocktail dress saunter drunkenly across the room.

"What's wrong with Raffaella?" he asked.

"Nothing. She has been carousing with your mother. They seem to get along splendidly. One good word I can say for your kin is that your mother is a sweet and gracious woman, though she does drink like a sailor. No wonder she was unable to tell I was not her son."

"That's disturbing," Rodney said in earnest.

"And another thing: a waif… 'twas a girl, I think, did threaten me today!" St Amour complained, "This girl means us harm, and I know not what powers she possesses, but I fear she will make good on her threat. What manner of a world is this?!"

"One in which you have no place, St Amour. But I'm going to be a graceful winner. Surrender while you still can, and I'll return you to your century."

"Surrender? Captain St Amour will not surrender. I am, however, willing to negotiate a temporary ceasefire."

"Oh, is that it?"

"I would like to be returned to my century and my ship, and I will keep the time boat, and in return I will never molest you again so that you may regain the dreadful company of your father and live in peace, as far as you're able, with all these emails."

"A good offer," said Rodney, "Only I'll make a small amendment: you'll be returned to your ship but you will definitely not get to keep the time boat."

"All right, I will be provisioned with those wondrous guns then, the automatics."

"Out of the question."

"A pistol?"

"Maybe... No! It will disrupt the space-time continuum or some such thing. I've done it once, but I've learned the folly of my ways."

"You offer me nothing that would entice me to accept your terms," St Amour declared.

"Except freedom," Rodney said simply. "Think about it."

He clicked the "hang up" button and St Amour disappeared from the screen.

Only then did it dawn on him: he had seen the name Reilly on his family tree. He had a document of the whole thing stored somewhere on his computer, and he rifled impatiently through various virtual files until he found it.

There it was: Roger de St. Amour m. Raffaella Reilly.

Rodney got up from his computer and walked slowly and deliberately down the hallway to a spacious, mirrored bar. He tried to avoid thinking altogether before he poured the whiskey in the glass. When its burning sting hit his throat and he had swallowed it down, only then did he begin thinking, very slowly and carefully, trying not to panic.

He took a breath.

"So St Amour is my ancestor," he pronounced.

He took a second shot of whiskey, and lowered his glass to see Solena walking into the room.

"He's my ancestor," Rodney said to her in utter consternation.

"You mean St Amour?" she asked.

"Yes. And Raffaella too."

"What?"

"At first I thought they were just messing with my head. If he had managed to figure out email and Skype, St Amour could also have figured out so many other things..."

"Such as your family tree? But what does Raffaella have to do with it?"

"I just discovered her last name was Reilly."

"But that's nonsense. Dryads don't have last names."

"Exactly. But that's what she chose to call herself. I guess she needed some kind of last name in order to live in our world. At first I thought she and St Amour may have broken into my family records and simply copied the name from there… But then I realized, how on earth would they have been lucky enough to find a record of someone named Raffaella who married Roger de St Amour. And then there was the name itself."

"It's the name of the priest!"

"Right, Father O'Reilly," Rodney said, "She had been close to him. So it makes sense she took his name. Now, there are two 'coincidences' concerning both the first name and the last name. This can only mean that they're not coincidences at all. My family tree does have a Raffaella in it. It's the Raffaella we know!"

"She married St Amour?!" Solena exclaimed.

"Or she's going to," Rodney said, pouring a drink for her.

"Thanks," Solena said, and she downed the whiskey. "Well, we always thought he might be your ancestor."

Attracted by the sound of voices, Anastacio peered curiously into the room.

"Would you like a drink?" Rodney offered.

"Yes," Anastacio said, still curious, sensing that something interesting was going on.

Rodney filled them in on his entire conversation with St Amour, and both dryads listened with growing excitement.

"And you know what this means?" Rodney concluded. "I'm part dryad!"

"I'll drink to that!" said Solena.

"To dryads and humans!" Rodney offered a toast.

He poured another round and all three drank and grinned happily at each other.

"Maybe…" Solena said, "all those pirates from St Amour's crew who stayed behind in the forest mated with the female dryads. Maybe I'm part human…"

"Great, we're both pirate offspring!" Rodney laughed.

"But come, we must go outside," Anastacio said. "I had forgotten to tell you the knights are preparing a feast."

***

Jackson and the knights had piled up a huge bonfire on the beach. They had taken out Rodney's small sail boat and caught several fish, which were now being expertly prepared in the manner of buccaneers.

Rodney, Solena, and Anastacio came over to the fire, bearing several bottles from the billionaire's stash. Here was French Armagnac, Italian grappa, and the finest of Spanish red wines.

Soon the entire party was feasting and drinking on the beach, oblivious to their uncertain future and the gathering forces of fate.

"You will never guess it to look at me, but I'm part dryad!" Rodney told the company. He was rather tipsy at this point. He related his conversation with St Amour to Tyler, Jackson, the knights, and the Professor.

"I'm going to change everything about the company," he continued, "There will be lots of replanting of forests. In fact, we can focus entirely on planting... but then there won't be any timber. Ok, just a little bit of cutting, but no clear-cutting whatsoever!" he finally came to an agreement with himself.

Solena felt elated. It seemed the whole adventure had been worthwhile after all. Perhaps her mission was complete? Here was the son of the head of Timber Corporation discovering his dryad roots.

"I'm so glad you see it that way, Rodney," she said. "I hope you'll be able to convince your father as well."

"My dad! He's going to go nuts when he finds out!" Rodney cried, both joyous and apprehensive. "Wait a minute... this means he's a dryad too! He's going to flip his lid."

"But as yet the company languishes in the hands of that devious pirate," Sir Lancelot reminded. "Are you sure we shouldn't wrest it from him in this moment of his weakness?"

"We've been talking the matter over," added Sir Gawaine, "and thought, why not gather a company of sturdy lads, much like that driver who conducted us hither?"

"We'll fight our way to your father's castle, and then—"

"It's not possible," said Rodney, "As much as I appreciate your enthusiasm, I don't think I want to use force anymore unless I really have to. You don't realize the amount of bloodshed modern weapons can cause – it's not like a few knights duelling or jousting. It could kill hundreds, maybe even thousands, including innocent people as well."

"Truly, it is a dark age in which you live," said Sir Gawaine.

"I know," Rodney replied. "But I think that with time it can be changed for the better."

"What about St Amour?" asked Sir Lancelot. "Is there anything that will induce him to surrender?"

"As Teddy Goldman advises, there comes a time when the wise man should do nothing and let his enemy bring about his own defeat," said Rodney.

Tyler lifted his head.

"That's right, I've read some of his works," Rodney winked at the alligator and then at Solena.

"I'm proud of you, boss," Tyler said.

"And you'll be even prouder when you see that mangy old pirate surrender to me just as I predicted. I'll have the time boat back, and then all of you knights can go home."

"In sooth, Sir Gawaine and I would rather continue onto other quests," Lancelot remarked.

The rest of the company looked at him in astonishment.

"Aye, we need not hurry to return to Camelot," Gawaine agreed casually.

"But I thought it was an amazing place," Solena said, puzzled. "Why would the most famous knights of King Arthur not wish to return to their famed castle and tell their tales at the Round Table?"

"Our tale is scarce to be believed!" Sir Gawaine lamented. "It is not an ordinary adventure, and there could be some who would think we are merely idle braggarts."

"Besides, who wants to be a knight to that craven churl, Arthur?" Lancelot exclaimed.

"Wait a minute! This is—What?" Solena, Tyler, and Rodney, who had all been avid fans of the Arthurian legends began to protest incoherently.

"Wasn't King Arthur the noblest, bravest, and wisest king Britain had ever known?" Rodney finally formed a complete sentence.

"Aye, so he would have everyone believe, and so the minstrels proclaim since he pays them handsomely," Sir Gawaine agreed. "In truth, though he is my uncle, I would be the first to admit that he is a rascally, land-grabbing villain."

"No matter how much land he has, he still yearns for more. He fights, cheats, and steals from his neighbours all the while calling it chivalry," Lancelot confirmed.

"He's the biggest arsehole in all of Britain, and maybe beyond." Gawaine concluded.

"Well, that is very odd," was all Tyler could manage to say.

"His wife, however, is a beautiful, virtuous lady. He's not worthy of kissing the hem of her robe," Lancelot suddenly said.

He said it more to himself than to anyone as he stared into the fire, his black hair gleaming in its light.

Solena remembered the legend of that fateful love triangle in which Lancelot falls in love with the wife of King Arthur, supposedly his best friend and liege lord. So, it seemed at least one part of the legend was true.

Things would not end well for all concerned. The rift between Lancelot and Arthur would leave their kingdom exposed to the Saxons. The affair would be discovered, the queen would forever retire to a monastery, while Arthur would be killed in the ensuing battle. According to some legends, he would be borne away to the enchanted isle of Avalon, whence he would return if England ever had need of him again. But according to the knights' opinion of him, perhaps this legend was merely wishful thinking since the thieving king hardly deserved such a ceremonious death and afterlife.

Solena, Rodney and Tyler all exchanged looks. For a while, they were silent, but finally Solena said, "Perhaps then it's better if you don't return to Camelot at all. Your quest will live on in legend, while you could occupy yourselves with something even more interesting. Professor, you would find something for them to do?"

"I am positively sure of it," said Professor X129.

But the professor's mind seemed to be occupied with something else, as much as humans could infer such things about a machine. His internal fans hummed in a strained manner, but otherwise he remained mostly silent.

Solena felt as if it was somehow connected with her thoughts and feelings, but she couldn't understand why that would be. Every time she looked over at Rodney or Anastacio, the professor hummed like a race car revving up its engines. She also noticed that Lancelot sighed more than usual, Jackson smiled faintly, as if recalling some fond memory, and Rodney flirted shamelessly.

She realized it had to be her dryad aura that was affecting the humans, and even the computer in such a strange fashion. Her feelings transferred over to them, and they felt an echo of what she felt, each in their own way. She wished she hadn't drunk so much whiskey; her emotions were becoming uncontrollable.

Would the Anastacio that she had known disappear now that this Anastacio was here? She wondered, while stealing glances at him. And was this one better than the old one? And if so, would he want to be her friend, or maybe...

The unruly part of her mind was pondering these questions while the disciplined part tried to supress them as much as possible, for it would mean admitting that she was in love with Anastacio. But would he stay here or would he go back to his time? She was now dependent on his decisions! It left her feeling weak and powerless. Surely, this is not what Teddy Goldman would have advised. And yet this desire was so delicious and irresistible!

Her thoughts were interrupted when the professor revved up his fans once again, only this time to break into song. It wasn't exactly him singing, it was an audio recording of a country singer, one who was considered ancient in the professor's time, but just slightly out of date as well as timeless in the early twenty-first century, singing an American folk song.

Down in the valley, the valley so low
Hang your head over, hear the wind blow
Hear the wind blow, dear, hear the wind blow;
Hang your head over, hear the wind blow.

Build me a castle, forty feet high;
So I can see her as she rides by,
As she rides by, dear, as she rides by,
So I can see her as she rides by.

If you don't love me, love whom you please,
Throw your arms round me, give my heart ease,
Give my heart ease, dear, give my heart ease,
Throw your arms round me, give my heart ease

Write me a letter, send it by mail;
Send it in care of the Birmingham jail,
Birmingham jail, dear, Birmingham jail,
Send it in care of the Birmingham jail.

Roses love sunshine, violets love dew,

Angels in Heaven know I love you,
Know I love you, dear, know I love you,
Angels in Heaven know I love you.

"Professor!" Jackson exclaimed when the song had finished. "I knew it, I knew there was some feeling buried deep down in you somewhere."

"It was buried very deeply," the professor replied. "I had an emotional circuit but I had shut it off due to disuse. Now it seems to have self-activated. I once liked that song, when I was human and had a taste for such morbidly sentimental cowboy music. Now I no longer recall what a cowboy is. A kind of minotaur creature perhaps?"

"Actually it's a boy who herds cows," Solena informed him.

"Oh, that's right. It's coming back to me. This is very ancient history indeed."

"But why now?" Jackson asked.

"Some strange electromagnetic waves are in the air," the professor replied mysteriously.

Solena said nothing. She wondered if the professor could tell these waves were coming from her and was covering for her. She looked over at him, but his screen face wasn't looking at her. It was looking off into the distance.

"Once, I knew a woman," the Professor said, "She was a graduate student of mine, so I felt it would be unethical to pursue a relationship with her. So I never did. This was back when I had a human body, of course. Ah, these emotions! They're drowning me. No wonder I had chosen to deactivate the circuit!"

"I rather like that you've reactivated it, professor!" Jackson said.

"Yes, good man," confirmed the knights, who didn't know what a circuit was but understood the general gist of things.

30 SISSY STRIKES (AD 2013)

The morning after the great feast found Rodney feeling rather exhausted. He lay face down on his bed, trying to summon up the strength to stand. He needed water.

Suddenly his computer made noises that hurt his aching head, noises indicating that someone was trying to reach him by Skype.

"I hope you're surrendering, St Amour," Rodney muttered, getting up, "I really can't handle bad news right now."

He smiled when he saw that the call was indeed coming from JollyRoger2013, and when he answered it, he expected to see that strange likeness of himself again.

Instead, he saw a chaotic blur of action. It looked like the desk on which his computer in Boston sat was pushed roughly as if someone had fallen against it. The room was filled with uniformed soldiers, but Rodney could not tell what nationality this army belonged to. Their green camouflage suits looked similar to the American army's but were not quite the same. He could hear the sounds of heavy breathing and blows being struck but couldn't see what was happening.

"Rodney!" he heard St Amour shout off screen, "They're taking us back to the forest!"

There were more sounds of a struggle. Then a green-gloved hand turned off the computer monitor on the Boston end, and the call disconnected.

***

"How perfect," Sissy remarked. "You've led us to the hideout of the real Rodney Love."

Dressed in the Greenpiss uniform, Sissy looked slightly more adult-like. She commanded these troops, who had never seen her in person but accepted her as their leader. She had an air of authority, not hard to achieve for someone whose IQ was higher than all the others' combined.

Sissy leaned down to the monitor and saw the town of Nuqui in Colombia as the current location of Rodney Love.

"Perfect," she said again, "We'll get the real one as well. Leave a clean slate."

St Amour and Raffaella were held by the green-uniformed Greenpiss troopers while being handcuffed in a corner of the room to which they had retreated in their futile fight.

"You'll not succeed," St Amour said, "Rodney Love is much better equipped to fight you than we are. He knows the ways of this century."

"Well, it will make no difference to you," Sissy retorted, "Whoever you are. You *will* find that medicinal plant for us."

"And why should I?" he asked proudly.

Sissy didn't say anything threatening, but gazed at Raffaella in a meaningful way.

St Amour's eyes glowed with ferocity at this implied threat, but he said nothing as the troops led him and Raffaella to the Greenpiss helicopter.

As soon as she entered the cockpit, Sissy gave the pilot the command to take off. She then took out her tiny laptop and checked her list of possible suspected residences of Rodney Love. One of them was just on the outskirts of Nuqui on a fantastic surfing beach. She picked up the radio receiver.

"Treehugger One to Treehugger Two, do you copy?" she said.

"Treehugger One here," Alex's voice replied on the other end.

"There is one high priority mission you must accomplish, Treehugger Two. Eliminate Rodney Love."

"Copy that," Sissy thought she could hear the glee in the environmentalist's voice.

"I'm sending you the coordinates and location maps," she said, "Treehugger One out."

***

"What the hell was that?" Rodney yelled. "Who would dare to

kidnap me from my own home?! Of course, it wasn't me personally, but they didn't know that."

Alarmed by the sound of his voice, the knights, who resided closest to his room, soon rushed in, swords at the ready. They looked a little the worse for wear since the party, but they were ready for action.

"You called for help?" Lancelot asked.

"No," Rodney said, shock still apparent in his face. "But thank you for coming."

"We heard strange sounds…"

"I just talked to St Amour again," Rodney explained. "I believe someone may have kidnapped him… and probably Raffaella too. He said 'they're taking us back to the forest.'"

"That is passing strange," said Sir Gawaine. "But if the maiden is spirited away, we must rescue her, even if it means possibly rescuing that scoundrel St Amour."

"Not to mention that he's my ancestor," Rodney reminded, "If anything happens to him, who knows… I may suddenly never have existed."

"Let us assemble the others," Lancelot reasoned. "We shall decide on a plan."

At that moment, Solena was sitting on the sunny porch watching Tyler swimming and splashing in the surf. Anastacio came over to sit beside her. His proximity didn't make her feel uneasy or nervous anymore. She had gotten used to his presence and his current non-aged state.

"So these are the times in which you live…" he said, pensively.

"It must seem odd to you," she said.

"Not so much. I suppose one shouldn't be surprised that humans have built up even stranger machines and have made incursions even into the dryad lands."

"They haven't, yet," Solena said. "But the threat seems imminent."

"I wonder that more dryads have not joined you to oppose this threat," Anastacio remarked.

"They don't understand the human world," Solena sighed, "That's why I was chosen."

Anastacio shrugged scornfully. "I think they're lazy. It wouldn't hurt them to learn more about the humans, as you did. As for me, I don't feel at home in the human world, but I am here since I must fulfil my duty."

"Your duty to Raffaella?"

"Or to any one of the tribe. I think if someone else had strayed or been stolen away, I would still try to find them and bring them back."

Solena looked up at him suddenly. "Even if they weren't as beautiful as Raffaella?"

"Even if they weren't as beautiful as Raffaella," he confirmed.

Rodney appeared on the porch, flanked by the knights. "I'm afraid I have some bad news," he pronounced.

After everyone gathered on the porch, Rodney re-told his story. Contrary to what Solena thought would happen, Anastacio stayed very calm. He was of course distraught at the news, but he stayed quiet and didn't say anything accusatory to Rodney, who had evidently been bracing himself for something of the sort.

Rodney now felt guilty about his somewhat blasé attitude in dealing with St Amour, so he brought up the subject himself.

"I think I've handled this poorly," he confessed, "If I had come up with a more actionable plan, maybe we could have ensured Raffaella's safety."

Everyone was silent. It was Anastacio who spoke up first.

"No," he said, "your plan was not a bad one. You couldn't have accounted for what happened. Besides, now is not the time to think about what went wrong but how to make it better."

"Hear, hear!" said Jackson.

"We are with you," Lancelot confirmed. "We will help in whatsoever way we can."

"We've got to get back to the jungle, to the dryad lands," Rodney proposed. "I presume that's what St Amour meant."

"Why would someone want to take him there?" Anastacio asked. "And who would have the power to steal him away?"

"I've been trying to figure it out," Rodney confirmed. "He did mention earlier that he had been threatened by a child. It made no sense…"

"Does your father have any enemies?" Lancelot asked.

"Oh, quite a few," Rodney replied, "But I very much doubt they would dare to kidnap me. It must be someone I don't know about, maybe even someone my father doesn't know about… Well, it doesn't matter! We'll find them, whoever they are. I'll call for reinforcements. The Timber Corporation's private army should be enough to take care of it."

"How quickly will they be deployed?" Solena asked.

"Three or four hours, I should think," said Rodney, "I believe some of them are still stationed around here to protect the time boat. I'll contact them and let them know we're here."

The company was in agreement, and Rodney quickly dialed a number on his cell phone to call one of the security teams.

"No, I have not been kidnapped," he replied to the voice coming from inside his cell phone. "I'm safe and sound; however, someone very close to me has been kidnapped, and I intend to go after them."

The answer on the other end of the line was evidently affirmative, as Rodney hung up with a satisfied expression.

"Well," he said, "They'll be here in two hours. We had better get ready."

But how does one get ready for unforeseen forces that had swept away a scoundrel as devious as St Amour? That was the question on everyone's mind as they gathered their meager supplies and tried to rouse themselves for the coming rescue.

Solena saw that Anastacio was meditating on the beach not far from the house, and she didn't want to disturb him. She too was worried about Raffaella but she couldn't help thinking that this was rather bad timing. Anastacio was just beginning to make sense to her, and now they were both distracted once again.

She went back to sitting on the porch, where she found the professor, sighing in a whir of fans.

"I can't turn it off!" he said.

"What?"

"The emotional circuit. I'd have to get back to the main computer and reroute all my programming. But I'm afraid I'll never be able to get back to my proper time period! What if I pine away like this for the rest of my life?"

"Professor, having emotions isn't so bad," she began. "Oh, what am I saying, it's terrible! I wish I could turn them off too!"

"Really?" the professor asked, forgetting his own troubles for a moment. "But if you don't mind my saying so, you were sending out very positive emotions. They were radiating at such a high frequency that it must have activated my own circuit."

"I'm sorry," Solena muttered, blushing.

"No, it's not something you should be sorry about."

"I just don't know…"

"Whether he loves you back?"

Solena had not expected the professor to know the exact nature of her emotions, and she blushed again. She didn't know whether he had meant Rodney or Anastacio.

But at that moment Rodney himself appeared, accompanied by the knights and Jackson.

"I thought I heard a helicopter sound," Rodney said. "This should be them, though they're a little early."

Everyone looked up into the cloudless sky and saw a small dot appear, but not from the South as Rodney had expected. Anastacio rose up and came to join them.

"Hmmm, maybe not," Rodney said.

They looked on as the helicopter flew directly towards them. It looked like the helicopter had the intention of approaching Rodney's seaside residence, for there was no other habitation for a few miles around.

"Get back into the house!" Rodney yelled suddenly.

They all stood in shock for a moment, but seeing his worried expression, they obeyed. As soon as they were inside, they rushed to the windows to see what Rodney had already noticed.

"These are not Timber Corporation choppers," he said tensely. "They're green, not black. And they're the wrong model. I don't like this, guys."

"Do you suppose…" Solena began. "It's those same people that kidnapped St Amour? And now they're coming for us?"

"In that case, I hope my reinforcements arrive sooner rather than later." Rodney said grimly.

The noise from the helicopter grew rapidly more and more deafening. The plantain trees outside the house shook anxiously at its approach. The company remained silent, gathering round the window, but trying to stay more or less concealed.

The helicopter landed just in front of the house, but no one emerged from it, and it sat there for a while with its engine still running.

The company in Rodney's house waited even more tensely.

Suddenly, a man's voice grated on their hearing with its unpleasant sound, carried to them via megaphone:

"Where is Rodney Love? Come out!"

"I'm Rodney Love," Rodney shouted through the open window. "Who the hell are you?"

"Die, you capitalist scum!" said the voice.

A rain of bullets descended from the helicopter. Rodney sprang back as they ricocheted from the stucco of the house and a few lodged themselves in the opposite wall, narrowly missing him.

"Who are they?" Rodney asked, bewildered. "The more important question is, does anyone have any more guns? I only have this Glock."

The knights had their bows handy, and acting as one, they stationed themselves by the two front windows on either side of the window at which Rodney stood, ready to let fly.

"I guess it's the next best thing," Rodney shrugged.

"I have a pistol," said Jackson resolutely.

He doubted it would be of much help against these warriors, but he knew he could make every shot count.

Rodney dared to look outside with a corner of his eye. The helicopter was lifting into the air but three of the commandos remained on the ground. One of them lit a smoke grenade and ran towards the house, ready to throw it. At once, two arrows hit him but bounced right off his body armor. Rodney cursed. He fired his pistol.

The man with the smoke grenade was thrown back, but evidently not wounded as he began to get up painfully. The armored vest had saved him again. In the meantime the smoke kept billowing out, eclipsing the scene as the two other mysterious commandos rushed towards their fallen comrade.

"Are you thinking of any spells?" Solena whispered to Anastacio.

"Yes," he replied, "but it's hard to know what to do about that metallic bird."

Solena found herself quite at a loss too. To harm the helicopter would probably mean killing those inside, and although she felt quite desperate, she wasn't desperate enough to risk it.

"But that smoke... we could try to dispel it."

Although the smoke grenade had been rendered highly ineffective, some of the smoke did drift into the house and caused light coughing all round.

"Are you thinking of?..." Solena asked.

He nodded. "A simple wind spell."

"Right."

They both concentrated and a tiny wind vortex formed inside the room. It unfolded itself, taking the smoke with it. Solena felt a kind of wordless connection with Anastacio as they worked the magic together. As if they had agreed on it in advance, they both began to strengthen the spell until the wind became more of a hurricane. It blew away all the smoke outside, allowing them to see the three commandos retreating behind trees. The wind pulled violently at the three men, making all their movements awkward and difficult.

In the meantime, Jackson scouted the back of the house with his pistol. He could see the metallic bird swinging away in that direction and could only surmise that it meant to outflank them.

He opened the door to the back porch and slammed it shut at once, seeing that three more soldiers were descending from the bird on lowered lines.

If there was one thing Jackson was good at it was picking off moving targets such as men swinging on ropes. He dashed over to a small kitchen window, knocked out the glass with the butt of his pistol, and fired at one of the men, aiming for the neck since every other part was armored.

He heard a muffled scream and saw the man fall the short remaining distance to the ground, but he didn't stay long at the window as the other two began firing on him at once.

Jackson locked the door, but he doubted it would hold these intruders back for long.

"Two more coming from the back of the house," he reported to the rest of the company.

He closed the door to the living room behind him, and the dryads helped him barricade it with as much furniture as they could drag over. Bookshelves, dressers, and tables all went into the pile.

An angry knocking was heard on the other side of the door.

"This is Greenpiss! Open up and surrender Rodney Love. The rest of you will be free to go."

"Nay, we will not surrender Sir Rodney." Sir Lancelot replied at once.

"Besides, I trust not that they will keep that bargain," Gawaine added.

"What is Greenpiss?" Anastacio asked, puzzled.

"It's an environmental group," said Solena, "they're supposed to protect plants and animals. I don't understand why they're trying to kill us."

"Everyone, get down!" Rodney warned.

It was just in time, for machine gun fire from the other side of the door tore through the walls just as the whole company fell flat, showered by chunks of plaster and furniture. Tyler was already low to the floor, but he also tried to curl up into a ball.

"Any dryad magic?" Rodney yelled over the noise of gunfire.

Solena was at a loss; it would be very hard to do another spell similar to the one she had done in the forest when she turned a pistol into a branch. It was impossible to concentrate, and she couldn't even see the machine guns on the other side of the wall. Anastacio was similarly discomfited, for he had only the vaguest notion of what machine guns were.

"Anything?" Solena asked Anastacio.

"We should flee through that window!" he said.

It was not much safer outside with the three other shooters, but at least their aim was rendered terrible due to the continuous wind spell the dryads had launched at them.

But it was too late to flee. The door cracked, giving in to the blows of the commandos.

One of them stumbled into the room, and Solena saw in astonishment that a man from another military team was attacking the Greenpiss trooper.

This strange man was attired in a colorful uniform with designs of wild flowers and grasses on it. It was largely done in shades of pink.

"WE BRING YOU LOVE!" a voice that seemed to be coming from the heavens sang out.

Upbeat music blasted from some unseen speakers, and Solena looked around, trying to discover its source.

As soon as the Greenpiss man fell into the room, Anastacio wrestled him to the ground and knocked him out with one powerful punch.

Beyond the broken-down door a strange fight was taking place. The Greenpiss soldiers shrieked in outrage and fear as the newcomers in colorful uniforms sprayed them with some sort of gunky pink liquid from their strange paintball-like guns. After staggering their opponents with the force of the pink liquid, they easily defeated them in hand-to-hand combat. The Greenpiss men lay in a heap, unconscious but alive.

"I don't know who you are," Rodney said, "But thank you."

The three strange soldiers, two men and one woman, grinned at him in a friendly way.

"That's all right," one of the men said. "Come on, we've got to get you all to safety."

Glancing outside, Solena saw that the three remaining Greenpissers were just as easily dispatched by the pink army.

Somewhat dazed, Solena and the rest of the company followed these soldiers out to the back porch, where they beheld a pink helicopter hovering just above the house. It was dousing the Greenpiss helicopter with pink liquids until the entire thing was covered up and the Greenpiss pilot had to perform an emergency blind landing.

Then the pink helicopter quickly landed at the front of the house, and its soldiers ushered the company across the expansive lawn towards it.

A man emerged from the cockpit, beckoning them. He looked fairly ordinary, rather slight in stature and thin in his physique. He wore the same predominantly pink uniform, and he limped as he stepped towards Solena and her party, his hair fluttering in the wind of the propeller. Though he didn't look particularly warrior-like, it seemed he was the leader of this strange band of commandos.

For a moment, everyone was silent as the leader eyed the newcomers and they eyed him.

There was something strangely familiar about the man. His eyes… Solena thought. Where had she seen his eyes? Before she could place him, Tyler plunged forward, exclaiming:

"Oh my God this is so great – I wonder if you would autograph – damn I don't have any books here – I've read all of your books and you're the smartest human on the planet – I'm so excited to meet you I'm an alligator who learned how to speak and all because of you!"

Tyler ran forward towards the man yelling these disjointed phrases like some religious fanatic possessed by the Holy Spirit.

Most people would be terrified or at least alarmed on seeing an alligator rushing so precipitously towards them, albeit uttering words of adulation, but this was far from the case with Teddy Goldman (for it was he).

He smiled, squatted down and shook Tyler's hand, or rather his foreleg.

"I'm pleased to meet you too," he said in a deep, mellifluous voice.

CHAPTER 31 FAMILY REUNION (AD 2013)

"We'd better get a move on before more of them come out of that helicopter," one of the pink soldiers said.

Solena and the others were safely in the pink helicopter as it tilted away from the ground and took off, leaving Rodney's cottage behind. One of the pink soldiers took over the controls of the helicopter and Teddy Goldman joined the others in the passenger compartment.

"I know what you're thinking," he said, "Pink is a color better suited to a little girl. But if you look back in time, even to about one hundred years ago in the Victorian era, pink was considered a manly color."

"Actually, we were more curious as to how you found us and why those 'Greenpiss Berets' were after us," Rodney said.

"I found out that a section of Greenpiss has gone rogue. They are under the command of someone named Sissy Maynard."

"But how did you get such intelligence?" Rodney exclaimed.

"My spirit guide," Teddy Goldman replied nonchalantly.

"I suppose that's one way to stay current on today's events," Rodney shrugged.

"You'd be surprised how much you can learn from meditation. All sorts of info comes flowing in. Recently my spirit guide told me it was time to go on my first humanitarian mission, to rescue a few innocent people – and alligator – from the clutches of Greenpiss. I did a bit of research on the current state of Greenpiss, and I also heard about your kidnapping, so putting the facts together, I hurried over here with my team."

"I never knew you had a private army," Rodney said. "For that matter, I didn't know Greenpiss had one!"

"This is not an army, really." Teddy replied, "All the people you see here are volunteers. They're mostly martial arts students from my gym, as well as a few friends of mine. I can't stand the concept of an army, and as you've seen, we try to avoid killing people. We call ourselves the Peaceful Warriors. Allow me to introduce Karpos, Alison, Domingo, Tyrone, Hallvor, Pariss, Myron, Leslie, and Dusty."

Solena was much shyer than Tyler in approaching her idol, but finally she said:

"Then you share that dislike with dryads. We try not to kill anyone too."

"Dryads!" Teddy exclaimed, "You are a dryad?"

"Yes," Solena said in a tiny voice.

She was rendered even more shy by his excitement.

"I've never met one!" he continued, "I supposed you've taken on a human form now."

"Yes, I've been living as a human for quite some time," she replied, "And I'm also a huge fan of your work, your self-help books."

"Are you?" he exclaimed, "Well, thank you. You have no idea how much it means to me."

Meanwhile, the knights were looking about them with a mixture of awe and exultation. They kneeled on a bench that ran almost the entire length of the helicopter, along a large window through which they could see the expanse of blue, cloudless sky and the scenery below.

"We are *inside* the dragon!" said Sir Gawaine solemnly. "I dare say no other knight has ever done such a deed."

"'Tis probably not a real dragon, but yet another one of those machines," Lancelot allowed.

"It matters not," said Gawaine.

"You're right, it matters not," Lancelot agreed, looking down on the sea of vegetation sweeping by below at an outrageous speed.

"Good sir," Gawaine addressed Teddy Goldman, "Let me once again add my thanks to those of our fair company, and congratulate you on the taming of this beast, or machine, or whatever it be."

"It was my pleasure," Teddy Goldman said, taking his archaic language in stride.

It was when the knights introduced themselves that he looked a bit stunned.

"You're putting me on, right?" he said. "Sir Lancelot? Sir Gawaine?"

"You doubt us, Sir Teddy?" Gawaine asked.

"He has some reason to doubt us," Lancelot reminded, "for there are no knights in these times."

"They really are the knights of the Round Table," Solena chimed in.

"It's a long story," Rodney added.

The story was then recounted by the entire company, each taking turns to tell the part that the others might not have witnessed. The Peaceful Warriors gathered round, and Teddy Goldman listened to the story with fascination. The more Solena watched him the more she could see the real person behind that wise, serene voice that had spoken to her through her beloved books. She saw that it was truly him, despite the fact that he looked nothing like the muscle-bound tough guy with the fashionably shaved head who usually appeared on the book covers.

"Well, this explains a lot of things," Teddy finally said when they had finished, "I understand now why my spirit guide brought me here."

"But there is something I don't understand," the professor spoke up.

"What is it, professor?" Teddy asked.

"Historically, the Rise of Sissy doesn't happen until the mid-twenty-first century. As I understand it, we are now only in the year 2013. It is much too soon: she must still be an adolescent!"

"The Rise of Sissy?!" Rodney exclaimed. "You mean she's going to win?"

"I have seen it myself," Jackson confirmed, "In the future."

The professor replied solemnly, as if giving a lecture, "The dawning of the twenty-first century would bring forth two great geniuses: Teddy Goldman and Sissy Maynard."

"Sissy," Teddy Goldman said. "I have seen her in my visions. Though I've got to say, I'm hardly a genius," he added humbly.

"The two would direct the course of events to come," the professor continued, "but it would only be after Teddy Goldman became president of the United States that Sissy would begin her campaign of terror and cause the Great War between the Environmentalists and the Citizens."

"Well, I have thought of becoming president," Teddy admitted, "but it seems a little too grandiose…"

"Maybe it's not the history that's wrong," Solena said, "maybe it's just changing because we went back in time and brought St Amour here."

"Then we've made it even worse!" Rodney exclaimed. "Whoever this Sissy is, she's going to take over even quicker than before."

"Not necessarily," said Teddy Goldman. "Although bringing St Amour into the present may have enticed Sissy to act sooner, this could also be her downfall. She is just a callow schoolgirl. I don't want to make the mistake of underestimating her, but maybe a younger Sissy is less of a danger than an older one? Having you here is a great boon to us, professor. You're well informed about Sissy, and this information could be the key to stopping her."

"You mean to say that you think you could prevent the Great War and the Rise of Sissy?" the professor exclaimed.

"I've got to try, at least," Teddy Goldman said. "It sounds like I'm her nemesis, or she is mine."

"I will help you as much as I can," said the professor. "These emotions that I had forgotten for so many years have now returned, and they tell me that it's the right thing to do. I had observed distant history and seen it as the inevitable course, but I feel now more strongly than ever, that it was not the right course."

"Maybe you can tell us why Sissy is so interested in the rainforest?" Teddy Goldman asked.

"That's an easy question. The way she proceeded in starting the Great War was to stir up resentment between the environmentalists and the corporations. I believe she may be drawing this Greenpiss towards such a conflict by arming and leading them on an imaginary crusade to protect the environment. Her real mission is simply to start a battle, or at least a skirmish. Sometimes she would let the environmentalists win, sometimes not. This could be just the beginning. After a few such encounters in different corners of the globe, two great movements would emerge, the Environmentalists, who would of course back organizations such as Greenpiss; and the Citizens, who would stand up for law and order, protecting the corporations. Both would be blind to the fact that they were completely breaking down the social order as well as national boundaries. A global-scale civil war would begin."

Everyone was uneasily silent.

"So the cause of the war is unimportant," Teddy Goldman said at last. "That's good to know. Still, I wonder what Sissy wants in the rainforest. It seems suspicious that she would wish to go to the exact place where your adventures so recently occurred."

"Such details have escaped recorded history," the professor said with a sigh.

"I know what she wants!" Tyler exclaimed. "The miraculous medicine! This would enable her to live forever; how else would she still be alive in your time? We can't let her get it!"

***

Sissy got off the radio with Treehugger Two after hearing his confusing report regarding an ambush by a pink helicopter. Despite the disjointed nature of his account, she understood who had rescued the erstwhile executive of the Timber Corporation.

"I knew you'd show up sooner or later, Teddy Goldman," she thought, "and I know you're coming for me. But you can't take me by surprise like you did those clueless idiots."

With her was a team of commandos who were better armed and much more ruthless than Goldman' "pink" army. Her helicopter was swooping down over the tangled waves of rainforest, heading for the narrow strip of beach that separated the aquamarine ocean from the ocean of trees.

Looking down, St Amour recognized it as the fateful place where he had first met Rodney Love and his crew.

St Amour wondered how this devil child could possibly know about this location. He was usually not given to superstition, but he couldn't help suspecting occult powers. There was no way for him to know that Sissy had traced the location of the online video she had seen of the time boat taking off.

Here was the beach again. This beach had been so fateful that it seemed intimately familiar to the pirate, as if he had spent decades there instead of minutes. He felt weary.

Raffaella must have noticed his despondency, for she subtly touched his foot with hers just as the helicopter landed on the sand. He looked up to see her brief but meaningful wink.

"This is not the place you are looking for," Raffaella said, "It's further inland."

"All right," Sissy responded. "Then you've got to guide us there."

The helicopter veered away from the beech and headed deeper into the continent, towards the dryad lands. St Amour found it strange to think that the distance he had traversed while chasing Rodney Love for days could be traversed in a matter of hours in this flying machine. Nevertheless, the swiftness of their approach was relentless, and they soon arrived in the area to which Raffaella directed them, in the heart of the dryad lands.

The helicopter found a clearing to land on, and they were led outside at gun point, their hands still handcuffed behind them.

St Amour couldn't get much more of a clue from Raffaella as to what she was up to. There was no opportunity to talk, for the relentless girl watched them so closely he could practically feel her small brown eyes boring into him.

"Now, find me that plant," she commanded.

Raffaella seemed to obey. She plunged onward into the jungle, and the soldiers followed.

***

"Another Greenpiss helicopter has been reported just 50 miles south of here," Teddy Goldman told the company as he emerged from the cockpit, "I've also made contact with Gregory Love. He's going to rendezvous with us. He sounded anxious as to your well-being, Rodney, and I assured him that you are still in one piece."

"Thank you," Rodney said uncertainly, "Wait, did you just say my father is on his way here?"

"Yes of course," Teddy replied, "He heard about the kidnapping and dispatched his people to find you, then he was told it was a false alarm and that you were at your cottage in Colombia. Then he got another report saying you were nowhere to be found. No wonder he was worried."

They met on the beach, the pink helicopter landing like some strange tropical bird beside the black Timber Corporation helicopter. They were a few miles north of where the original time boat launch had occurred, for they wanted to avoid the Greenpiss troops – for now.

A few Timber Corporation soldiers were waiting around on the beach, together with a small but lively elderly man who paced back and forth impatiently.

"Rodney!" he called, as the varied crew of the pink helicopter began to emerge, Rodney being one of the first.

It was his father, looking about ten years younger, and sounding actually glad to see him.

"Dad!" Rodney ran over to him.

He wasn't very comfortable hugging his father, so he stopped before getting too close, and they both looked at each other, looked at the changes that had been wrought on them so recently. Rodney realized he must look much more tanned even than he had been in California, and somewhat more scruffy. His father, however, was the one who took the prize for being the most changed.

"Dad, are you cured?" Rodney asked.

"Yes!"

"I'm so glad to see you healthy again!"

"I thought you'd been kidnapped and I'd never see you again." Gregory replied.

"The guy who was kidnapped wasn't me," Rodney explained, "Ever since we got back from the 17th century he'd been posing as me."

"But who the hell is he?" Gregory asked.

"He's our pirate ancestor," Rodney said wearily.

"Oh… so you're not going to marry that nice Columbian girl?"

"No, but I guess he will," Rodney sighed.

"She's the one who cured me, you know."

"I'm glad," Rodney said. To bicker over taking credit for the recovery seemed petty to him. "I wish I'd been the one who brought you the cure, but it doesn't matter."

"It does," his father said, "I know it was your idea all along. I haven't forgotten. I may have been hard on you before, but things are going to change from now on. I wanted you to know that I love you, son."

Rodney never heard his father say that in many years, perhaps twenty or so. It felt extremely scary and awkward, but he staggered over to his father and felt that the old man picked up on the same impulse. They hugged, and Rodney felt the strength in his father's embrace, a warm, positive energy that had long been absent.

"I love you, dad," he said.

"I love you, Rodney," his father replied.

Teddy Goldman looked on in a humble but slightly self-satisfied way, feeling that he had had a small part to play in this happy reunion. Solena observed them out of the corner of her eye. She knew how much Rodney had struggled to get to this point. The others, slightly embarrassed, pretended to observe the scenery, as if trying to find the elusive birds and monkeys calling from the depths of the jungle.

"So who is that other fellow again?" Gregory asked.

"He's our ancestor, Roger de St Amour, a French corsair."

"Well, you've opened up a whole can of worms there," Gregory didn't say this in his old accusatory tone, but rather in a slightly amused way, as if Rodney had invited an unwanted guest to one of his mother's fashion shows. "I've read about him. I think he was quite the troublemaker."

"You don't know the half of it. We've been chasing each other all across South America for the last few weeks. Now I've got to rescue him and take him back to his century where he belongs."

"Well, I'm with you on that," Gregory assured him.

Teddy Goldman chose this as a good time to introduce himself. Then the Peaceful Warriors and the entire company of dryads, knights, and alligator introduced themselves to the bemused billionaire.

"It's good we have so much manpower," Gregory Love said, "I understand this rogue section of Greenpiss doesn't mess around. They're highly trained and out to get us. Fortunately, I've brought some of my best soldiers."

"Actually, Mr. Love, I wanted to ask you to let me and my associates handle this," Teddy Goldman intervened. "I know that you have every reason to deal with this crisis yourself, and that your family has been attacked... but I believe that if you pursue Sissy now, you'll be doing exactly what she wants you to do. She wants to create a violent conflict, and we must not let her."

"What do you suggest I do, then?" Gregory asked somewhat stand-offishly.

"I will go and affect the rescue together with my team. Maybe you and your soldiers would be so kind as to stand by in case of any trouble?"

"Stand by, huh?" Gregory said.

He really seemed to be considering the idea. Rodney would never have thought that the old Gregory would have accepted such a course of action for even one minute. But it seems times were changing...

32 GAINING TRUST (AD 2013)

It had been an anxious day for the dryad tribe. The sentries posted on the outer boundaries reported the presence of humans, which was unusual in itself since humans hardly ever ventured into these wild forestlands. And these were not just humans but aggressive military humans, and they were looking for something. They had two captives, one human and one dryad.

"I fear this bodes ill," the priest said, "but the Great Tree has whispered that there is still hope."

The dryads were gathered round the Tree as usual on public occasions of importance. The priest wanted to calm them, but he could see now this was an impossible task, and he couldn't blame them for being agitated.

"They're here to cut down our forest!" voices in the crowd shouted.

"They're looking for magical plants. If they find them, they'll send hordes of humans to raze our forest to the ground!"

"That will not happen," said the priest.

"But they are invading our forest as the Great Tree foretold. And what has Solena done to help? Nothing! She's disappeared, probably ran away from doing her duty!"

"Maybe she's joined with the humans!"

The priest raised his hands to quiet them.

At this moment, the dryads gathered around the Great Tree heard a faint roar, which turned into a kind of rhythmic whirring sound, coming closer and closer. They gazed into the sky and saw a pink helicopter hovering into view. It swooped down closer and closer until it was almost touching the treetops, and the perplexed and terrified dryads heard the upbeat and contagious strains of "WE BRING YOU LOVE!"

The dryads saw Solena climbing down a rope ladder from the helicopter, and shouts of wonder filled the air. A male dryad, one they had never seen before, followed her down the ladder, then a group of humans armed with pink guns and finally an alligator. The latter was lowered down in a secure harness, in which he looked very comfortable, lounging even.

Solena saw at once that their dramatic entrance was receiving a mixed reaction. As she jumped down onto the fragrant, grassy turf of her native dryad land, she could see that some dryads, especially the young ones and the children, were looking at her with hope and excitement in their eyes; others glared with suspicion and contempt.

She glanced back at Teddy Goldman, who in turn was staring transfixed at these amazing creatures the likes of which he had never seen before. With their wild, flaming hair and their fanciful leafy attires, the dryads were quite a sight. Solena remembered one thing she had read and found wonderful in Teddy's martial art book: "Instead of fighting my opponent, I simply align myself with the Universe. This way I am invincible, for my opponent is striving against the entire Universe itself."

She had been tempted to react angrily to those accusing stares and shouts, remembering all the insults she had had to suffer, but suddenly she felt amazingly calm and at peace even in the midst of the general hubbub and confusion.

"Dryads!" she began, "the danger that threatens our forest is great. But it is not too great for us to face together."

"An army of humans are in our forest!" a dryad in the crowd shouted. It was Magdalena, old and wrinkled as Solena was used to seeing her, always stirring up trouble. "You've led them here!"

"You know that's not true," Solena said, remaining calm.

A few other dryad voices rose up, some to oppose her, some to support her.

"How do we know we can trust you?" they cried, "you've been living among humans, and you even brought humans with you."

Here, suddenly Anastacio stepped forward.

"I have heard enough!" he declared. "You dryads don't

understand the forces you are facing. Now listen to us."

He had the kind of commanding presence and voice that made everyone stop shouting and listen, if only briefly.

"Who are you?" someone from the crowd asked.

"Anastacio."

There were un-encouraging replies such as "Never heard of you!" and "That's a stupid name!"

"I hope you're happy with yourselves. Here you are moaning and whining while Solena faces countless dangers to save you." Anastacio yelled back.

The dryads wanted to counter that, but were temporarily flummoxed, for in their heart of hearts they found some truth to what he said.

Solena seized this moment to jump in.

"What Anastacio is saying is that there is so much we can all do to prevent disaster. What those humans want is to start a war, and then the forest really will be in danger. All we have to do is overcome them – without violence, through magic and superior knowledge of the forest. The young ones can easily hide in the forest and be safe; you know how to make yourselves invisible to human eyes. Everyone else who is willing to join us, please do! We need your help."

The dryads shuffled about uneasily. There was muttering and whispering.

One male dryad stepped forward.

"I was on sentry duty today when I spotted the human invaders. I can show you where they are."

"Good!" Solena exclaimed. "Thank you."

She felt an amazing feeling washing over her. She had won the trust of at least one dryad! It made her heart race, and she was almost overcome with tears when others joined the sentry and started gathering round her little group.

The young dryads and their parents began to retreat to the depths of the forest as Solena advised. Some of the most fearful and suspicious dryads did likewise, but the majority remained, seeing that the priest stood silently but firmly beside Solena. The dryads massed around her, excited, slightly frightened, but ready for action.

***

Raffaella stumbled along, the handcuffs which still bound her wrists making her feel less than graceful. She had been leading the hapless army around the rainforest for the last two hours. For a dryad, the heat was nothing, but the humans were beginning to show signs of fatigue. Sissy was especially affected, not having been very physically active aside from the occasional gym class. Her Greenpiss uniform was soaked, and her hair clung to her forehead, a sticky irritant.

"That's it!" Sissy yelled suddenly, and threateningly.

She was huffing and puffing, but through sheer will power she had kept up with the rest of the party.

"You're leading me on a wild goose chase, aren't you, missy?"

Raffaella admitted nothing. She looked defiantly at Sissy, and suddenly everyone realized that some sort of magic was happening.

"What are you doing?!" Sissy yelled in consternation.

She wasn't a big fan of magic.

The soldiers began to look around, distracted by various cries and songs of birds, animals, and insects. Sissy tried to find the source of the distraction, but couldn't see anything in particular. Then she realized that this *was* the spell.

"Hey! Focus!" she shouted at her soldiers, but they couldn't hear, and they were slowly wandering off in different directions, pursuing sounds or visions of their own. Sissy had to concentrate very hard to shake off the confounding call of the spell, but her mind was strong enough to resist it. By the time she was completely free, she saw that her two captives' handcuffs had somehow melted away, and that they were running off into the jungle.

Furious, Sissy drew her pistol. She aimed at the running target that St Amour presented. She pulled the trigger, and the sound of the shot echoed through the vast forest.

Raffaella froze for a moment. She looked to see that St Amour had fallen but was still alive, cast one brief wild look at Sissy, then began casting a spell.

It was a similar spell to what Solena had once used for turning guns into branches. The soldiers, who were brought back to reality by the sharp report of the shot, looked terrified. The machine guns in their hands began to shake violently. But they did not change into branches or anything else.

"Magic-proof guns," Sissy bragged. "That's right, I expected some underhanded voodoo-type stuff."

St Amour groaned and tried to rise, but his strength was quickly fading.

Raffaella tried not to let desperation take over. She looked down to where St Amour had fallen, the blood seeping from the wound in his back. She knew she couldn't save him alone, she needed other dryads to help, and she could feel they were close at hand.

***

Solena heard the gunshot. It sounded frighteningly close, and now she was certain of Sissy's location. She signalled for the others to follow silently. A few minutes later, they sighted Raffaella facing off against Sissy and the soldiers.

Of course, neither the soldiers nor Sissy had heard or seen them yet. Rodney, Jackson, the knights, and Teddy Goldman' team hung back, for they were not as adept at masking their presence. The dryads, however, were remarkably close to the invading army, yet invisible, blending with a clump of moss here, a flowering shrub there. Some even climbed up into the branches and crouched directly above Sissy and her men.

Anastacio was there too. From his lofty position in the tree, he was looking down on St Amour's prone body and trying to figure out a way to snatch him up without being seen. So far, it was impossible, as the body lay just in front of Sissy.

"And now," they heard Sissy saying, "You will show me the way. You have no other option."

Raffaella could sense the presence of the dryads all around her.

"No," she said. "I would never give such a powerful remedy to someone as evil as you."

At this moment Solena stepped forward from behind a tree to confront Sissy.

The girl was a little startled to see a dryad so unexpectedly close, and the soldiers raised their weapons nervously. Solena stood her ground, but didn't dare approach. She was just a few feet away from St Amour but there was no way she could reach him without being shot.

"Sissy, you're surrounded," Solena said. "Surrender now."

"Why should I?" the girl replied.

Solena was just thinking of what to say next when Teddy Goldman also stepped out into the open, recklessly facing Sissy and her well-armed team. He had no weapon as he limped forward to face his young antagonist.

"Sissy," he began.

"Teddy Goldman?" she asked.

"Yes, it's me. And I'm here to offer peace."

"Peace?" she snorted in an angry and amused way, "Why peace? Is your position so untenable?"

"I think the battle could go either way, but that's not the point," he replied, "Peace is what we all desire, even you, Sissy."

"And how do you know me so well?" she asked mockingly.

"I have seen you in my visions. Your soul is filled with darkness and sadness. I know that many of your fellow students have wronged you, rejected you, and you feel the need to revenge yourself."

"Do you feel sorry for me?" Sissy suddenly asked, "Well, don't, because I hate you most of all, Teddy Goldman. I'm glad you're here because now I can shoot you down myself. You and your so-called self-help books filled with bullshit! You make it sound like any regular person can be like you: attractive, successful, loved. Look at me! I will never be attractive, no matter how hard I try. I am a plain, ugly girl, and yes my fellow students let me know it, but you are the one who, for a time, gave me false hope. And look at yourself: *you* don't even look like you. Aren't you supposed to be this great big hunk? You've fallen for your own bullshit!"

"I will be honest with you, Sissy," Teddy Goldman sighed. "The portraits on the covers of my books are of my twin brother, Freddy. He's the attractive one. It was a marketing ploy to help me break into the publishing business. I think you're right, I shouldn't have done it. But the essence of my books still remains truthful, as I see it. I was once like you, Sissy. Having a brother who was an overachiever in athletics and martial arts made me feel like the runt of the litter, unloved, with no friends, no one to care for me. I became good at martial arts too, but never as good as him. My high school crush didn't even know or care that I existed…"

Sissy's lips trembled with some mysterious emotion.

"I guess you had a similar journey," Teddy Goldman continued, taking a few steps toward her, "But that was just high school, Sissy. Real life is not like that. It gets better, much better."

"I don't believe you," Sissy said. "And now, Teddy Goldman, you will die."

Before anyone could react, she raised her gun and fired. No one had thought she would do it. Even the Greenpiss soldiers were startled. Sissy was more affected by Teddy's speech than she admitted: as she fired the shot, her hand trembled. She had aimed at his heart, but the bullet hit the ribcage below it.

The impact knocked Teddy Goldman to the ground. At this moment, Anastacio, hanging on to a vine, dropped down to the forest floor, grabbed hold of St Amour, and swung back up into the trees so quickly that Sissy didn't have time to react.

Sissy and the soldiers aimed high into treetops, trying to see the quickly disappearing Anastacio, and the explosion of machine gun rounds disturbed the forest. While they were thus distracted, Solena lifted Teddy Goldman off the ground, slung him over her shoulder and took off at a run. She knew Anastacio was running in the same direction, for they were both going to where all dryads go when in dire need: the Great Tree.

33 THE GREAT TREE

Solena ran on, the human she was carrying a fairly light burden on her shoulder. His body was warm and sticky, its blood and sweat soaking through both their clothing, but still she could not believe she had just witnessed the one and only Teddy Goldman shot in cold blood. It was as if everything she had learned, everything she had read about had been undone in the cruelest way possible. No matter what else happened, she could not let him die.

She wasn't sure, but she felt the dryads and the rest of the crew were following. She knew that even with the extra encumbrance of carrying Teddy, she and the others would outrun Sissy and her soldiers. But sooner or later, the humans would be able to track them. Why was she leading them to the Great Tree? She didn't know, but it felt like the right thing to do, as if the Tree itself was sending her a secret message.

Solena knew that Anastacio would be there too, and just as she came in sight of the giant tree with its ever-sprawling canopy, she saw him hefting the wounded St Amour under one arm, while climbing gracefully down from the treetops across which he had journeyed.

Breathless, he approached and laid down the human underneath the shelter of the Great Tree. The two dryads stood so close beside it they could see the minute patterns in its bark, the meandering cracks, the bits of lichen, the small bumps, the gullies and crevices. It was mesmerising. It was as if the Tree was trying to distract them from the matter at hand.

St Amour was barely conscious, struggling to cling to life with obstinate will. He was panting from the pain his wound caused while he was being carried through the tree branches. Teddy Goldman, on the other hand, was completely unresponsive and deathly pale.

"I have a piece of Poniato root," Solena said, finally breaking away from the vision of the Great Tree.

"It can't work," Anastacio objected. "They can't eat it raw: it would kill them."

He was right, Solena thought. The raw power of the plant was at times too strong and filled with life force even for dryads. It needed to be specially prepared, but they had neither the times nor the means.

"Give it to me," St Amour whispered hoarsely, "I must have it."

Solena considered giving in to this demand. Perhaps it would save him after all. But if it killed him, it would mean killing Rodney too.

Again, the tree seemed to call to her... It seemed that the patterns on the barks were moving like ripples on a lake.

"We must get them to safety," Anastacio said uncertainly. He seemed affected by the same strange trance. "I think I hear someone coming."

"Yes," Solena said absently.

She lifted the unconscious Teddy Goldman from the ground in a fireman's carry, but instead of heading away from the Great Tree, she stumbled towards it, as if it were a magnet attracting her. The rippling effect of the bark increased. Curious, she reached out and touched it.

The bark felt soft and liquid: her hand passed right through it. Suddenly, she knew what she had to do. She took a step forward, and the tree bark began to look transparent. She stepped right into it and then she was inside the Great Tree, still carrying Teddy Goldman over her shoulders. Anastacio followed close behind her, carrying St Amour, and now all four of them were submerged in a kind of liquid greenness, with channels of some unseen substances flowing, gushing, and pulsing all around them. She could feel the energy of these invisible things, and somehow she could tell they were passages, mysterious passages through time or space that the Great Tree commanded. The space she was in seemed vast and eternal, yet compact and comforting at the same time.

She could see Anastacio vaguely through the green liquescent substance that was like water, yet they were suspended in it and were able to breathe. Anastacio reached out and grabbed her hand, as if he feared them being separated in this vastness. As soon as he did so, they were both suddenly caught in an upsurge of some huge energy. It rushed them upward, or so it seemed, at enormous speeds, but it was gentle and wonderful.

At last, all four of them emerged on the other end of this strange passage. The liquid domain of the Great Tree disappeared, and they were standing outside of it once again. The two dryads were speechless. They looked up into the intertwining branches, and saw that the Great Tree was the same as ever, but everything around them had changed.

They were no longer in the rainforest. Nothing but primly mowed grass stretched out all around them. The Great Tree towered all alone above this level, sterile terrain. The sky, empty and cloudless with its lonely sun looked down sadly on the scene.

The dryads put down their burdens onto the soft grass.

"What abomination is this?" Anastacio queried. "Where are all the trees?"

St Amour groaned. "This is the future… I have been here…"

"I believe he's right," Solena muttered, "This must be Sissy's future."

"Help me!" the pirate wouldn't let up, "Give me the dryad medicine."

"You're doing just fine on your own," Anastacio said none too gently, "I can tell, you're the type who survives anything, like a rat."

"A rat?! How dare you?" St Amour, despite his grave wound, launched himself at the dryad. He tried for a low tackle but failed miserably.

"You see, there is life in you yet," Anastacio confirmed, stepping away.

"You are not getting the dryad medicine," Solena said to St Amour, "but you," she turned to Anastacio, "must not taunt him."

They turned their attention to Teddy Goldman, who was still not showing any signs of coming to. Solena found a tiny first aid kit in one of his pockets, but it held only a couple pieces of gauze, which were soon both soaked through with blood. She wondered whether perhaps Teddy had been overly optimistic when organizing his Peaceful Warriors. She tried to feel for a pulse. But if there was any, it was very faint. It was obvious Teddy would not last much longer.

Desperately, she listened for a heartbeat. It was soft, and growing inaudible. Then it stopped.

"I can't believe this," Solena said. "This can't happen."

Anastacio put a comforting hand on her shoulder. "Even if Teddy Goldman is dead, his ideas will live on. You said you've read all his books…"

Solena felt the sting of tears in her eyes.

"But this means Sissy won…" she said. "She exposed him for being a fraud… and now he can't even fight back or do anything. It's too late."

"She didn't expose anything that we didn't already know about humans," Anastacio objected. "They all have weaknesses, vanity not least of them."

"Well, I guess you're right. But this means we must fight on alone…"

"I hate to say this, but we should try to find a way to help this scoundrel," Anastacio reminded, indicating the fuming St Amour.

At this moment, a strange sound invaded the deathly stillness of the lawnland.

It sounded… like a siren! Solena couldn't believe it. From the east, across the impossibly level terrain, a vehicle approached. It was a weird, futuristic vehicle that hovered above the ground, but it still had the general look and sound of an ambulance.

"I hope this is really an ambulance!" Solena cried.

"A what?" Anastacio asked.

"It's… well, it means we may be able to save St Amour and Rodney."

The vehicle came to a stop before them, making Anastacio slightly nervous. A few robots emerged, and without greeting or otherwise acknowledging the dryads, the mechanical creatures began to carry St Amour and Teddy Goldman inside their vehicle.

Solena and Anastacio exchanged looks. Then they rushed towards the ambulance and squeezed inside between the two stretchers. The robots ignored them and went on with their work as the vehicle took off.

These mechanical medics bustled around the prone bodies and applied some sort of medication to both. St Amour winced as a syringe pierced his arm, and a liquid began to flow into it from a tube. Strangely enough, the same was done to Teddy Goldman.

Solena held her breath, not daring to hope that somehow these futuristic doctors could revive the dead.

"Can you bring him back?" she asked the robot doctor, not really expecting a reply.

A mechanical voice said, "Organic human. Under three minutes of dead status. Must be brought back to living form."

When the fluid injection was done, the robots began to shock his heart back into rhythm.

***

Solena carefully poured boiling water from a disposal unit into an improvised vessel made from a futuristic beaker. She was brewing the Poniato root to help speed along the recovery of the two wounded humans.

They were already recovering with amazing speed, but Solena trusted the dryad medicine more than the scientific stuff.

With the combination of technology and Poniato root, in just two days' time the mechanical doctors allowed the patients to walk about in the hallways and in the perfect garden outside. Solena found the plants in there were real, though they looked almost too pretty and symmetrical to be true. Anastacio couldn't stand the garden and kept running off trying to find trees to climb, so far, unsuccessfully.

St Amour, though well-recovered, was in a foul temper and spent most of his time trying to find information on how to get back to the Great Tree or to some other time travel device. He was not the only one burning with impatience. Solena and Anastacio were both eager to get back to their time, but they understood that Teddy needed to recover his full strength. They trusted that the Great Tree would bring them back to the right moment in time and not let the forest fall into Sissy's hands. Still, the wait was excruciating.

In the afternoon of the third day, Teddy Goldman felt he was almost back to his usual self. Teddy was using the hospital bed more as a couch, being fully dressed and sitting atop the sheets, scribbling something on a small notepad. He had been writing a lot since his brush with death.

Solena came in alone, as Anastacio was out, having sworn to find the Great Tree, which should guide them back to their time period.

"I've brought you a bit of tonic," she said.

"Ah, thank you," Teddy replied.

He tasted the tea and suddenly said. "So this is what all the fuss was about?"

"I'm afraid so."

A computer attendant entered, announcing suddenly:

"The Great Sissy arrives!"

Solena was seized with panic. She looked over at Teddy, but he was fairly calm.

"It's all right," he said. "Surely, she must have known we're here, being Great and all. I don't think she means us any harm."

The person who entered did not look particularly great, but she did look like Sissy. She looked like what Sissy would grow up to look like, and since Sissy was one of those people who looked perpetually forty years old, she hadn't changed much.

Her voice was almost toneless, as if she had not talked to real people for so long that she had forgotten how to add any expression to her words.

"Hello," she said, in that robotic voice.

"Hello," they replied, dumbfounded.

"There had been other organic humans here recently, but I was afraid to face them," she said without any introduction, "I've got such low self-esteem, as you, Teddy Goldman, would say. I'm always afraid someone will mock me or tease me, an old habit from my school days. These old habits are hard to shake. You are time travelers?"

"Well, yes," Solena said, "How did you know?"

"Because I'm the only human left alive on the planet. Everyone else is converted to computer form. So, you must be from another time."

She sighed, and continued in the same monotone.

"I convinced them to do it, saying how the environment was too harmful to their bodies. At first it was true. Following the War, there was too much pollution. Now, I've restored most of the environment, I've made it even better with more perfect plants and animals. It's so much easier to do when humans aren't around. I've lived in solitude for nearly fifty years. Computers are around, sure, but it's not the same as people."

"So you really did start the war between the Environmentalists and the Citizens?" Solena asked.

"Yes," Sissy replied indifferently, "I once believed I would get satisfaction from all this. There will always be someone to take advantage of people, whether it's environmentalists or anti-environmentalists, doesn't really matter. What matters is who can inspire the masses to the highest devotion and then milk them dry. Thus spake Sissy.' A foolish girl, for all her intelligence. Now I know that even though I have achieved what I set out to do, it's all worthless. It really taught me the meaning of the saying 'be careful what you wish for.'"

"Sissy!" Solena exclaimed suddenly, "Maybe you could go back in time with us and tell your younger self to put a stop to this plan!"

"I'm not going back into that," Sissy motioned vaguely with her hand, probably indicating the disorder and chaos of a human-filled world. "Besides, I suspect with all your time traveling you've completely disrupted the past. The young me might be hatching a different plan altogether. I had lots of different ideas, you know."

"Can you give us a clue as to how we can stop her?" Teddy Goldman asked.

"Not really. I think you *could* stop her, Teddy Goldman. But even if you win, you will lose."

With that, Sissy got up and left the room, precluding any more questions.

"I think I know what she meant," Solena said. "You can't make it a battle between Sissy and Teddy Goldman. No matter who wins, it will be a loss to humanity."

Teddy nodded. "I've let my ego have too much influence on me," he admitted, "Running for president? Trying to win some sort of battle? It's all wrong. We need a new plan."

"Right. I think you were on the right track when you tried to talk to Sissy, make her feel like she can be loved," Solena said.

"But I failed miserably and got shot for my efforts," Teddy objected.

"Still, there was something about it… Maybe we could adjust our method a little bit, and it will work. I can't help but feel sympathetic for Sissy too, especially now having seen how she's turned out to be. I can't help but think that love and compassion should be our weapons of choice. And don't forget your 'we bring you love' theme song!"

The thought of love brought her back to a question she had been meaning to ask.

"Teddy?" Solena suddenly said. "You know how in your book *How to Get a Man and Keep Him* you advise the women not to be the pursuer, to let the man do the pursuing?"

"Yes," he confirmed matter-of-factly.

"Well, imagine a scenario where there isn't much time for the man to make up his mind whether he wants to do the pursuing. Such as, for instance, this man is from a different time period and he may have to travel back to his own time and then they would never see each other again?"

She felt all her blood rushing to her face, and her heart pounded as she awaited his answer.

"Well," Teddy Goldman said thoughtfully. As if he could feel her anxiety, he deliberately avoided eye contact so as not to upset her further. "I wouldn't presume to give advice on such a complicated matter. But I can say as a general piece of advice, if a man proves himself worth pursuing, then he must be pursued."

At this moment St Amour strolled in. His moustache and beard were now almost grown back to their original form, and he looked less like Rodney Love and more like himself.

"*Sacre bleu!*" he began, "When do we depart from this rat-infested port?"

"I think the time is nigh," Solena replied. "Have a little more patience, captain. Anastacio has gone to seek the way to the Great Tree, and he will return soon."

"We must betake ourselves to the armoury nearby before we leave," St Amour declared.

"There's an armory here?" Teddy Goldman asked doubtfully.

"Aye, this is the very city where I had delivered Lieutenant Jackson before. It boasts a grand armory."

"Oh no!" Solena burst out laughing. "Is this where you got that 'weapon of the future'?"

"Aye, but why is that funny?"

"Well, that weapon was in fact… how shall I say it in 17th century terms? It was a device for a lady's toilet. It was a laser hair remover."

Now Teddy Goldman too started laughing, and Anastacio came in to find St Amour fuming and the other two rather giddy. Suddenly, on seeing him, Solena was more than giddy. She was spellbound.

Appearing in that cold, neutral world of the hospital, Anastacio was like the essence of the forest with the feral scent of his sweat, his flowing hair, and the wild gleam in his eye.

"I have found the way back to the Great Tree!" he announced.

34 THE SHOWDOWN

Sissy and her army tracked Solena back to the Great Tree. Exhausted, as they reached it, they were extremely puzzled to find no trace of Solena, Anastacio, or the two humans they had rescued.

Sissy sat down on the ground and took a great gulp from her water bottle.

"They must have climbed this gigantic tree," she reasoned. "I can't even see to its very top. There could be a hundred dryads sitting up there and we wouldn't even know it."

"What do we do, Commander?" her lieutenant asked.

"I've got just the thing," Sissy replied.

She unpacked an object from her backpack. At first glance, it looked like a metallic lunchbox, but it was in fact a very powerful explosive which Sissy herself had designed.

But as she began to set up the bomb at the base of the Great Tree, the dryads and humans who had been up until that moment hiding in the thickets, drew closer, preparing to face Sissy's army.

The Peaceful Warriors aimed their pink guns and fired, catching Sissy's soldiers unawares. A scattered burst of machine gun fire was the response, but the pink army had already ducked back into cover. Three of the Greenpiss guns were disabled by the pink goo. There were still dozens of well-armed soldiers peering into the branches, trying to scope out their invisible assailants.

The dryads watched on from their hiding places, waiting for their chance to pounce. They had been scared and vaguely angry before, but now that the humans were trying to mess with the Great Tree, their fury knew no bounds.

"Don't waste your rounds," Sissy cautioned the men. "Only shoot the creatures when you can see them."

A tense silence ensued. The Greenpiss soldiers were edgy, ready to pull the trigger at a moment's notice. Knowing to be wary of dryads hiding in the upper branches, they lifted their heavy machine guns upward to scan the upper reaches of the trees but saw nothing until it was too late. The well-camouflaged dryads, who had borrowed the pink goo guns from their allies opened fire.

The place quickly became a mess of pink, where pink blobs blossomed explosively like strange flowers, covering the Greenpiss troops from head to toe. This rendered their machine guns useless, and a strange stillness and silence fell over the jungle for a moment or two. Only Sissy's bomb was still in working condition – she had pulled out a parasol to protect it in the nick of time.

**

Solena stood once again before the Great Tree. This time, St Amour and Teddy Goldman were in much better shape and Anastacio was in good spirits, seeing that he would soon return to his beloved forest.

"Are you ready?" she asked her three companions.

"It's hard to be ready for whatever unknown moment in time the Tree will put us in," Teddy remarked.

"I know," said Solena, "but I trust it will put us in the right moment."

She was first to step into the Tree, and soon she was floating once again in the ethereal chamber of its strange passageways. The others were beside her, but suddenly Anastacio floated away on some strange current that was perhaps taking him back to his own time, as if someone, perhaps the tree itself, had pushed him down and away from the others.

Solena felt her heart was about to burst, beating faster and faster. The sudden thought of losing him was too much. She reached out towards him and all at once some strange current brought him back. They clasped each other's hands, and she felt relief wash over her at once as she pulled him level with her and the others. Suddenly, she couldn't resist it. In the strange, unreal, yet earthly and beautiful world of the Tree, everything moved slowly as if in water. Ever so slowly, she drew closer to Anastacio, or maybe he pulled her towards him. Her arms enclosed his powerful shoulders desiringly. His scent was like the wildness of the forest, sun-drenched greenery and wild jaguars, or maybe that was the fragrance that reigned inside the Great Tree.

They could read in each other's eyes the exact timing of the imminent kiss. It was very slowly that they came together, and she felt the surprising softness of his lips as they offered a gliding touch. The next kiss was deeper and longer, letting her taste and smell the dizzying wild scents that were as enticing as life itself.

When they broke away, they saw that St Amour and Teddy Goldman were gone. Solena laughed, then she could see the bark of the tree, its translucence, and she knew they would soon emerge back in the 21st century. She saw Anastacio grow serious as they were about to face the unknown. She hoped they were prepared for whatever was on the other side.

***

"I'm going to do the death roll. I'm going to do it!" Tyler said to himself.

Everyone else had already joined in the fray. As soon as the machine guns were disabled, the dryads screamed a ferocious battle cry and sprang down from the branches upon their foes. Teddy Goldman's soldiers followed, yelling their *kiais* as they assumed martial arts stances and advanced upon the resolute commandos. Rodney, Jackson, and the knights were not ones to dawdle either. So great was Rodney's anger at Sissy for kidnapping his ancestor that he tried to fight his way through the masses of highly-trained paratroopers to reach her. He wasn't sure what he would do to her when he did.

But Sissy was not easy to reach, as she had now set up her bomb and was retreating away from the Great Tree, surrounded by her best troops. The dryads tried to pry the explosive device away from the Great Tree, but it was no use. There was some sort of magnetic field around it, which repelled the touch of any dryad. And soon, the dryads were swept away from the Tree in the general torrent of the fight. Tyler approached the bomb and tried to dig under it. He nudged it with his nose, but it was immovable. He decided instead to join in the fight.

"Come on, Tyler, you can do it," the alligator persuaded himself. "Yes, but I haven't done it in over a year. It's instinct; you can't forget how to do it… Those Greenpiss soldiers still have their knives… It doesn't matter. Here I go!"

But here suddenly Teddy Goldman sprang forth from the Tree. Seeing their friend alive and well, the Peaceful Warriors cheered. For them, it was just another typical Teddy Goldman miracle. Everyone else looked astounded.

St Amour appeared next, followed by Solena and Anastacio. The dryads rose up as one, cheering the appearance of their kin, and some new light seemed to shine from their eyes, as if they regained their hope and confidence.

"All right, that's enough!" Sissy cried. "I've had it with all of you dryads and pink losers! I've got a live bomb here. Like all my weapons, it is protected by a magic-proof field. This tree, which you dryads seem to value so highly, is going to be blown to smithereens unless someone brings me that miracle plant right now!"

The dryads didn't move, but their dilemma showed on their faces. Solena said nothing, but simply advanced slowly towards Sissy. As if on cue, Anastacio, Teddy Goldman, and even St Amour did likewise. The pirate looked menacing, but Teddy and Anastacio appeared only calm and serene. Solena knew they were picking up on her aura, which was getting out of control again, just like that time when the professor had burst into song. She could feel Anastacio's reassuring presence beside her, and she was still thrilling with the ecstasy of their kiss.

She knew she was attempting something very similar to what Teddy Goldman had done just before he got shot. Sissy was not to be defeated with strength of arms or clever ruses. Sissy had to change her mind of her own free will, or she would forever be feeling thwarted and bitter towards the world. Solena knew that feeling. It had encroached upon her when she was ostracised by her tribe. The feeling of not being loved and accepted. It made her current state ever more ecstatic after having been love-deficient for so long. These wordless thoughts were whirling through her mind, powerful yet gentle, much like the currents of the Great Tree. She knew she could never express them in words, so she walked slowly onwards towards the girl, gradually letting the magical aura that was almost palpable in the air wash over everyone.

"W-what are you doing?" Sissy asked uncertainly, trying to remain calm.

Solena didn't reply. She took another step forward, and suddenly the dryads and the humans watching uttered exclamations of wonder. A small flower sprang up at her feet. It didn't exactly just spring up. It followed all the normal progression of a plant, sprouting its first tiny leaves, then growing and developing new buds from which bright red petals sprang. But it did so almost instantaneously, like a video of a flower filmed over a long period of time and then played in fast-forward. The dryads all issued a collective gasp. They recognized the powerful and ancient magic that was at work.

Solena felt she was in a sort of trance. She saw the flower rise up out of the earth, and it seemed like a natural part of the unfolding events. She took another step forward, though she was still not far from the Great Tree and would be in range of the blast if Sissy were to press the trigger. A few more shoots of greenery blossomed all around her, forming a kind of retinue for her and her three companions.

Sissy was wide-eyed and tense. Beads of sweat were forming on her face, and the hand holding the bomb's remote trigger was visibly shaking.

Solena stood her ground. She and her companions were still just about ten feet away from the Tree. Together, they walked forward as if the four of them were an advancing army. But they did not look antagonistic, just certain and fateful. Neither Anastacio nor Teddy Goldman knew what Solena was up to, but they sensed the irrevocable workings of fate, and even St Amour stood firm.

Finally, Solena spoke. "The Great Tree cannot be killed by such a feeble weapon."

All of a sudden not just one flower but a dozen blossomed all around. There were bold red bromeliads with their juicy, shiny leaves opening up, orchids of all colors unfolding their elegant petals, and passion flowers with intricate little "thorns" perching atop their purple, white and yellow leaves. The flowers, which would normally take weeks or days to mature, whirled up in a fanciful parade of color. They were followed by other growing things: shrubs, grasses, and vines that dropped suddenly from the nearby trees, enfolding Solena and her companions in beautiful mantles.

As Solena stepped forward again, new growths of plants sprang forward before her, as if rolling out a carpet of greenery. She walked on slowly and gracefully, flanked by her companions. They waded through the waist-tall grasses and flower stalks and shrubs, and Sissy was finally thrown into complete terror at this inexplicable advance.

"I'm going to do it," Sissy said, taking a few steps back, putting herself out of range of the bomb.

Sissy squeezed the lever, and everyone except the four who were facing Sissy leapt away in a last-ditch attempt to avoid the explosion.

Nothing happened.

Sissy tried to press the trigger again, several times.

"But... that bomb was magic-proof. I put a special magic proof field around it myself!"

Solena smiled. "Nothing is magic-proof."

She glanced back to look, but there was no bomb, only a small mound of earth overgrown with greenery.

"Aaaaargh!" Sissy threw the remote in a fit of rage. "Greenpiss troops, retreat!"

Some of the Greenpiss troops were still pinned to the ground by the Peaceful Warriors, but all those who weren't backed away slowly from the Great Tree and its defenders.

"Let them go," Solena said.

Everyone did as she said. It was not so much that they were obeying Solena, but that they were listening, and agreeing with her. The aura had engulfed them as well, and they were filled with love and compassion. The pink soldiers and the dryads who had managed to wrestle down some of the Greenpiss troops now released them without the slightest reluctance.

Sissy backed away hesitatingly at first. Then she realized that no one was going to stop her. A malicious grin crossed her face.

"I'll see you all later, suckers!"

She broke into a run and disappeared in the shadows of the rainforest.

Solena had brought along some of the Poniato root distillation, and she now began dispensing it to all who were wounded. A few of the dryads had suffered bullet wounds, knife cuts, and bruises, but there was no one mortally hurt. As Solena walked over to each patient, flowers continued to spring up all around her, and she was followed by a sweet-smelling breeze that carried the scent of these fresh blossoms. Some dryads who weren't injured watched in wonder while others rushed to follow her example and help their wounded friends.

She got so caught up in helping the injured that when she was finished it was a bit of a surprise to come face to face with Anastacio.

He stood there before her, still demoralizingly handsome, but now she felt she would possibly never be demoralized again. Flowers continued to grow all around, enclosing them both in a fragrant circle of colorful blossoms.

"I want you to stay," Solena said.

"I don't want to go," Anastacio replied.

They said these sentences almost simultaneously, and they both blushed and laughed.

"Then I suppose…" Solena murmured.

"I must stay."

"Yes."

Rodney and Tyler came over to them.

"That was really awesome," Tyler said, "Instant plant miracle! Beats even reality TV!"

"Thanks for keeping my buddy St Amour alive for me," Rodney added, winking.

Solena laughed. "I know how much you like the guy."

"All I can do now is offer you and Tyler pay raises," Rodney continued, "You've both saved my life. Despite the fact that you're completely undermining the Timber Corporation with your Alligator Alliance and dryad magic, I think the life of the CEO is worth something. And I've got a new plan for the company. It will require you both to work out in the field more."

"What is it?" Tyler asked. "I've been dying to work in the field. I was getting so tired of having an office job."

"You two could act as liaisons with the local dryads or alligators or what have you, making sure we don't destroy the environment," Rodney proposed, "What do you say?"

"But isn't logging going to automatically destroy the environment?" Tyler asked.

"I don't know… Maybe not always," Rodney said, "I need you guys to help minimize the damage."

"Well," Solena replied. "This will take some serious thinking."

She hadn't really expected to work at the Timber Corporation after the secret mission was over. Yet this offer seemed a welcome one to her.

"Come on, let's go talk to Teddy," she suggested.

They went over to her hero, who was surrounded by his pink crew, waxing congratulatory and jubilant.

"Well, what do you think about the future, Teddy Goldman?" she asked.

"I think we have seen that the future can be changed, and I really hope that what we did today has changed it for the better," he replied. "I'm curious… I wonder if it will all be different now that Sissy is defeated. If only we could have another glimpse."

"Maybe we could," Solena offered. "I believe we'll need to take the professor to his own time period, as much as we'll miss him here."

Soon the helicopters of the Timber Corporation hovered overhead and Gregory Love descended via rope ladder to investigate the latest developments.

"I guess you've got it under control," he said to Rodney, though his tone betrayed a hint of doubt.

"As you can see," Rodney confirmed, "Greenpiss has retreated."

"I'm going to have a long talk with their leaders, letting youngsters run around like that," Gregory grumbled. "Now about that pirate… Can we get him back to his century and be done with him?"

They looked over to St Amour and Raffaella, resting among the dryads, and looking overjoyed at their reunion and the pirate's miraculous recovery.

"I guess we'd better take them back sooner rather than later," Rodney said, "According to our family history, he does end up marrying a dryad."

"Oh yes I know," Gregory said lightly.

"You know?! You know that we're part dryad?"

"I just don't think it's *that* important. You always exaggerate things, Rodney. You're about 0.1 percent dryad at the most. Whoop-de-doo! I never told anyone because I don't want it to leak out to the media. They would just love that story: dryad descendants cutting down forests."

"I don't know, dad. Maybe we have some magic powers that we don't even know of… Have you ever thought of that?"

"Do I look like I think about things like that?" Gregory asked.

"You got a point there," Rodney admitted. "I guess I'll round up my collection of knights and we'll be on our way…"

As Rodney approached the knights, he found them talking with their favorite professor.

"If time traveling boats become the norm, I would like you to help me obtain more visuals of the past. What do you say, gentlemen? I could offer you a position as field researchers. Perhaps I could collaborate with my engineering colleagues and construct a similar time boat."

"It sounds like a worthy cause," said Sir Gawaine.

"Aye," said Sir Lancelot at length. "But what does Sir Jackson think?"

"I would like to join you," said Jackson.

"Maybe I can get my dad to donate the boat to your university, professor," Rodney offered. "It might take some persuading. I think it would be better used for research purposes than for... whatever it was we were using it for."

Jackson looked away for a moment to where St Amour was waiting. "I shall bid adieu to the Captain."

The knights didn't hear what Jackson and St Amour said to each other, but they saw them shake hands solemnly.

Then Rodney ushered St Amour and Raffaella into the waiting Timber Corporation helicopter.

"This is it, St Amour. You're finally going back to where you belong."

"With pleasure," the pirate replied. "I am weary of this century, and I long to return to my *Belle Catherine*. My crew awaits!" He turned to Raffaella, "I know, my dear, you must be sad to leave. You liked it here..."

Raffaella looked a little wistful, but suddenly she gave a radiant smile. "I like being with you, Roger, wherever we may go. I have seen a fascinating human world, but that's not what I need to be truly happy."

Everyone who had been in the original expedition – Solena, Tyler, Jackson, Sir Lancelot, Sir Gawaine, and of course the professor boarded the time boat a few hours later. That eventful day was drawing to a close as the setting sun lit up a beautiful array of clouds on the horizon. Rodney piloted the boat. He was enjoying himself, though he hoped this was the last time he would ever have to travel through time. They had already dropped off St Amour and Raffaella in the 17th century, and now that everyone was relieved to be rid of the pirate, they were having an enjoyable, though slightly sad time, knowing that they would have to say goodbye to the professor soon.

Everyone sat on the benches, but Solena got up and walked over to Rodney.

"I'll take that job," she said softly, "as long as it means I spend most of my time in the dryad lands."

"Of course," Rodney said. "That's the whole point."

He sighed. "I guess you want to be closer to… him."

"Well, there's that too," Solena said. She placed her hand over his as it held the steering wheel. "Rodney, we're friends, right?" she asked.

He turned to her with that engaging smile she had come to know. "Haven't we always been?"

She smiled back.

As they traveled through the blinding streak of light and emerged on the other side, they found a calm and boundless ocean, not much different from the one they had left.

Suddenly, Solena and Rodney heard shouts of jubilation. They turned around to find a new character entering the day's drama… only he wasn't really new. Instead of the robotic computer, a middle-aged man in professorial tweed stood among a group of his overjoyed friends.

"I knew it, the enchantment would break eventually!" Gawaine cried. "Professor, you're free!"

"I am quite amazed," the professor replied. "This must mean that my physical body did not succumb to critical illnesses, and I did not have to be transferred to a computer. And that can only mean one thing: we have made a change for the better. There was no War! No pollution! Ah, the air, it tastes so sweet!"

On a sudden impulse all except Rodney who was still at the controls went out into the fresh air, feeling the rushing wind as the time boat raced over the low waves. They were heading toward a lush, green shore.

The future was assured – for the moment.

35 EPILOGUE

Boston, Massachusetts...

Some make peace with old age and live with it as with a friend, and others surrender to it, as to an enemy. Gregory Love did the latter, for he was too much a man of action to accept his fate easily. He felt that this world was no longer familiar to him with its fast-changing beliefs and technologies. No matter how much he tried, he would never catch up to the pace of the younger generation, and he didn't really want to anyway. Of course, he never officially retired. But he did leave Rodney in charge of all the important decisions, while he himself instead played golf with his billionaire friends and took long swims in his Olympic-size pool.

Occasionally he looked with pride at the latest reports from the company as he sat in his gloomy office. Rodney wasn't doing half badly. Sometimes the play of sunlight of the leaves would beckon him outside, and he would sit on a bench in the meager New England sunshine, reading about his son's latest work.

Los Angeles, California...

"I know that our first and foremost mandate is to make money for our shareholders, some of whom are with us today," Rodney turned his charismatic gaze at them.

He had made speeches to the board of directors before, but these speeches had been more about what his father wanted. Now, it was all in his hands.

"So you may be wondering what new changes I would like to introduce and how they will affect profits. First of all, I would like to implement more environmentally-conscious practices, such as selective logging and reforestation. This would be a first for our company. It will not be easy, but I will ensure that the environment is respected and that there is minimal impact on local wildlife. Tyler will liaise with the Alligator Alliance and other animal organizations to help us with this mission."

Tyler sat at Rodney's right hand, smiling his alligator smile, so no one dared argue that point.

"Why am I so concerned about the environment, you might ask? It's not my job as the CEO of this company. Let's just say I had a bad dream... a dream in which I met one of my ancestors from several centuries ago. He treated me very unkindly, tried to rob and kill me, in fact. It was just a dream, but it made me think, am I not doing the same thing to my potential descendants down the road? If we cut down all the trees, what will be left for future generations? We can't go on robbing them. We've got to leave the earth a better place than we found it, as the environmentalists say. And I pledge to do that. I hope all of you will join me."

Rodney paused, looking around the room. "Are there any questions?"

Some board members looked disgusted and scared; others just stunned; yet others, hopeful. They were silent, still digesting what they had just heard. Rodney seized his opportunity.

"Well, if there are no questions... let's go surfing."
***

Sissy did not feel defeated for long. Yes, there had been a defeat, she had to admit it, but the new challenge of facing a magic-wielding opponent only sparked up her imagination. Moreover, Teddy Goldman and the others had the advantage of time travel, which Sissy did not. She would have to level the playing field. Of course, it would be hard if not impossible for her to build her own time machine. Although she was making good headway in particle physics and other useful fields, the engineering knowledge required to build such a thing was beyond her. It probably took a team of the highest-ranking professionals to put that boat together.

And Sissy was, after all, just one person. Still, she reasoned, she could always obtain a boat by other means...

She sat in an LA café sipping a hot chocolate. It was one of those dimly lit exotically decorated places with cheesy, vaguely Eastern knickknacks. Some instinct had told her to come here. Usually, Sissy did not follow her instinct, but the crushing defeat in Colombia put her a little off kilter. Yes, she had felt something, some dryad magic had engulfed her then, whispering the promise of love and acceptance by others, not just her parents who were supposed to love her unconditionally, so that didn't count. But as the feeling wore off, Sissy realized that it was just that, a feeling. There was no proof that she would ever be loved. She decided to keep an eye out for it, but not to bank on it.

She had an idea. Opening up her little laptop, she checked the Skype messages, and sure enough there was one from Maxwell of the Timber Corporation. She called him back, and he replied after just two rings.

"Hello!" he said, snidely cheerful.

"What did you want to talk about, Maxwell?" Sissy asked.

"That was rather embarrassing, wasn't it?" he asked, ignoring her question. "But I imagine you quickly got over it and are now thinking of a new plan of attack."

"Maybe," Sissy allowed. "Now, I want to know, were you the one who masterminded that time boat operation?"

"Maybe," Maxwell replied with a sneer. "But I quit working for Rodney Love. He's getting out of hand, and his father is letting him have the run of the place. They've donated the time boat to that stupid professor in Colombia."

"That's interesting..." Sissy said.

"The reason I called," Maxwell said, "was that the Dark Elves see a lot of potential in you. That operation in the rain forest may have been a failure, but the planning that went into it was ingenious."

Sissy beamed, "I like it when my work is appreciated. But I prefer to be a free agent."

"The Dark Elves are fine with that. We would consider you an ally rather than a subordinate."

"Okay... I've got to think about this. We'll be in touch," Sissy said.

She hung up and looked around the café. At a small table in the corner sat a middle-aged woman who seemed to be some sort of fortune teller, though she could have just as easily been an Avon saleswoman. A tea cup, a deck of cards, and a crystal ball were arranged before her on the colorful tablecloth. All at once the woman realized that Sissy was looking at her, and she turned a mysterious smile towards the girl.

"Would you like your fortune told, Miss?" the woman asked.

***

A very tall, muscular man dressed in pirate costume was walking down Ocean Street. He walked with a purpose and a passion and energy, but gracefully, with that swaying seaman's walk that stood out at once to any who were paying the slightest attention or had the slightest interest in people-watching. His strides were long, and it was a while before the squat, pudgy talent agent caught up with him.

"Excuse me, sir?" he began. "May I ask which show you're in? Is it Pirates of the Raging Sea? Or is it a theater show? Either way, your costume is amazing. Real authentic stuff."

The pirate glanced back at him briefly.

"I am not in a show," he said.

"Well, you should be!" said the agent, "I'm Phil Jenkins, I work for the Salvatore Agency."

"I'm Jackson."

Jackson stopped walking as the man offered his hand and he shook it.

"Just Jackson! No last name or anything, just like Fabio. I like it!" Phil continued, "If you're looking for work, I could find you something tomorrow. Okay, maybe not tomorrow, but next week for sure. I'm talking big-budget films here!"

"I'm already employed," Jackson said proudly, "I am a researcher."

"Brains and beauty both! Very good. I see you'll go far," Phil got even more excited.

"And now I must meet my fellow researchers at the dock. I do not wish to keep them waiting. Adieu."

Jackson resumed his determined walk.

"I'll walk along with you," offered the agent.

"If you must…" Jackson sighed.

"Look, I can't promise you the lead," the dogged man continued, "but definitely a speaking part. You've got that authentic historical look. Audiences will love you! What do you say? I'll give you my card, and you can think it over, huh?"

"If I take your card, will you go away?" Jackson asked.

"Yes! Absolutely!"

"All right, give it here and be gone."

The man thrust the flashy, gold-bordered card into Jackson's hand and ran off, in compliance with their accord. Jackson stuck the card absently into his hat band.

After fending off the Hollywood talent agent, Jackson continued on his way, musing on the vicissitudes of his life.

It had been a month since the end of their adventure and the professor's return to his true form. In that time, Rodney Love had managed to convince his father to get rid of the time machine by donating it to the Ancient History Research Institute of Colombia. Now, the Timber Corporation had brought it here, to Los Angeles, to be taken over by the "research team" which consisted of Jackson and the two knights, who in the meantime, had been Rodney's guests.

At length, Jackson reached the harbor where he had agreed to meet the knights. Among hundreds of pleasure boats, some more humble and rusty, others more like miniature cruise ships, the time boat rested on the waters of the bay, looking clean and well-tended if not the most ostentatious of the lot.

Not far from where the knights met, a heron was standing on the wooden walkway of the docs, balancing perfectly still like a statue of a bird.

"Greetings, Jackson!" said Lancelot. "This heron is a good sign, methinks, though the voyage ahead bodes to be perilous."

Jackson grinned. "And I thought we were simply embarking on a research voyage. We still have to visit ancient Egypt and write that article for *Time Travel Geographic*."

"Nay, Sir Jackson," Lancelot came over and put a hand on his shoulder, "We know your heart's true purpose, and we're with you to the end."

"Yea, we're with you!" said Gawaine.

"Thank you, my friends," Jackson replied. "You move me to follow my better nature."

Together, they boarded the time boat and cast off. The water was golden with the setting sun as the heron pushed off from the wooden planks of the dock and flew away over the gentle waves.

Jackson stood at the controls and entered a new date into the time boat's programming.

"I have been afraid long enough," he said, "But now, no matter what lies ahead, no matter what hardships I must face, I will save my parents."

Somewhere in Colombia or Venezuela

Solena was returning to her forest, the newest issue of *Narcissism Carnival* clutched in her hand. It was colorful and glossy and had that fresh magazine smell.

On the cover was a photo of Teddy Goldman, the real Teddy, with his warm smile, lean build, and mousy brown hair. "TEDDY GOLDMAN COMES CLEAN!" ran the headline, "Will the king of self-help literature lose all his followers with this risky move?"

She hadn't read it yet. She was waiting until she got back to her tree house to savor the whole thing and tell Anastacio. But before reaching the tree house, she ran into Theodoro, the priest. He greeted her with a beaming smile.

"How goes it in the human world?" he asked.

"Much the same," Solena replied nonchalantly. "Reputations are made and undone. Business deals are concluded. The fight for the forest continues."

"I am confident that you will not let us lose," the priest said. "And I wanted to apologize for doubting you before. Many of us did, but being the priest, I should have had a little more faith."

"It's all right," Solena said with a smile. She was so joyous, had been since the showdown with Sissy and the miraculous aura magic. She suspected it might also have had something to do with Anastacio's deciding to stay in her time. The suffering of the past, her exclusion from the tribe was all but a memory, and she didn't dwell on it. She still wasn't certain about how the other dryads would relate to her now. They didn't try to avoid her, but also didn't seek her company. Anastacio said it was because they were in awe of her.

"Well, I shouldn't keep you. No doubt, you must be anxious to see Anastacio and tell him your news. I think you'll find him by his old tree."

Solena agreed with the priest: she had been away for a week, tending to Timber Corporation matters, and she couldn't wait to see her favorite dryad. As she was about to walk on, the priest said, "You know, it's a funny thing. I have been taking care of that tree for him for a couple of centuries. The former priest, Venicio, had told me that he had been entrusted with it when Anastacio left the dryad lands several hundreds of years ago. Before I took over as priest, Venicio asked me to accept this duty from him. He said that it was important, and that he believed Anastacio would come back one day, for his heart would always remain in the dryad lands. He said that the reason he was going away was because of a very special and extraordinary female dryad."

"Oh yes, he left to save Raffaella," Solena admitted with reluctance.

"Actually," the priest replied with a twinkle in his eye, "that was not the name he said."

After leaving the priest, Solena hurried on, running through the forest and feeling the freedom of its wild ways. She was back in her dryad form now, though still wearing human attire. The smells of the forest filled her nostrils with their flowery, mossy, and animal overtones. Such a multitude of intermingling scents almost made her dizzy as she ran full out towards her beloved.

The priest's words had finally put to rest the doubts she had been having. After all, Anastacio was not obliged to stay in their strange time. He could always go back via the Great Tree or some other way. But now she felt this had been merely a delusional thought.

She found him sitting with his back against his tree, perhaps reviewing in his mind the changes that the centuries had wrought. Although he usually preferred roaming about the forest, these moments of stillness and reflection were also one of his favorite habits.

Anastacio must have felt or heard her approach, for he opened his eyes and sprang up to greet her. After such a long absence, he was always fiercely affectionate, and he lifted her off the ground in his strong embrace.

"What is it humans say… 'How was work, honeybee?'"

"Something like that," Solena laughed. "Look at this: the latest issue of *Narcissism*."

They settled down beneath the tree, as she leafed through the magazine and Anastacio gazed at it with a mixture of wonder and irony. He found humans' need to take pictures of themselves rather amusing.

"It says there's a new novel coming out called *A Lumberjack's Tale: Romance and Adventure in the Amazon*." Solena pointed to a glossy page that showed the book cover: a square-jawed lumberjack surrounded by menacing pirates and scantily-clad dryads. "And…" she flipped to a different page, "Check this out!"

The photos were of a gala held by the Timber Corporation. There were a few different groups of guests photographed, including Solena, Rodney, and Tyler talking and drinking champagne.

"It's rumored billionaire Rodney Love was dating Solena Rodriguez, the first dryad to ever reveal herself to humans," the article reported, "Though the relationship may have fizzled out, something tells us that this handsome billionaire will have no trouble finding a new flame. Meanwhile, Rodney and Solena seem to be having no troubles in their professional relationship as their work to make the Timber Corporation more environmentally friendly has garnered praise from the global community."

"Well," Anastacio grinned, "You are *in* your favorite magazine."

"Kind of exciting, isn't it?" she said. "But really, what makes me even more happy is being able to make friends with other dryads again."

"*Have* you made friends with them?" Anastacio asked quizzically.

"Um… not exactly. But I think they're more open to it now."

"All right, that does it. I will introduce you to the ones I know," he said threateningly. "This older Anastacio, didn't he introduce you to anyone?"

"He tried… but I just want's good at socializing."

"Foolish old tree stump! He could have done much more to include you in dryad friendships, but it sounds like all he did was mope around."

"You know you're talking about yourself, right?"

"Well, no more," he continued heatedly, "In fairness, *they* should approach *you* after all you did for them. But they are idiots, and of course now they probably feel ashamed for the way they've treated you. I guess it's up to us now to approach those ungrateful bamboo shoots. And if they don't want to be friends, I will socialize them with my fist if need be."

"There won't be a need," Solena laughed. "I think I will be able to make friends now. The Coconut Festival is coming up…"

"Yes," said Anastacio, suddenly looking serious. "The Coconut Festival. It's an important event, you know."

"I know," she said, suddenly aware of his sober demeanor. "We could gather a few coconuts to take with us."

"Yes, but that's not it… I mean that is part of it. But the more important thing I wanted to tell you is that it is a time when one may choose a mate."

"I know," she said, but this time with astonishment.

"I wanted to wait until the Festival to ask you," he continued, his nervousness mounting together with her astonishment, "but I can't wait. As soon as I saw you, I wanted to say it. I love you, Solena. Just as 'Sol' means 'the sun,' you are like a warm sun that makes all the world come to life around you. Will you let me stay by your side and be your friend? Will you and I be together forever?"

"And that means we'll dance together at the Festival?" she asked.

He erupted in a hearty laugh. "Of course."

"I mean, yes," she said. "I will be your dryad. And you will be mine."

They kissed, and finally both were assured that they would never be separated again.

Suddenly, Solena sprang up.

"There is so much to do!" she exclaimed. "We have to find only the most delicious coconuts. But never mind that for now… I just want to feel what it's like to be in the forest again."

Usually, he was the one who initiated their forest wanderings, for there was nothing he liked better than simply to roam the forest, looking at each and every part of life that inhabited its great and tangled domain. But now Solena felt the urge to see as many things in the forest as a dryad could, which was quite a lot, as she felt part of the great forest now.

She took his hand, and they wandered off between the slumbering trees that seemed frozen in time. Though she enjoyed the human world with all its excitement, the forest beckoned her, and Solena finally felt she was not just comfortable and content but also overwhelmingly joyous with being who she truly was. A dryad.

ABOUT THE AUTHOR

Sonya Solomonovich is a writer with several published works including film reviews, online articles, and translations of novels and short stories.

She is also the author of a romance novella, Very Much Alive.

She has traveled and adventured around Europe and earned a Master's degree in English from University College Dublin, Ireland. She currently lives in Vancouver, BC, Canada.

Bonus: Excerpt from Sonya Solomonovich's upcoming historical novel, *Count Morelli.*

CHAPTER 1

With a Cossack at the reins and a scrawny young servant hanging on for dear life at the back, a four-horse carriage was wreaking havoc on the Via del Leone. It had appeared unexpectedly from around a corner, startling unwary pedestrians who had no choice but to leap to safety to avoid being trampled. Then it sped on, the driver and the servant both ignoring the shouted curses of the respectable citizens.

Florence's fierce heat was as relentless as its smells, but the elegant Russian officer seated in the carriage did not mind these discomforts, nor was he concerned by the sudden lurches of the vehicle. All that did concern him was reaching his goal with the utmost dispatch. The carriage emerged onto a square, and the Basilica Santa Maria Novella was revealed to him in all its beauty. The mesmerizing geometric lines standing out against the pure white marble of its façade made his forget-me-not blue eyes widen a touch.

"Mikhailo, slow down! " he shouted to his coachman, then added softly to himself, "I want to see this city."

Of course, the mission was important, but the messenger was not just some assiduous flunky. He was a gentleman, and a gentleman sometimes needed to exercise his right to amuse himself.

The carriage slowed, allowing the officer to observe not only the splendour of Florentine architecture but also the loveliness of its female inhabitants. The carriage passed a pair of modest housewives who lowered their eyes and blushed at his intense gaze but then looked after him with curiosity. The officer waved to them without any particular objective, but he was rudely interrupted in this activity when the carriage came to an abrupt stop.

Picking himself up off the floor, the officer stuck his head out the window to find a large gathering of townspeople blocking the entire width of the street in front of an inn called "Beviamo." The officer's limited knowledge of Italian allowed him to understand that this meant "Let's Drink," a suggestion that most of the crowd had obviously followed.

"What's happening, Mikhailo?" he asked his coachman, who had stood up for a better view.

"It looks like a fight," the latter drawled after the languid manner of his countrymen.

"Is it a good fight at least?"

The Cossack stroked his long moustache, shrugged, and said "Hmm. Not bad."

"I'll go see." The officer descended from the carriage with a slight groan at the stiffness in his legs and glanced at his servant, still clinging white-knuckled to the back of the carriage.

"I'll need you to translate, Lorenzo," he said as he began to push his way, with some distaste, through the sweaty crowd. He parted the sea of people, pushing them aside unceremoniously while his servant, a small but agile fellow, glided forward in his wake, offering charming smiles and apologies.

Emerging in the front row of the throng, the officer cast a quick appraising look at the situation while the townsfolk eyed his foreign uniform with some curiosity. Dressed in the short, blue, gold-braided jacket of a hussar captain, he also wore some small marks of affluence in the form of a golden pocket watch, a diamond ring, and a velvet-covered scabbard that sheathed his sabre. It was a long, slightly curved blade, which the Russians and Poles called a *szabla*.

At first glance it seemed the coachman — or rather the Cossack acting as coachman, for he was hired mostly as a bodyguard against the hazards of the road — was wrong to call it a good fight, or even to call it a fight at all, for three sturdy ruffians were setting upon a dishevelled, panting wretch. Then a fist, swift as a pouncing snake, sent one of the assailants reeling, while a second, who looked the most dangerous of the three, judging by his enormous size and a notable lack of teeth, was toppled over with a solid right on the jaw.

The hussar surmised it would have been an even better fight if the curly-haired man in the centre of it had been sober. He was tall, young, with strong arms but, as he had obviously acted on the advice of the inn's straightforward name, very lousy aim. His next punch missed by at least a foot, and he collapsed with his own momentum, raising a small cloud of dust and a burst of laughter from the crowd.

"Is no one going to stop the fight?" the Russian asked in broken Italian.

"Why should they? It's a good spectacle!" a lad beside him replied cheerfully.

"What about the watchmen? I think I see one over there!"

"They won't do anything," the youngster paused in his explanations to cheer as the drunkard took another bad fall, "These are Don Leopoldo's men. They can do whatever they like around these parts."

"*Don* Leopoldo? What is he, a Cardinal?"

"No, not a Cardinal, but he likes being called Don."

Meanwhile, drunkenness had won out over pugnaciousness. The three assailants could see this; they slapped their victim, and, from what the Russian could tell, mocked him cruelly.

"Stop that!" shouted the officer, coming forward. "Lorenzo?"

The servant repeated the order in Italian.

The biggest of the three assailants turned a gap-toothed face to him, "Who are you to give orders?"

"Captain Palashov, envoy of His Most Serene Highness Prince Potemkin. Stop this fight and clear the street so that my carriage may pass."

"Balls to your prince, shorty! We work for Don Leopoldo Fontana. He is a prince, of sorts." His companions chortled at this remark. "And this swine owes him some money."

"What does he say, Lorenzo?"

"He says the inebriated gentleman is indebted to Don Leopoldo Fontana, who is their employer. He also said some uncomplimentary things about your stature."

"Uncomplimentary?" Palashov's lack of imposing height was now more than made up for by an air of pugnacious bravado, "I merely wanted to clear the street, but now I see I have to teach this fellow a lesson."

The drunkard was now struggling to get up and still attempting to punch an opponent who was no longer in front of him. All three of the ruffians were now facing Palashov.

"So you will not desist?" the officer asked, beginning to unbutton the uniform that he could see did not inspire any respect in them.

The gap-toothed one spat out a few words, which Lorenzo translated as, "We cannot do so on the grounds that your prince whatever-his-name-is has no political clout here."

"Did he really say all that?" Palashov asked.

"Well... I couched it in more elegant terms," Lorenzo admitted.

Palashov paused in his unbuttoning. He did not entirely believe his new servant's constant declarations that he was the grandson of a Chinese ambassador, but there was certainly an oriental curve to his eye, and his speech and actions never ceased to startle him with their refinement. But this was not the time to consider that matter.

"Is that so? Tell him he is about to feel the prince's political clout right now."

Palashov unclasped his sword belt, and dropped all of his accoutrements into the arms of his astounded translator.

"Sir," Lorenzo whispered, "Don Leopoldo is really like a prince around these parts — a former pirate turned merchant. He holds the justice system in his pocket."

Palashov smiled and gave him a pat on the shoulder.

The ruffian decided to end the conversation with a left hook, but Palashov dodged it. Unbalanced by his own strength, the bandit left his ribs exposed to be pummelled by the envoy of a prince he had never heard of. Then, even more embarrassingly, he was seized, by the scruff of the neck, spun around, and tossed into a rubbish heap. The other bandits were finally subduing the desperate drunk, who was near unconscious. When they saw Palashov approach, they dropped their victim to the ground and backed off a few steps.

"We were finished anyways," one of them muttered.

"Don Leopoldo will find you," the other warned, edging away to pick up his fallen comrade.

"Let him find me, if he can," Palashov declared.

The officer looked down at the fallen drunkard, who groaned feebly, a few of his black curls pasted to his face with drying blood, as the innkeeper attempted to revive him with a cup of water.

"It is not even noon," Palashov checked his golden pocket watch with an elegant flourish of his wrist, "A fine time to be drunk!"

"He is a good man," the innkeeper interjected, "Just a poor violinist a little down on his luck."

"Here then," Palashov thrust a couple of coins in the innkeeper's hand, "Feed the poor bastard. Mikhailo, the coach!"

The crowd parted to let the carriage pass, and Palashov hopped inside as it rolled by, then extended his arm and pulled his servant onto the seat across from him. They picked up speed again, followed by the astounded gazes of the crowd.

CHAPTER 2

"My coat please, Lorenzo." Palashov seemed refreshed by the adventure.

"How old are you, sir?" the servant blurted out. "If I might ask..."

Palashov laughed. The dirty blonde hair was untouched by grey, but a few lines that highlighted rather than spoiled his features revealed his age to be most likely a little beyond forty.

"Too old to be a hussar, too foolish to quit."

"That was well done, sir. After last night's carousing I thought you would be in as pitiful a state as I am, but you were sprightly to say the least."

"A trifle for a hussar," Palashov boasted. "We may be in the light cavalry, but we are heavy on the drinking and dueling."

"But between the two of us we upended five bottles of Brunello, no less!"

"In truth I am not in my best form today. But last night was nothing! I will tell you sometime of the Eagle Cup... But come, try to pull yourself together, Lorenzo. We must look presentable for Count Morelli."

Soon they left the towers and cathedrals, and thankfully, the rotten meat, sweat, and garbage smells of Florence behind, and the carriage was flying along, careening around the odd hay wagon. They stopped once, when Mikhailo wanted to ask for directions from a passing peasant. The Cossack had absolutely no knowledge of Italian, but this did not bother him in the least. He simply spoke his native tongue, asking where the Palazzo Morelli might be found.

The peasant understood at once, hearing the familiar name of Morelli, and explained the directions in a few gestures and many words. Palashov reasoned that they must be somehow comprehensible to Mikhailo by dint of having a languid musicality strikingly similar to the Ukrainian's speech. After that, they did not stop at all, only once slowing down enough for Palashov to blow a kiss at an olive-skinned milkmaid.

Despite never having been to Tuscany, or indeed to Italy in his life, the Cossack seemed to have perfectly understood the directions he was given. He steered the carriage towards the palazzo as surely as if he were heading for a familiar village in his native Ukraine.

They entered the wrought iron gates crowned by the heraldic crest that bore two crossed lion's forelegs beneath a chess rook. The count's summer residence was shielded from the sun by luxurious greenery. The entire structure was grand, but also tasteful, with two wings extending forward as if to welcome visitors. However, the visitors were not greeted with strains of beautiful music but rather with what sounded like a heated argument coming from somewhere inside.

Palashov alighted from his carriage, followed by Lorenzo. The officer knocked decisively on the front door.

After several minutes, an impassive butler with heavy-lidded dark eyes set in a bald head appeared in the doorway and made it clear that Count Morelli was not home. His tone was so forbidding that Palashov understood him without Lorenzo having to translate.

What the Russian officer and his translator did not understand was how the maestro could be absent from his home and yet screaming out an exasperated tirade — throughout which they could distinguish quite a few obscenities — from somewhere on the top floor of the left wing.

The ferocious staccato of his high-pitched voice was blasting from all the windows, which were opened to admit a nonexistent breeze.

"Truly, only a genius, a virtuoso of the violin can get away with throwing such tantrums," Palashov remarked.

"It doesn't hurt that he's a count either," Lorenzo added.

"Not at home," the butler repeated, his gleaming head about to disappear into the murkiness of the hall.

"Just wait," the officer grabbed hold of the door, forcing it open.

"Tell him," he demanded, turning to his translator, "That I am an envoy of His Most Serene Highness Prince Potemkin, which is as good as saying I'm sent by the Empress of all Russia."

The message was relayed in a voice shaky from the previous night's carousing.

"I don't care if you're sent by the Empress of Russia or the Great Khan of Mongolia, the maestro will not see you," was the irritated reply. "Look," the butler added, his expression softening momentarily, "I'm sure if you come back tomorrow, he would be delighted, but today," he shrugged with stoic resignation, "the maestro is in one of his moods. I'm sorry for you, but there is no other choice."

"I don't need the man's pity!" the officer exploded; his cheeks, already reddened by the stifling heat, flared up even more, "The nerve of the fellow! I'll show him."

But the butler, sensing danger, heaved the door shut. Palashov was just quick enough to snatch his hand out of the way.

"The nerve of the fellow," Palashov repeated with a hint of grudging respect, "Closing the door on the prince's envoy."

They stood about uncertainly for a moment, and just as they began to walk away, the butler suddenly reappeared in the doorway, shouting, "Here is what I think of you!" and making a rude gesture. Then he disappeared, slamming the door shut once again.

Instead of increasing Palashov's anger, this exhibition elicited a chuckle.

"If that is the butler, what can we expect from the man himself?" he asked, "I can see that dealing with this Morelli is going to be something of a trial. But then, if it was easy, the prince wouldn't have sent Captain Palashov."

"Perhaps we should go, sir?" Lorenzo suggested, "Tomorrow might be a luckier day for us, as the fellow said."

"No." Palashov strode around the blooming flowerbeds and approached the side of the building from which the yelling seemed to emanate. He stood beneath the window and shouted, "Signor Morelli!"

He could now make out a female voice, not quite as loud but equally ferocious, arguing with the male one.

"Signor Morelli, I am Captain Palashov, envoy of Prince Potemkin!"

"I know, I could hear you bellowing at my butler!" a ruddy, long-nosed face appeared in the window.

"You could hear *me* bellowing?" Palashov muttered after Lorenzo relayed the message to him. "Then what was it you were doing?"

"Only disciplining my daughter, signore, not that it's any of your business."

"I'm sure it isn't, Count. I'm here on different business altogether. Perhaps you'll recall your correspondence with His Most Serene Highness Prince Potemkin? The prince invites you to display the glorious art of your violin for our beloved empress. My carriage awaits to whisk you away in excellent style to our beautiful capital, Petersburg, the Venice of the North."

"Don't talk to me of Venice!" two bulging veins suddenly swelled up on the count's forehead, "As you can see, I have a daughter who has set her mind on a Venetian merchant. I can't be bothered with all these petty concerns now."

"But Count—"

"Do you have a daughter?"

"No."

"Then you're a happy man. Let that suffice for you. Out with you now!"

A red-headed female face with the same oval shape and long nose as Morelli's poked out of the window.

"It isn't fair, signore! Saying that his own daughter is a curse just because she wishes to marry for love."

"You are, you are a curse, Rosa!" Morelli tried to push her away from the window, "Now don't interrupt while I'm arguing with the officer."

"I love Benicio!" she shouted, pushing back, "and you will never be able to keep us apart!"

"You are too young to know what love is," Morelli objected.

"Signore," she appealed to Palashov as a neutral third party, "the Morellis have always been a merchant family. How can my father look down on the Collegarias?"

"We have been ennobled centuries ago," Morelli protested, "These Venetian so-called gentlemen will never be truly noble. They're no better than hawkers at a market."

"But Count, the prince—"

"The devil with your prince! I told you I am furious enough

already. You expect me to jump into your carriage and travel to the land of bears upon a minute's notice? Out, signore, out!"

"But—"

"Another word out of you and you'll be pummelled by my dogs and bitten by my servants!"

Palashov decided not to risk it and turned to leave.

He could see that Lorenzo ached for a drink. Ever since Palashov had recruited him in Trieste, the two had migrated happily down the coast of Italy from one tavern to another, paying their hefty bills with Prince Potemkin's generous funds.

"Not to worry, sir. We take this Morelli and turn him into *vermicelli*."

"I came here looking for a musician, only to find a poet," Palashov muttered, "All right, let's go get a drink then."

Once they were back in Palashov's carriage, Lorenzo tried to restrain his chatty nature, mistaking Palashov's pensiveness for moodiness as the officer gazed intently at the sumptuous greenery of the rolling hills. Of course, Lorenzo could not stay silent for very long.

"Do you know, sir, what my grandfather would have said at this moment?"

"I've become very well acquainted with your grandfather's sayings over the last few days, but no, I'm not yet familiar enough with his philosophy that I could predict his utterance word for word."

Mikhailo swung the whip, and they were off, flying back to Florence as fast as the horses would go.

"He would say that in China," Lorenzo raised his voice over the clatter of horse hooves, "they have a custom. If you wish to invite some high-ranking person to your home, you don't simply send out an invitation. You send one invitation, then the next day, you send another, then the day after that you invite them again. That way you assure them that your invitation is in earnest and that their august presence is supremely important to you. It flatters them."

"There is just one problem with that."

"Which is?"

"Your grandfather has never met Morelli."

"He doesn't have to."

"I think he does. He couldn't have accounted for the man's contrary nature. What worries me is the more we invite him, the more he'll be set against going. Now there is a puzzle I'd like the Chinese gentleman to help me solve."

"He would, but the Heavenly Kingdom is so complacent at the moment that it feels no need to actually send out ambassadors beyond its borders. Thus my grandfather resides happily in his own palace. It could take months for him to get here..."

"We can't afford to wait for him, even if your grandfather really is a Chinese ambassador. I give Morelli another night. Tomorrow morning I'll have him sitting next to me in this carriage even if I have to kidnap him at gunpoint."

"Are you saying that in all seriousness, sir?"

Palashov grinned, white teeth flashing against lightly tanned skin.

"If you want, I can render him unconscious," Lorenzo suggested, "I know a practicable ancient method. I touch one pressure point..."

"We could try that. But hold off unless I give the signal."

***

It was early evening by the time the carriage pulled up to the inn outside of which the fight had taken place earlier that morning. As Palashov jumped down from the carriage, he could hear the restless strains of violin music, a skipping Scottish jig, coming from inside.

"This violin is mocking us, Lorenzo," Palashov exclaimed, "We went on a pretty jaunt in the countryside and we've nothing to show for it."

Nevertheless, the smell of roasting meat was welcoming to the tired travellers, as was the innkeeper himself.

"Excellent to see you, signore!" cried the innkeeper as they entered. "I'm glad you decided to dine here and were not frightened off by the threats of those ruffians."

The place was not yet crowded with customers, and Palashov chose a table in a relatively quiet corner, though of course the violin music teased him even there. He could see the violinist strolling about amongst the tables on the far side of the room. Bent toward the violin was a face framed by dark flowing curls, a face covered with scruffy stubble and colourful bruises – but it couldn't be.

"Lorenzo, is that not our friend from this morning?"

Lorenzo stared in amazement. "So it is. Who'd have thought he could play the violin? And not badly, either."

The fiddler approached them, and something in his dark eyes

seemed to say he recognized Palashov also.

He ended the jig standing opposite Palashov's table and, placing his right hand on his heart, gave a solemn bow.

"I'm in your debt, signore."

"Oh, so it *was* you who got a beating in the street this morning," Palashov said.

Lorenzo translated.

"It was me. But I needed that beating."

"What for, my dear man?" Palashov was intrigued.

"To awaken me."

"Have a seat. What is your name?"

"Enrico Rosatti."

"Captain Palashov."

"Lorenzo Liu."

"An interesting name!" Rosatti said, taking the seat that was offered, "What corner of the world are you from?"

"I'm half Italian and half Chinese," Lorenzo replied, "My grandfather is a Chinese ambassador."

Palashov rolled his eyes.

"I was born in Naples," Lorenzo continued eagerly, "My Chinese father married my mother, an Italian woman and settled down in that glorious city. But their trade did not flourish. When they died, they left me with nothing but my native wit and an excellent knowledge of languages."

"And your grandfather, the Chinese ambassador doesn't provide for you?" Rosatti inquired.

"He had never approved of my father's marriage. They had quarrelled then and never talked to each other since. But I am, after all, his only heir, so he seems to tacitly consent to my existence."

"How is that?"

"He sends me tea."

"Tea?!"

"Yes, a package of fine jade green tea from Yunnan. No matter where I am in the world – and I betake myself to many different places – the package always seems to find me each year."

"A fascinating story." Rosatti declared, "Glad to meet a fellow half-breed: my father was French and my mother Italian."

"He is half French," Lorenzo reported to Palashov, who had been struggling to follow their exchange.

"Do you speak French then?" Palashov asked.

"Very decently."

They continued in that language, and Palashov could finally join in the conversation more comfortably.

"But tell me why you wanted to be awakened," he reminded, pouring a cup of wine for the violinist.

"It's quite simple. I borrowed money from Don Leopoldo so I could drink. It was not much money to speak of. I don't think he would care about losing such a paltry sum. He set those bandits on me to prove a point about how low I have sunk. That those three fellows could beat me so easily is disgraceful, truly disgraceful. You have not seen what I was like in my prime, captain."

The innkeeper appeared, pouring more wine for all three of them. Palashov took a sip and nodded approvingly.

"It seems to me you are a complicated man, Signor Rosatti. You are like this Brunello de Montalcino, a wine that never ceases to surprise me with its many layers. For example, I have wagered against Lorenzo that you should be able to play something finer, something more deeply felt than this simple dance music we just heard. Lorenzo doesn't think you can do it."

That was the first Lorenzo had heard of this wager, but he tried to make a suitably sceptical face.

"You are a gambler?" Rosatti grinned ruefully, "Be careful lest you become destitute like me. Well, the least I can do for my rescuer is to reward him with a well-played melody and maybe help him win a wager. At least, I will try."

He got up from the table, making a slight bow, and moved back to the centre of the room.

"Are you in concert with my thoughts, Lorenzo?"

"In concert. Ha ha! No I can't say that I am."

"Listen to him play. Observe him. A musician, a good musician is always a bit of an actor. He portrays with his very being the music he plays."

Lorenzo did as he was asked, observing the sun-browned arm in a white sleeve raggedly ripped off at the elbow raising the bow, halting it above the strings awhile, still with concentration. Then it was moving, and Rosatti was grinning that rueful half-grin, but now a bit more warmly, as if sharing a joke with his patchy violin. The face, even marked with the recent beating, was attractive. Being like his own a blend of two races, it had its unpredictable edges and angles and a glow in the eyes that spoke of an intense passion for his music. The nose was almost completely straight, save for a slight bump, a memento of some other fight long ago.

The melody he was playing, contrary to Lorenzo's expectations, was not some sentimental folk love song. It was a sonata, beginning in energetic but not overly hurried allegro tempo, in a major key. Though the violinist himself must have been despondent, the music declared itself to the world bravely and nobly, and his bold posture and movements completed the impression.

"What do you think?" Palashov asked.

"Very fine. I don't know where he was taught to play, but it can't have been in a place like this. But not at an academy either. He's making up some ridiculously unorthodox variations!"

"Hand over my winnings!"

"We never made a bet."

"Just hand them over for the sake of appearance. I'll repay you double the amount later."

"I have no objection to that, sir."

"The important thing is, are you following me now?"

"What, one violinist is not enough for you? You must have two?"

"No, that's not it."

Lorenzo paused for a moment.

"Oh no! If it's what I'm thinking, then it is much too bold! Are you sure you wish to attempt it?"

"No, I'm not entirely sure. We will still see Morelli tomorrow morning. But if that fails..."

When Rosatti finished playing, the audience, which consisted of simple workers, mostly young journeymen who had come to spend the little they had on some much-longed-for revelry in the roughly convivial atmosphere, was a bit astounded but generally content. They applauded him and pounded the tables with their fists as he returned to Palashov's table.

"That was remarkable," Palashov said, "My intuition was correct about you. Where did you learn to play, my dear man?"

"Aboard a ship. A Scottish sea wolf taught me the workings of it."

"And that last piece? I'll wager it wasn't aboard a ship!"

"No," Rosatti downed the rest of his wine in one gulp, "That one just seemed to descend down to me from heaven."

"How is that?" Palashov asked.

"I was walking home one evening, and I heard that melody from the open window of a gentleman's house. Then I tried to play it and found that it was easy enough."

"You learned to play it from memory?"

"Exactly so. It's not perfectly right, but I have the general gist of it."

"Amazing! We must come back tomorrow to hear you play some more. Will you be here?"

"I play here every night."

"Excellent!" Palashov cried, "You will dine with us this evening."

The innkeeper, according to Palashov's order, brought them enough food for three, and Rosatti set upon the meat at once, gnawing frantically on a leg of lamb. It was obvious the man had not tasted such rich food in many days, if not years. Still, that was no excuse for such poor table manners, Palashov thought. And while Palashov stared disapprovingly at the violinist, Lorenzo stared disapprovingly at Palashov, for he was beginning to divine his master's plan.

www.ingramcontent.com/pod-product-compliance
Lightning Source LLC
Chambersburg PA
CBHW061603180626
46818CB00011B/2976